To all those with a dark side who love a bad boy.

Thank you.

And also to Shawn Mendes. I'm late to the party as always, but your songs are insanely inspirational, and your voice... *happy sigh*.

Angel xo

AUTHOR NOTE FOR READERS

This book is set in the U.K. and is written in British English.

Phoebe

I exited the car where I'd had to travel with my parents. It had been sixteen days since I watched my friend die in front of me.

Sixteen days since I experienced a horror the most expensive therapist couldn't help me with.

Approximately three hundred and eighty-four hours without one of my best friends. I'd slept only when exhaustion took me. Hours with nightmares. Flashbacks of so much blood. My mind imagining what the doctors had said, about how the broken fragments of Flora's own skull punctured her brain further, adding to the crush injury she never could have walked away from.

My parents took one of my arms each and walked towards the church. To the other mourners they looked as if they were supporting me in my grief while they processed their own. The tragic loss of one of their daughter's closest friends. The loss of a pupil from my mother's school. The loss of the daughter of one of my father's sailing club friends. My mother had secured my father 'day release' from rehab for the occasion and had warned me that should anyone ask he had officially been 'travelling for business'.

Of course. The show must go on, mustn't it, mother?

There had been no expense spared at the funeral. Flowers were everywhere. Elaborate displays of roses, lilies, hydrangeas, and foliage. Who were they for? The dead couldn't see them. Was Flora here? Present in spirit to see these people gather? To see the resolution of untimely and unfair death on earth?

My parents greeted people and muttered their sympathies. I wanted to peel their arms off mine using acid. I wanted their fingers to melt off painfully as they dared to make us look like a little happy family.

Twenty-three thousand and forty minutes and counting.

The ticking like a timebomb.

I'd allowed myself until midnight. As the new day dawned, it was time for Phoebe Ridley to wake up from this nightmare for long enough to wreak revenge on all those responsible and on all those who thought I was a pawn in their life.

To be played.

To be ridiculed.

To be harmed.

To be bereaved.

I was coming for them all.

If Liam Lawson professed himself a Bad Bad Boy, then a Bad Bad Girl should be born at midnight, and some people in Richstone would find themselves her target.

"Phoebe, for heaven's sake, can you please offer your condolences to people. They will expect you to have manners at your friend's funeral."

I beckoned my mother towards my ear, and she leant down. "Fuck you."

Her gasp was audible, and it gave me enough of a spark to break away from my parents for a moment and to greet my friends. Renee and Lucie's eyes were swollen. They were also broken souls, but at least they were left without the nightmare that lived in my memories. I wanted to see my friend's face the way I'd seen it most: smiling, happy, loving, and I hoped that in time, as I looked at videos and photos, this would return and erase what I saw every time I thought of her now. Car tyres weren't kind when they met skulls. They made quite the impact and as such had ground their tread into my brain.

Renee and I put our arms around each other first. Lucie stepping back in line to wait.

My mind had had so much time to think—too much— swirling around in what felt like thick, black tar. Thoughts I couldn't escape from, like imagining Flora's last minutes on earth where her heart went from full to devastated. Did she know things were going to be okay before she died? Had she listened to me? She did have hope, I was sure. She'd turned to come back. She'd been deciding who to talk to first: me or Daniel before *it* happened.

If Liam hadn't made the stupid pact *it* wouldn't have happened.

If Flora hadn't spied on Daniel *it* wouldn't have happened.

If I hadn't encouraged her to pick a rat *it* wouldn't have happened.

If Ulric hadn't put pressure on Daniel *it* wouldn't have happened.

If Daniel hadn't panicked and pressed the accelerator...

And on and on and on...

"I just can't believe it..." Lucie said as she released me from her hug. "There's a good turnout, isn't there?"

Our friendships laid in pieces, ready to be put together again, but in a different arrangement from before. We didn't know what to say to each other. I really did believe that once this service was out of the way, a line would be drawn where my friends and I would be able to speak more honestly. Where we could forge forward, knowing that we still had futures to grab with both hands despite one of us being missing.

I turned to look around me at everyone else in attendance. My eyes flittered over to Flora's parents, united in grief. His mistress was forgotten as they mourned their precious daughter and their unborn grandchild. The one they didn't even know was present until the doctors had informed them. I told them how their daughter had been in love, had been happy. Had, despite their differences, loved a boy from the wrong side of the river and been loved hard in return. If she'd been alive, they'd have raged —her father would have anyway—yet in death this provided them some comfort. That she'd experienced true happiness before she left the world.

I guessed even a half-rat bastard could be mourned if it didn't exist in anything but a sad memory. A fantasy grandbaby that would never exist to upset the balance of Richstone life.

But at least they acknowledged Daniel. Didn't act as if he didn't exist and that was something. Flora would be happy with that.

The words of the service could have been a reading of that day's newspaper for all the notice I took of them. My eyes focused on the rats of Sharrow Manor. Heads hung, a unit.

Liam hadn't looked my way since we'd arrived, his focus on his friends.

It was the right thing to do.

For the last sixteen days, I had stared at walls and lived in the dark, and at night I had crawled into the bed of a rat, who had put his arms around me without saying a word. Those same arms had pulled me back close when I woke in terror. Liam had soothed me by stroking my arm until I was calm again. In the morning I would leave. Sometimes when he was on my back, Liam's lips would press to my shoulder and I imagined I felt a tear fall against my skin.

Imagined, because it couldn't have been real.

Liam Lawson didn't do real emotion.

He'd told me so.

He'd said he'd ruin me.

And he had.

So I believed the man who told me he had a stone-cold heart.

I mean, I'd seen no evidence of anything else. I watched a man whose chin was taut. Whose body was coiled like a tight spring. One who was waiting for the first person to give him an excuse to beat the shit out of them.

He had no idea I knew of the plan.

I had Daniel's silence on the matter.

In any case, had we not set our own pact? Us girls were no better. Playing games with people's lives. The rats had seemed like new toys for us riches. But still, our bet didn't set out to trap people, to extort, to use someone in order to exploit.

Did my mother sit at night and write down the results of her psychological experiment? Did she still think it had the substance to gain her an award? *Look what happens when a rat meets a riches. Boom.*

She'd smirked while in the living room the day my father had beaten me outside the front door, and then told me that Liam had agreed to be paid a lump sum in return for persuading me that marrying a riches was in my best interests. Liam had declared that he'd told her what she wanted to hear, and maybe he had, because he'd had his own game plan all along. I even understood. I'd said to my friends as much in the beginning that the outsiders would try to gain from this. They had nothing of monetary value, of course they'd try to extort from those who did.

But I'd honestly believed what Liam had told me. That we were taking one day at a time. That I meant something to him.

Clearly, I'd been a deluded, gullible fool. But no more.

The service over, it was time to leave the inside of the church and to walk outside for the committal. Once again, my parents flanked me at either side, their arms through mine. What did they think I was going to do? Cause a huge scene? I had no power at the moment against them. None whatsoever. For now, I had to endure living in the same place as my abuser's accomplice. At least my brother was on a business trip and well out of here while he attempted to rescue my father's publishing company in the hope we could be freed from our parental imprisonment.

From me having to marry a riches to secure our financial future.

From him having to try to carry on with a business suffering via my father's ill-informed decisions.

Eddie had been trying to get me some money siphoned off so I could escape. The only problem was there didn't seem to be any surplus. Seemed my family really were in the shit. Not the kind that sent you bank-rupt, just the kind that eroded the image you'd built for yourself as the elite of Richstone. But reputations built on crumbling foundations were never going to remain standing.

As I felt my parents' arms either side of me, pressing against me as I walked towards the graveside, I wasn't sure I could wait much longer to get away from Richstone and the falsehoods it represented. I wanted to be some-where people lived honest lives and loved heartily. I still dreamed of the beaches my grandmother had told me about, and the love she and my grandfather had had for each other. She'd be turning in her grave if she knew what kind of person her son had turned out to be.

"I need to stand with my friends now," I told my parents and I moved away to join Renee and Lucie. I stood alongside the rats too because all eyes were on them. They should be on the parents mourning the loss of their child, but they were instead mainly fixed in judgement on the rats.

The pallbearers carried the mahogany coffin to the side of the open grave and the vicar stood ready to commit my friend's body to the ground.

I steeled myself and forced my fingernails into the palm of my hand in order to stay grounded and present. Not to be taken back to that fateful day where life had changed irrevocably.

"Please recite with me The Lord's Prayer," the vicar said.

"Our Father, who art in heaven,
hallowed be thy name;
thy kingdom come;
thy will be done;
on earth as it is in heaven.
Give us this day our daily bread.
And forgive us our trespasses,
as we forgive those who trespass against us.
And lead us not into temptation;
but deliver us from evil.
For thine is the kingdom,
the power and the glory,
for ever and ever.
Amen."

As I recited the words my arms were folded in front of me and my fingers crossed. I had no forgiveness within me and would not be forgiving those who trespassed against me and my friends. It was too late, vengeance had rung my doorbell and I'd invited it in, giving my solemn vow that there would be penance for the loss of life. But as they began to lower the coffin, I reached my hand towards the person standing at my right-hand side. Our fingers intertwined as the vicar spoke.

"All-powerful and merciful God.
We commend to you, Daniel, your servant.
In your mercy and love, blot out the sins he has committed
through human weakness.
In this world he has died.

Let him live with you for ever.
We ask this through Christ our Lord.
Amen."

Liam gripped my fingers as tightly as a delivering pregnant woman in a labour ward. I knew my touch was the only thing stopping him from leaving. From running from the grief we all shared.

The grief that within a week had caused us to attend two funerals. Because Daniel couldn't stay in a world where he'd taken his love's light. So he'd chosen to accompany her to heaven and send us all further into hell on earth.

Flora's parents had united with Daniel's in their communal grief and paid for him to have the funeral they felt he deserved.

And that's why today, several riches stood in a church, having crossed the river to Sharrow Manor.

I watched as Brett sunk to his knees, letting out his grief at the loss of the friend who had lit up their days like Flora had lit up ours.

Did God decide they were too pure for this earth and so took them to be angels? That's what the Prestons and the Chadwicks had agreed.

Liam's hand slipped from mine as he and Marlon stepped forward to lift up their friend, but instead of feeling sympathy, all I could think was that this was the result of their stupid pact.

They had blood on their hands.

Closing my eyes, I said a silent goodbye to the one rat who had defied his friends to fall in love with mine.

I hoped they were watching down on us now, Flora and Daniel, together with their little baby.

Staring down at my hands I wondered how long it would be before there was blood on my own.

2

Liam

This couldn't be fucking happening. It wasn't real. None of this could be fucking real.

Daniel's smile, his laughter, his *life*. The memories circled in my head like a zoetrope casting moving shadows on the wall.

That's all I had of Daniel now. Memories and shadows. The shadows were the darkness within me when I thought about what I had done and what I had seen.

I lifted Brett up off his knees, "Come on, man. Not much longer now. Keep it together and then we'll go get a drink."

We kept our arms through his, Marlon and me. It gave me a focus. Keeping the man whose legs didn't have the strength to support him, upright.

The coffin was lowered into the newly dug rectangular hole, the shovels of earth following, but I focused on Brett instead. My mind couldn't equate the body in the casket to that of one of my best friends. One of my 'brothers'.

Eyes were upon us. I knew it. Phoebe's fingers had touched mine, giving me strength, until I'd needed to reach for my friend.

We hadn't spoken one word to each other since it happened, and neither of us had been to school. None of us had: the three remaining riches and the three remaining rats. There had been a further week of the Easter holidays, and then the funerals. School started again for us on Monday, a reminder that life went on.

Now more than ever, I had to make the most of the opportunity because I wanted to make sure I could look after Daniel's parents as well as my own. An only child, his mother had loved having us all round when we were younger, seeing a house full of 'life', she'd said.

My eyes cast over to her now, seeing Josie huddled into her husband, shoulders hunched, dying inside. Daryl Preston looked like he'd aged ten years in two weeks. His eyes dark and shadowed, his face etched with lines of grief. It was as if their son being removed from their lives had took the sun away too, leaving them like the statues fixed amongst the gravestones, white and grey, and lifeless.

And then the committal was over. Our friend gone for good. "It'll bring closure," my uncle had said, and I got what he'd meant. That it was a stark reminder of the fact Daniel was gone. One you couldn't deny to yourself.

But I was yet to have closure. Closure would come when Ulric McDowell paid for what he'd caused.

———

"What's happening?" I yelled at Lucie as I arrived back at the table. Daniel had heard Flora sounding distressed and had gone after her.

"I don't know. Flora ran outside, Phoebe on her heels, and Daniel following. They took the Porsche."

Not waiting for more information, I took off out of the restaurant. By then the commotion was already starting. Something ahead. Screams. Distress.

It won't be them, I told myself, but my feet didn't believe me, picking up speed.

If only my eyes had been deceiving me as I eventually pushed past the bystanders and got to Phoebe, who swayed on the ground barely holding onto consciousness.

My arms folded around her back and I held her against me as my eyes took in my surroundings. The Porsche on the pavement. The blood. Flora.

Phoebe passed out. Sirens wailed, coming closer. Help was coming. Not for Flora, who I could only identify by the blood-soaked party dress clinging to her lifeless corpse.

Daniel staggered into my eyeline. I'd not even had time to get to my friend yet. Had seen him being helped by a passer-by, while I sank down to Phoebe on the floor.

"What the fuck happened?" I yelled. My eyes felt so wide, my voice a level of hysteria I had only experienced once before with my father's death, despite the ways we'd

15

made people bleed in our past. They had been deliberate. This here was tragedy. This was not supposed to happen.

This could not be real.

"Ulric startled me, coming past. Honked his horn, and my foot, the accelerator. Is she...? Is she...?"

I screamed for him to not look as his eyes fell to the car.

"Flora. Oh my god, Flora. I knew. I knew. I'm sorry. I'm so sorry."

"Dan, mate. It's an accident. She knows you'd never have done that on purpose."

But that's not what he was apologising for. I realised afterwards, when it was too late.

He looked at me again and mouthed he was sorry. Before he took the blade from his pocket and stabbed it hard through his own neck. I needed him to have missed his vital veins, but he hadn't. Blood spurted out covering me, covering the thankfully unconscious Phoebe in my arms. He dropped to the floor. Dead not twenty seconds later.

Renee had told Brett what had happened with Ulric. Phoebe had told her. About how he'd beeped his horn and wouldn't give our friends a minute. A minute where they'd have both ended up happy and alive. I wouldn't give him a minute either when it came to it. Oh no, he'd suffer at my hands for far longer than that.

We moved like the rats we were, following the Pied

Piper parents as they acknowledged those who were leaving. Brett had found the strength from somewhere deep inside to follow Mr and Mrs Preston.

I saw Daphne addressing her daughter. Then her eyes caught mine, a blank gaze before she turned away and moved with Maxwell towards their car. I was absolutely nothing to Daphne Ridley except a potential success story for her to gloat over and profit from. Phoebe waited for them to drive away and then she walked over to me.

"It's almost done. Come on."

Flora's wake had been held in the palatial home of her parents in Richstone. Daniel's was to be held in The Crown.

People who weren't at the funeral but who wanted to pay their respects waited outside the pub, lowering their heads or nodding. Faces solemn except when their eyes alighted on the riches. I could see it in their gazes.

If he hadn't crossed the river, he'd still be alive.

Richstone had taken one of their own. One of their best. Someone whose light had not been dimmed by the greyness of Sharrow Manor.

And it was true.

It was my crazy plan to trap a riches. My fault he'd met Flora.

A plan I'd called off just before the accident.

A plan Daniel had ignored anyway as soon as he'd met and connected with Flora.

He was still there because of you.

If he hadn't crossed the river, he'd still be alive.

17

Alive.

Alive.

Alive.

At the bar I demanded a full bottle of scotch. I scowled in reaction to the concerned gaze of Trev, the landlord. I didn't have a father and I knew his concern only ran as far as to whether I intended to trash his bar or not once I was wasted.

"Four glasses." I held up my fingers as if he didn't hear my words.

"I'm sorry, Liam. Daniel was a good one."

"Yeah, he was fucking awesome, and celebrating his life with a bottle of cheap shit scotch is the most pathetic moment of my entire existence." I swiped everything up. Bottle in one hand, glasses in the other, and strode towards the table where my friends waited.

I sat at the circular table with the other two. Phoebe, Renee, and Lucie were at the next table, and Lucie had gone to the bar for them. Their table was touching ours.

"Excuse me," I said, and I thrust my hip into it, moving it a foot further up. Grabbing a chair, I put it in the space so that now four chairs were around our table.

One of them glaringly empty.

I unscrewed the lid on the scotch and poured out four glasses. One I gave to Marlon, one to Brett, one I placed in front of the empty chair, and one I kept in my own hand.

I lifted mine in the air.

"To the rats," I toasted.

"To the rats," Marlon and Brett echoed, clinking their glasses with mine.

The reality that the other laid still and untouched and would forever remain that way tore through my insides. I could feel the anger begin to unfurl, roiling within me.

And then Phoebe lifted up Daniel's glass and held it in the air near mine.

"We shall vow to keep their memories alive. But you need to acknowledge that he's gone." She passed me the glass, and stood up, holding out her hand.

I wanted to throw the glass and shatter it like my sanity, and I knew Phoebe saw that in my gaze. She gave me an imperceptible nod before beckoning the others. On her instruction, Lucie went to the bar to get three more glasses and enough scotch to fill each with a decent amount of the amber liquid.

And then Phoebe walked us right back to the church. Right back to the grave that had now been filled with earth. A huge mound on the top.

"To Daniel," Phoebe shouted into the air.

"To Daniel," we all shouted back.

I poured his scotch—his final drink with us—into the mound of earth and put the glass at the top where his headstone would mark his final journey.

Everyone drank their own and put their glasses alongside his.

"Goodbye, my friend. I love you," I said. The first

time I had uttered those words since we'd buried my father. I thought I'd whispered, but that hand wrapped back around mine, fingers entwining, and she whispered back.

"He loved you too."

3

Phoebe

The last thing Liam needed to do was keep drinking, because the anger coiled inside him was dynamite and more alcohol would ignite the fuse.

"Go say your goodbyes now. This day isn't about you. It's about Daniel, and his parents saying goodbye. They don't need your drama; they need your strength. Go give them that and then we'll go back. There are better ways to work through that rage."

He quirked a brow at me.

"I meant a gym full of equipment including a punch bag."

Liam nodded, and gestured for the rest of us to make our way back to the pub for the final time. We all said goodbye to Mr and Mrs Preston, and it pulled at my heart when she embraced each of the other boys. She didn't want to let them go; they were part of her son.

We would never be the same. Irreversibly changed by the events of that fateful day.

———

A driver brought us back to the bungalow. The Porsche was gone but its vivid impact remained. The garage a reminder of it every time we walked past, because it used to be in there, the weapon of mass destruction.

We'd still barely said one word to each other and now I followed him through the house and out of the rear patio doors. The keys to the outdoor gym swung in his fingers as Liam strode purposefully towards the wooden structure.

But once through, Liam ran at the punchbag. His fists rained down on it like he was a maniac, reminding me of when he'd hit the waste-of-space guy his mother kept hooking up with. His knuckles began to split, but I didn't stop him. The only person he was hurting was himself. He was letting the inside out and if that was what he needed to do, to experience that pain on the outside to help him clear the inside, then so be it.

Plus, I wanted him to feel pain anyway. Both inside and outside. Because his stupid ideas had led to the death of our friends and for that he deserved to suffer.

My own mind was still a mass of confusion when it came to Liam Lawson. Because I understood his determination to try to benefit from the opportunity thrown his way. Maybe if what had happened to Flora had been a tragic accident it would have been easier to forgive. But it wasn't. It was a direct result of Liam + Ulric = death, and their part in the equation would be avenged. Daniel was the only person I forgave, because ultimately, he had loved my friend.

Finally, the punches stopped being thrown and Liam hugged the punchbag towards him, his head resting against the material. Blood poured from his knuckles, but I didn't offer to help him fix them. The thought of pouring neat alcohol into those cuts and making him feel agony was strong within me. To pull his hands down a cheese grater. To rain blows in his face with a hammer.

Yes, the old Phoebe was definitely dead, and the new one had issues.

But vengeance fuelled me. Made me feel alive rather than numb, and I'd cling onto anything that pulled me from the abyss of grief regarding my friend.

"How do I not end Ulric on Monday?" Liam had turned his head towards me.

"Because he needs to suffer before he's finished in Richstone," I replied, walking over and taking a seat on the press-up bench.

"Oh, he will suffer all right."

"He's not just yours to take down. I was there when it all happened. It was me he ignored. He chose to do what he did while I stood there. Ulric left me abandoned on the kerbside, watching helplessly as my friend got mowed down." My voice was getting louder and I felt my nostrils flare. "So don't you dare take away my chance of retribution. I need it to be slow, painful, and glorious.

Ulric not listened to and abandoned and then his life destroyed. An eye for an eye."

"You know I want to kill him, right?" Liam said, matter of factly, like he was telling me he needed to return a library book.

"I get that. My need for revenge is the same as yours. But I don't know how Ulric's story ends yet, just that each chapter will be a nightmare up until its epic conclusion."

"So are we doing this together?"

I stood up and moved closer to him. His hands dropped from the punchbag and he turned towards me.

"I guess we could," I said, lifting his hands to cup my cheeks.

I didn't care that blood ran down my cheeks. I felt like I was drowning in it anyway. When I slept at night it was to block out the images of that day. Daniel's blood might have been washed from my face and body, but it had stained deep.

I opened my eyes on hell. How could the concrete beneath my limbs be so cold, when all around me the fires of hell burned? I sat up, seeing Liam in front of me cradling Daniel's body in his arms. He was covered in blood. Covered. What the fuck had happened?

Water trickled from my chin tickling me and I wiped it away, but when I placed my hand back down in order to try to get to my feet, to try to help, my hand came away streaked with red. I wiped at my face and the red on my hands increased like the bloom of a blush.

Looking at Daniel, and at Liam who was now being told to let go and step back by the paramedic, I got to my feet and staggered forward. Daniel's body now laid on the ground just inches from my friend's. A knife was sticking out of his throat.

Liam's gaze met mine as understanding hit me. His look confirmation of what Daniel had done.

We stood there staring at each other, drenched in the blood of innocence, until paramedics led us both away to be checked over, the police hot on their heels to try to ascertain the chain of events that had occurred this fateful day.

A tragic, but accidental death, and suicide. That's what the coroner had ruled within days of their deaths. At least it meant no delay for the funerals. No question marks for the family. No, as far as the Prestons and Chadwicks were concerned, all they had to do now was mourn.

Liam's fingers trailed down my cheek and then his hand left me to fist in my hair. He pulled my face closer to his and kissed me like his life depended on it. Maybe right now his survival did? I knew what he was doing. Regardless of how he felt about me in reality, and whether he truly was falling for me, right now he wanted to lose himself in my body to feel and to lose more of the tension that still raged within him.

He could use me.

And I would use him right back.

Because it was a distraction that right now I needed more than air.

Liam bit the edge of my lip and then ran his tongue over the sting he'd caused. I climbed up his body with his assistance, my arms wrapping around his neck as my legs wrapped around his hips. He walked us over to the wall, pressing my back against the scratchy inside surface of the shed. But the splintered wood could destroy every inch of the black dress I wore with my permission. I never wanted to wear these clothes again, wanted them ruined, to burn as if they'd never existed. That's what I would do when I finally rid myself of them. Incinerate them.

But right now, I'd forget about my clothes and concentrate on what Liam Lawson intended to do with my body.

He moved my hair to one side as his mouth trailed kisses down the inside of my neck, nipping gently the further down he travelled.

My legs returned to the floor, and he stood back from me. Turning me around to face the wall, he unzipped my dress, knocking it from my shoulders and pulling it down and off my body until I stepped out of the material. He took my feet out of my heels and pulled my tights off next. He carried on until I was completely naked.

I heard his own shoes kicked off, and other clothing following. As he stepped closer, I felt his hard cock against my arse cheek. He pulled my hands behind me and wrapped material around my wrists. Was this his tie? Pulling the bindings tighter, it pinched the skin of my wrists, and made my chest thrust out more, my now pebbled nipples rubbing against the coarse tongue and groove cladding.

Liam instructed me to widen my stance without a word, just using his knee. Then his warm breath fanned against my neck, his hands back in my hair. He moved my hair over my left shoulder, leaving my neck clear for his mouth.

With a thrust he was inside me. His aim just slightly off at first, it dragged the delicate skin there, making me burn as he got situated and sunk deep. He withdrew from me oh-so-slowly and then rammed into me again, filling me to the hilt. My skin scratched against the wood with each deep thrust. I could do nothing to stop it with my hands behind my back.

With the next thrust he bit the side of my neck just above my collarbone. His teeth not gentle. I winced but that just seemed to make him harder. His hands settled around my hips as he drove into me over and over.

"I am Richstone," I said to him, breaking the sounds being only that of heavy breaths and groans. "I am everything you despise. Rich, privileged. I have everything you want, and now in your pursuit of bettering yourselves we've taken one of your own."

His hand came around my neck, squeezing as his thrusts became harder, like he wanted to tear me apart.

But every thrust, every single bit of pain, brought pleasure anyway. I was a mess of epic proportions. Happy that my chest and stomach would need splinters picking out of them. Happy it had abraded my skin. Delighted I was being fucked so hard I'd be sore for the rest of the day. Ecstatic that Liam's pressure on my neck was becoming dangerously close to restricting my breath.

Use me.

Hurt me.

Make me bleed.

But then make me come.

His hand dropped to the front of my body as his thrusts got faster. I was being lifted onto my tiptoes now. His fingertips dropped to my clit and they danced their little steps that had me exploding, milking his cock as he himself came undone.

He pulled out of me and as his cum ran down the inside of my thigh, I thought about the fact that had been his plan. That my being on contraception had thwarted his plan to impregnate me, and yet he'd stayed with me anyway. Was it because of the bungalow? My mother?

Of course it was, Phoebe. Don't be so stupid as to think it's because of you.

He's a liar.

So what would be next then? Blackmail? I would have to keep a close eye on Liam, and what better way to do so than to be his person, his confidante, his lover.

Keep your friends close and your enemies closer, right?

I reluctantly re-dressed myself in the black funeral attire. Liam had sunk down onto the floormat. Spent in more ways than one.

I left him there and made my way back up to the house.

My mother called from the sitting room as I walked down the hall. "Phoebe, is that you?"

Sighing, I changed direction and walked into the room. Thankfully, my father wasn't there.

"Has the puppet returned to the theatre?" I asked with a sarcasm-ladened tone.

"Your father is back at the clinic. These were just day releases as I told you, so that he could pay his respects."

"Oh, Mother, please. Save it. You mean so you could keep up appearances."

"Watch your mouth, Phoebe."

I tilted my hips, placing my hand on one of them. "Or what, Daphne?"

Her eyes narrowed.

"I thought so. See, you need me as much as I need you right now. Maybe even more. Because the rats being at Richstone can offer you kudos and the potential of fame and fortune. And you need my silence about the fact I'm fucking one of them or your back-up plan of my value as a trophy wife falls right off the charts. I need a nice, quiet roof over my head and my father in therapy. So we're at an impasse, where we have to call a truce. That is, until someone's power diminishes. So watch your back, Daphne. I'll sure be watching mine, and if you bring that bastard back home, you'd better keep him well away from me. Because the next time he touches me I'll knock him out with pills and push him down the stairs hoping I accidentally break his neck."

My mother remained silent, but her mouth hung slightly open. I guessed it was the first time I'd properly fought back.

"Thinking about it, you might want to make sure you keep an eye on your own drinks. Eddie and I would be rich orphans. All your life insurance policies and your personalities show me we're better off without you."

"Are you done?"

"Well, that's the million-dollar question, isn't it? All I want is to be out of Richstone after my exams. Until then we shall carry on with our clever chess-like game of life. Move your pieces, Daphne. I'll be moving mine, and we'll see who topples at the end of the summer."

With that I turned and walked out of the room.

4

_____

Liam

I should get up.

Look at the state of yourself. I enter the casket and you enter pussy, it's about right. I felt like I could hear Daniel in my head laughing, as I thought about what he'd say to me right now in his usual 'Daniel' way.

But the reality was he'd never talk to me again.

So I continued to lie on the mat awhile, my cock covered in Phoebe's and my own cum, my hands starting to knit their own sticky outpourings as healing came into force.

Healing.

Would I ever heal from Daniel's death?

I guessed, sadly, I would. Though I'd always be a different person from the after-effects of what had happened. The past assaulted me, as if being by a graveside today had somehow opened up a portal to the other side, to the memories I'd rather keep buried.

Four years earlier

I'd been in the kitchen making a sandwich while my ma cleaned up around me.

"Ma, I can clean up. Stop hovering. You've just emptied my juice into the sink. What's with you?"

"Sorry, love. You know how your dad likes a clean house though. I thought maybe if I keep it clean he'll get out of bed and come downstairs."

"The guy's been working hard all week. Let him have a lazy day," I shook my head at her while getting a fresh glass out and opening the refrigerator door to grab the orange juice carton for the second time that morning.

My dad had looked especially worn out over the last few days. He'd always been a quiet man, who liked to take himself off for walks in an evening. A man who considered every word he uttered before he said it. I figured work must be busier than ever as it approached the holiday season. Dad worked for the mail-sorting office, and I knew he had a physically demanding job.

"I'll go get some shopping and leave you in peace, but please clear up after yourself. I'll make a nice meat and potato pie for tea, your dad's favourite. That and some treacle sponge for afters." She began fussing around

writing a shopping list, but eventually the house became silent as the front door banged behind her.

I made my sandwich and then carried on with my day as usual. Went and met my mates, moaned about life. About my fussing mother, like kids do. The fussing mother who as a typical kid I'd never given much thought to as an actual person, because what kid did? Mothers fussed and gave you a slap or a handout depending on what mood they were in. They were just there when you needed them, right? Like a pint of milk. When you were young you didn't see them as an individual, didn't see that they put the pint of milk there. They just were there.

You didn't know they were on their seventh affair since they married your father.

You didn't know that your father had depression. That his periods of tiredness came from deep in his soul.

In the future you wouldn't know if the affair caused more depression, if the depression caused more affairs, or whether both things happened separate from the other. You'd never know for sure. All you had were assumptions.

That day we'd sat in the kitchen around the small dining table. Dad had got out of bed and sat at the table picking at his meat and potato pie. Then he'd refused his pudding saying he wasn't hungry.

"I shopped for this specifically because it's your favourite and then I spent all afternoon making it." My ma's jaw clenched, teeth grinding as she looked at my father.

"Ma, he's tired. Maybe he's coming down with something?" I protested.

"Well, you try to get him to go to the doctors then. I have and he won't listen to me. Never fucking listens to me."

"No, I listen to the gossip about you and that's enough." Dad fixed her with a look I couldn't read.

"We're not doing this now over the dinner table," she warned, her eyes flashing with sheer fury. Depending on his next words, a door was about to be slammed before she stomped upstairs or outside.

He nodded. "You're right." He stood up. "I'm going to go out to clear my head, grab some fresh air."

Walking past me, he squeezed my shoulder. "I love you, son."

I put my hand on his and squeezed it back. Didn't say the words. Teenage boys didn't do that.

Not until what remained of my father's body was lowered into the ground and I whispered I loved him into the wind to be carried to him.

That night he'd put on his shoes and his coat and he'd left the house.

And then he'd thrown himself under the express service to London Piccadilly that passed through Sharrow at seven twenty each evening.

It had been my first experience of death that mattered.

Sharrow was full of gossip about why the nice-mannered Mr Lawson had killed himself. Rumours about my mother's infidelities reached my own ears.

My ma's booze binges went from weekend binges to all day 'all you can drink' specials. You didn't have to think while you were drunk. That's what she told me, as I cleaned up her vomit and made sure she didn't choke to death, while I stood over her wondering if her affairs were the reason Dad had decided to leave us both.

The older I got, the more bitter I got, to the point where I left her to it, staying at my friend's houses, letting fate decide if that night would be the night she killed herself too. By falling downstairs. Choking on her own sick. Liver failure.

She thought the alcohol made her numb, but it didn't. It loosened her tongue, and I was told all about her affairs, what she hated about my father. How he wasn't ever good enough for her. Why she should now be free of him and his morose ways, but instead was the talk of Sharrow, called a whore for her behaviour when she'd just been letting loose from the shackles of marriage and motherhood.

That she wished she'd never fallen pregnant with me. That I was the reason she'd had to marry my father. That ultimately the blame laid with me because they never should have married in the first place.

Jekyll and Hyde. My ma would wake from her binges and not remember a word of what she'd said. Would become the mother who loved me. Made me packed lunches and my favourite teas. Encouraged me at school. Got my uncle to take me out to his garage because she knew I needed a replacement male influence in my life.

But now I was older, wiser. 'Grown up beyond your years', Uncle Karl always said. You had to be when the payment of bills often landed at your own feet, depending on whether your ma was managing to get to work or not.

My limbs had started to stiffen after my being laid down for so long and all I could see now as I looked down at my body was the Sharrow boy who was desperate to throw off the shackles of his upbringing and do better.

Rising to my feet, I strolled out of the gym not bothering to lock up, and straight into the shower where I let the water scald me and I washed away the sins of the past that clung to me.

Once dried and dressed I didn't know what to do with myself. Here I was in this place that had been home for two-and-a-half months while back in Sharrow, Mr and Mrs Preston now sat with nothing but photographs and memories of their son.

Marlon and Brett had probably stayed together to carry on drinking until they passed out and no longer had to think. I grabbed a bottle of whisky and sat down on the sofa. As I opened the bottle and took a swallow, I realised maybe I wasn't so different to my mother after all.

Maybe I judged her when actually she was just pissed off with life and the hand it had dealt her. Perhaps she'd had wishes of escaping Sharrow herself and one stray sperm had taken that away from her?

My friend was fucking dead.

Dead.

Dead.

Dead.

We'd come to Richstone in an attempt to be able to live the dream and it had turned into a fucking nightmare.

What had I done?

For my ma her life had changed the moment she'd missed her contraceptive pill or the condom broke, or whatever had happened for me to make my appearance.

For me my life had changed the minute I'd told my friends we should get to Richstone and do whatever was necessary to secure our futures.

Daniel had been the first to say he was in.

Not necessarily because he'd wanted it, but because that was who he was. He'd jump in, like the brother I'd considered him to be. He'd had my back.

I took another swallow.

His falling in love with Flora had been the subject of the rest of the gang's mirth. Typical Daniel. You asked him to get a riches pregnant in order to blackmail her and he didn't play the game. But she got pregnant anyway and they loved each other and planned a happy ever after regardless of where it happened.

And the crazy impulses of one Ulric MacDowell swiped both off them out of existence.

The more I drank, the angrier I got.

The angrier I got, the more I drank.

I imagined my hands around his neck, squeezing the last vestiges of life out of him. Watching his eyes turn from fear-filled to dull as the spark left.

But then he'd have peace, and I still wouldn't.

Phoebe was right. Ulric had to suffer. A long, painful suffering where he'd welcome death, but I wouldn't give it him. It would be more of a punishment for him to live a tormented existence. Hell on earth.

So, yes, I would talk more with Phoebe and we would hatch a plan.

I wondered what she was doing now up at the big house with her mother for company. Picking up my phone to send her a text, I stopped and threw it across the carpet.

I'd learned from my mother's rancid drunken mouth to never communicate when drinking. Because you might say things you'd later regret.

And I might let Phoebe know that she was under my skin. That when I was with her, the darkness wasn't so bad.

She was an addiction worse than my mother's alcohol issues.

There was no facility where I could check myself in because a woman had managed to bury herself deep in my soul and maybe even my heart.

No. I would carry on drinking and carry on thinking for the whole damn evening and then at some point before school on Monday, I would speak to Phoebe about how we handled our return to Richstone Academy.

Because my reasons for being in Richstone had changed.

No longer was I here to trap a 'riches'.

I'd get my education and while I was at it, I'd get retribution.

I'd pay my penance for bringing Daniel to Richstone with every day I lived with the guilt of a life without him, and I'd serve justice via the destruction of Ulric MacDowell and any other Richstone brat who thought me and my friends weren't good enough to shine their shoes.

I'd destroy them all and then throw a party as I left the ruins of Richstone behind me.

Holding up the bottle in the air, I shouted out.

"To the ruination of Richstone." Then I drank a damn load more.

5

Phoebe

It was a warm morning. The sun was shining so brightly I had to grab my shades from my bag and put them on as I walked across the driveway to my car. I was glad to be wearing a soft, light-blue t-shirt with a pair of cream cut-off trousers instead of the funeral wear of yesterday. As the gravel crunched beneath my feet, each sound brought thoughts of my father back. I would have him on his own knees, begging for a second chance he wouldn't be getting. I shook my head to cast thoughts of him aside.

Last night after far too much to drink, I'd taken the black clothing I hated because of what it represented out onto the back patio, had emptied alcohol on it courtesy of my father's liquor cabinet, and then I'd used my candle lighter to set it all on fire. I guessed my mother had gone to sleep courtesy of sedatives because no one stopped me.

I'd left a charred mark on the patio, but I didn't give a shit. I had charred marks on my heart and those who should didn't care about that. She'd have someone make it look like it never existed. She was good like that was Daphne.

This morning I was meeting Renee and Lucie at Café Renzo. It was the first time we had met together outside of the funeral in a public setting. Seeing as we were back at school on Monday, we'd agreed it was time to get back to a 'normal' routine, even if none of it felt like it would ever seem normal again. Our bistro was our safe space and Renee had suggested we start there.

We usually met inside and yet this morning I found both my friends waiting outside the entrance for me. They stepped forward and enveloped me in a tight hug in turn, desperation and non-complacency in a hug that seemed fearful that there might never be another. We were forever changed, and yet, I knew as time went on, we'd find a new normal.

"Let's grab a table then, I'm thirsty," I said, pushing open the door and hearing the familiar ring of the bell as it heralded our arrival.

The bistro was moderately busy and the noise of cups clinking as they were cleared from tables mixed in with the smell of baking and coffee. Petula saw us and pointed to a table with her index finger before using the same finger held aloft to say she'd be over in one minute.

We took a seat each and just like at the funeral it was obvious to us that someone was missing, even more so amongst this familiar environment.

"Hello, girls," Petula joined us, tucking an escaped wisp of her dark-blonde hair behind her ear. "I am so very sorry about Flora. What can I get you girls? This morning's is on the house."

She insisted after we said it wasn't necessary and then she left to prepare the coffee and pastries we'd asked for.

"Does anyone else need at least two coffees this morning because they have a hangover from last night?" Lucie asked.

Both Renee and I nodded.

"I burned my funeral clothes on the back patio at some point. I was so wasted I'm surprised I didn't set myself alight," I confessed.

"Is your dad back?" Renee asked.

"No. He was sent straight back to rehab from the burial. It wouldn't surprise me if he's just in a rental somewhere and they've decided to live apart for a while. I don't trust anything they do anymore. Roll on passing my exams and hopefully getting to university."

"Have they gone quiet on your future marriage to a rich man?" Lucie raised a brow.

I shook my head. "It's still their main focus, but hopefully I can extricate myself from that and get to university. I need Eddie to take Dad's company into another stratosphere so they become so rich they no longer care about my potential marriage prospects and say I can have a few extra years. Then hopefully I can find a way to escape their clutches and opinions."

Petula came over at that point with a tea trolley and

she passed our coffees to each of us, followed by not only the pastries we'd ordered, but a few extra selections.

"Now you're spoiling us," Lucie admonished her good naturedly.

"Yeah, well, I've known you all a long time now." I watched as her eyes filled with tears. She sucked in a breath to compose herself. "I'd better get on, we're quite busy today," she added and then moved away.

"I wonder how long it will be until everyone can approach us again without deep looks of sympathy?" I asked the others.

Lucie's eyes went wide as the bell tinkled again. "Keep calm, we have incoming, and hold that thought, Phoebs."

I turned my head to see the Queen Bee herself, Ivy, walking towards us. I had to push my nails into my palms as she pulled out the fourth chair and sat down in it. Mentally, my hands were dragging her off the seat and punching her straight in the nose. Instead, I gave her nothing. Keeping my face a mask of blankness and calm.

Her face wore a false mask of sympathy while her eyes glittered in triumph at her actions. She knew exactly what she'd just done. I quickly flicked my gaze to Lucie and Renee and shook my head slightly. Whatever her game, this wasn't the time to deal with her. She seemed to have forgotten however that Liam had told her to back off from baiting me. That, or somehow, she had new ammunition herself. She made my skin crawl.

"I'm so very sorry about what happened to Flora," she simpered. "And to have seen it happen. To have not been able to protect your friend. It must be eating you up inside."

I wanted to stick my fork in her eyeball and while I stared at her I imagined doing exactly that. Twisting the tines while the blood ran down her face.

"Thank you for your sincere apology," I said in return. "You can slither back away to where you came from now."

Her head tilted to one side as she straightened up so she could attempt to look down on me. "The fact your friend's death was linked to her relationship with a rat means there's not as much support for your mummy's great idea now. There are rumblings in Richstone about whether it should be halted."

"You mean your father is stirring the pot again. Don't you get tired of being his puppet, Ivy?"

Her nostrils flared. I'd got to her with that insult. I'd note it for future reference. "I'm not his puppet. I'm his protegee. His empire will be my empire. I don't have to play second fiddle to a brother. I'm not offered out like some kind of whore to all the wealthy men of Richstone."

Her barbs landed where she'd aimed them. I inwardly felt a wince and knew my jaw had set, giving away the fact she was getting to me.

"You and your family won't be around here much longer. There are so many rumours circulating about your father. Has he left your mother? Tired of her games? Or has he been drinking too much of all that scotch he buys?"

"He's away on business," Renee stuck up for me.

"Is he? My father has been keeping a close eye on your family business and the rumours are it's not doing so well of late. Could this be a nail in another coffin, but this time it's the Ridleys?" She wrinkled her nose up. "Anyway, I must go. I don't want to be seen hanging around with you. See you Monday at school."

She pushed back her chair and gave a little wave. It was triumphant and she clearly thought she'd excelled in her little act.

"That fucking bitch. Why didn't you just let me throat punch her?" Renee almost growled.

"Because that's not how I'm dealing with her." I took a sip of my coffee. It was black, strong and much needed. I called Petula over asking her for a fresh cup for us all. Then I turned back to my friends.

"Ivy is all about image, status, and her role as Queen of Richstone. It's time she was forced to abdicate."

"Ooh, tell me more," Lucie said, and I began to see a spark of excitement in both my friends' gazes. Where the thought of vengeance began to push grief back just a little.

"Let's just wait for our fresh drinks and then we'll plot."

With hot new coffees on the table, I began to share my thoughts. "Our dear Flora always loved a makeover and I know that she is watching over me now getting excited about what I'm about to say." I swallowed because the thought brought a lump to my throat. "I'm going to finally stop being meek little Phoebe who just hangs with her best friends and sits on the sidelines hoping for a quiet life and to escape from Richstone. I think it's time I channelled my inner diva and took over Richstone Academy as their new Queen Bee. My mother heads that school and I shall rule the halls."

Lucie clapped her hands together. "Yes. Oh my god, yes. And we will be your ladies-in-waiting, or your princesses."

Renee chewed on her bottom lip. "Ivy's going to come out fighting and it'll be dirty."

"And we'll be ready for her. First though, I need a whole new look. I'm thinking highlights, and where Ivy has always modelled her fashion choices on Serena from *Gossip Girl*, it's time to pull out my inner Blair Waldorf."

"Anything you need from me, you got it," Lucie said. "And you're right, Flora would have loved this."

I gave a regretful nod. "All I need from you is your friendships. You stand by my side and I love you both hugely."

"Right back at you," Lucie said.

"I love you both. You're my lobsters," Renee added. "We need to brainstorm how we take over the rule of that school and I think I know how to start. With the party to end all parties. I'll book a private function room for a week on Saturday. I'll call the sports lounge or the sailing club. If all else fails, I'll hold it at my house. We'll call it a celebration of Flora's life and we'll use it to remind people of just how powerful we are."

I hesitated a moment. "Do you think people will find it weird if I go back to school on Monday with a new hairstyle and image? Should we have a period of mourning first?"

"Absolutely not," Renee replied. "Flora would be all over this makeover and while we're at it, please tell me we're going to ruin Ulric too."

"Oh for sure." I smirked. "But one at a time and hopefully when Ulric sees what we do to Ivy, he'll be watching over his shoulder. I said to Liam, Ulric needs to suffer. No quick take down for him."

"Did you see Liam yesterday? After the funeral?" she asked.

"Yes, for a short time. He's like we are: angry, grief-stricken, frustrated, lost. But he's determined to pass his exams. He now wants to be able to provide for the Prestons too."

"For a bad boy he sure seems to have a good heart," Lucie said.

"He thinks he doesn't. Believes he's broken, and the thing is he shouldn't be underestimated. Liam has shared with me what life in Sharrow was like. Knife crime, drugs. I think he's hurt people in the past. But he wants better. I just hope what has happened with Daniel doesn't cloud his future judgement."

It didn't feel right not being able to share with my friends the truth about the accident, and Liam's role in it all. But I just couldn't bring myself to add to their stress and grief. So for now I'd continue to let them think everything between Liam and myself was perfectly fine, even though bitterness burned through my veins.

We drank the rest of our coffee. Lucie and Renee

decided they'd have a restyle too, so while we were there we called Emily from *The Look Book*. It was her weekend off, but when faced with the prospect of a fantastic bonus for three urgent bookings, she agreed to visit us in turn over the weekend for restyles.

With more hugs we parted company and I made my way home, ready to call Bells, the Ridleys' personal shopper, to arrange the brand-new wardrobe to go with my new look.

Liam said he wanted to be left alone that night and in my fucked-up mind it stung a little as it would be the first night I'd not slept over there. I shouldn't care, but it had been the way I'd been able to sleep. Why was the man who'd started this tragedy the one person who I also found solace in? What was wrong with me?

I wanted to hate him.

I wanted to hurt him.

But he'd been by my side through what had happened with my father and this blurred my vision of vengeance.

6

Liam

When I woke with yet another headache from drinking, I cursed for more than one reason. Alcohol was not the answer to the hatred festering inside me. I needed healthier ways of letting out my grief and anger and from today I was done with the pity party for one.

Though I had to clutch my temple as I flung myself out of bed, I ignored the pain of the hangover, and took myself into the kitchen where I fixed myself a hearty breakfast and drank what felt like a gallon of orange juice, swallowing two painkillers while I was at it. I then opened windows, though I hissed as the bright sunlight hit me square in the eyes. I put the bottle into the recycling bin and tidied my shit up.

Then armed with a large bottle of water and a semi-fresh towel, I went across to the gym and put myself through a gruelling session, running on the treadmill, lifting weights, and doing boxing moves, although I didn't punch the bag given my knuckles were tender after yesterday's frenzy of my fists.

My mind flickered back to Phoebe as I'd taken her pressed up against the wall. That was another thing I needed to sort out. I'd promised Phoebe we'd take one day at a time, but since Flora and Daniel's deaths, nothing had been the same. We'd barely spoken to each other. I sent her a message saying I wanted to be on my own tonight. Phoebe needed to receive the message that I was no longer a warm body she could curl up with at night, and then leave in the day as if 'we' didn't exist. It was hard enough for me to try to put my trust in a person. I could feel my walls coming back up, rising against her, because she herself had shut down.

I understood. Probably more than anyone. But to shut me out after it took me so long to let anyone in, hurt. And Liam Lawson didn't do vulnerable. While I processed the loss of one of my best friends, I needed Phoebe either by my side, or away from me. I had no middle ground to offer her. No mental capacity for half measures.

We still needed to discuss what we were doing about Ulric, but it could wait for tomorrow. Because I'd decided that as soon as I was showered, I was going to Sharrow to talk to my mother. I'd not seen her since the day at my uncle's place when I'd beat up Vin. I'd refused to talk to her and instead checked in on things via my uncle. Last week she'd moved into a small studio flat. It was time for me to go see her and find out how she was doing and somehow try to form some kind of relationship with her again. She was my ma and despite the fact I'd said I was done, I couldn't turn my back on her. Losing Daniel and the resurfacing thoughts about my father's death had made me think of my mother a lot over the last two weeks.

Before I could change my mind, I picked up my phone and called her.

"William?"

"Yeah, it's me, Ma. How's the new place?"

"Small, but I'll make it work. It's not our home though. If you come back, they'll get us a bigger place."

I didn't respond to that. I hoped I'd never have to go back to Sharrow permanently.

"I thought I'd come say hi. If you were free for a visit today."

I heard the slight tremor of emotion in her voice as she said, "I'd love that."

"He won't be there, will he, Ma?"

"I've not seen Vin since you..." her voice trailed off.

"Is one o'clock okay? I could bring fish and chips."

Her laugh came down the phone. "You live in that fancy place now and you're bringing me fish and chips?"

I thought about Marjorie, the Ridleys' cook. She was incredible and kind and would make me anything I wanted. "What do you want, Ma? Lobster? Caviar?"

Another laugh. "Just you would be fine, but fish and chips sounds good too. You have endless possibilities, William, but I am and always will be a Sharrow girl."

I ended the call and went to get ready.

Being alone and in my own head gave me a lot of time to think. Walking over to the other side of the river I noted how much I'd changed in that small amount of time since I'd left. I might still wear my old clothes, but I didn't hold myself in the same way. I was more confident and less defensive. I didn't straighten myself up to let Sharrow know I was a force to be reckoned with. I walked straight because I knew what I'd put up with and other people's shit wasn't it.

I said hello to those who knew me and acknowledged me. Most acted like I'd never been anywhere else. A couple made smart-arsed comments about where my new Cartier watch or gold crown was, and a few looked at me with a new suspicion in their gaze. I didn't give a fuck. Their opinions weren't important or required. I was here for one reason only. To talk to my ma.

I called in for the fish and chips and grabbed a bottle of water and a couple of cans of coke to go with them and then went to find her new place. It was in a block of flats near an empty ex-industrial unit and thankfully away from being in walking distance of Sharrow's pubs. Not that it would stop my ma drinking if she was determined.

Her flat was on the ground floor and I went through the door to the main concrete lobby and knocked on the cheap, flimsy, red front door that I could break into with not much effort. She needed extra locks.

When she answered the door, I was pleasantly surprised. Ma was clean, presentable, and still sober.

With a hesitant smile she beckoned me inside, taking the offered bags from my hands and heading to the corner kitchenette area. It was one large room with the kitchenette and a small circular dining table at the far end, and a double bed and a small sofa at the other. A door led through to a tiny bathroom with a shower and small basin.

"It's not much, but it's my own and God only knows, Karl had certainly had enough of me by the time I left," she said.

I didn't comment. I just waited while she plated up the fish and chips. She took them to the table and grabbed salt, vinegar, and tomato sauce out of a small cupboard. "Do you want a cuppa with it? Bread and butter?"

"I'll drink a can of coke, but yes to a slice of bread and butter."

As she busied herself, I could almost pretend she was cured, normal, and my loving mother again. But it wasn't true. She was on her best behaviour right now and I'd bet if I looked in those kitchen cupboards I'd find a bottle in there.

I took a seat at the small table.

My mum looked at me with fondness. "Jeez, you can barely fit your legs under the table. I birthed a giant. I remember you laughing when you grew taller than your dad."

"Yeah, my six foot to his five foot ten. I remember the day I noticed, and he measured me and then I tapped him on the head and said I was the man of the house now."

"And he made a quip that you could work and pay the bills then."

"Yeah." It hadn't been long before he'd taken his own life. At fourteen I'd shot up like a runner bean plant.

"I miss him, Liam. Every day."

"Do you though?" I asked the question I'd always kept in my mouth, but it was like holding vomit in and I needed it out of me. "Because when you drink you tell me you regret him and regret me. Regret that pregnancy trapped you into marriage."

Her mouth fell open revealing small amounts of mushed chip. She swallowed it down. "I said that?"

"Many, many times."

"I'm sorry."

I shrugged.

"No, don't shrug, William. It's clear I've hurt you. You have to understand. I was young when I got caught with you. I'd had aspirations of working my way up to being an office manager. I'd been a receptionist when I'd met your dad. But instead, I became a mum and no matter how much I love you and loved your dad, I resented it in equal measure, because my life was no longer my own. I had to be a good wife for your dad, providing his dinners and keeping a good house, and a mum to you. And I disappeared. And then so did your dad. No matter what I did he stopped seeing me. Stopped seeing a lot of things..."

"We don't have to talk about this, Ma."

"I think we do. I think we should have had this conversation a long time ago. You're an adult now and you wouldn't have brought the subject up if you didn't want to know."

"If you loved him, why did you cheat on him?"

She sighed. "Because when I had a drink out with my friends away from your father and from you, I remembered the carefree girl I used to be. And I got attention from men where your dad had largely stopped noticing my existence beyond me handing him his dinner. And though I know now it was exhaustion from his job and his battling with depression, I was still young and foolish, Liam. I justified it as a way of coping. And when your dad came back to us, when his depression wasn't bad, I'd stop sleeping around. But eventually his periods of melancholy got longer and my reputation became more knowledgeable."

I watched as a tear ran down her cheek. "Even now, I don't know if he threw himself in front of that train because of what I did, my cheating, or whether it was his depression that was too much for him."

"The fact he didn't leave a note feels like it was more that he was tired of it all, Ma. That he'd gone down there on one of his walks and he'd just had enough."

"And it made me feel that I wasn't enough. We weren't enough for him to stay." Ma's cheeks were tear-ridden now and she used one of the chip shop's paper napkins to dry her eyes, though more tears fell to take their place.

"But that's the illness, isn't it?" I'd done my homework on the subject of depression while trying to make peace with my dad's loss.

"That's what they say, but I'll always wonder if I drove him to it. I did love him, Liam. It's just I wish we could have done things the right way. That I could have had my career first and had you when I was ready. When we were more secure, had the chance of a better future."

I stared at my mother. Maybe she'd also had her own dreams of leaving Sharrow behind?

She blew her nose and then got up. "I'm going to make a fresh cuppa. Sure you don't want one?"

"Go on then," I said. I didn't particularly want one, but I knew she needed to make the drinks while she composed herself.

When she sat back down sliding my cup of tea towards me, I expected her to move onto more banal subjects, but she didn't. "So I suppose you want to know about my drinking."

"I'll always hope you've stopped, Ma, but I'm beginning to think you probably won't."

"I'm still on the waiting list for treatment. I still drink a large bottle of cider every night. You've seen this place. I'm shit scared someone will break in and I've never lived alone before. The cider helps me sleep. But I'm not drinking in the day and I'm managing to get to work. Bernie understands. I told her about my alcohol issues a long time ago. She rosters me in and keeps me on a casual contract. I'm grateful to that woman because without her I'd not have kept a job and I know things would have been even worse."

"Well, it's not perfect, but it's a start, Ma. I'll go grab

some locks and shit after lunch and we'll get this place fixed up so you'll feel safer, okay?"

"That'd be grand, but you know it's likely I'll still drink myself to sleep, right?" Her voice was thick with emotion, and it twisted my stomach.

"One day at a time, Ma, hey? Let's get you feeling safer and let the doctors advise you."

"Just don't expect a miracle. I have a problem, an addiction."

"I know."

She took a deep swallow, clearly gathering herself together. "This talk has been good. For me anyway. Felt long overdue."

I nodded.

"Don't be a stranger, will you? You've always been too big for Sharrow. I hope you achieve everything you've ever wanted but be careful. I can't imagine being in Richstone has been easy."

I told her a little about my new life in Richstone, and then we spoke of Daniel. Finally, I left and bought the things she needed from the hardware store and I added a can of pepper spray and an attack alarm to my purchases.

I spent the rest of the afternoon fixing locks to her doors and windows and doing a couple of other DIY jobs she needed doing, like fixing a new blind up in the bathroom, and then I left. I hugged her as I went and her eyes filled with tears once more.

"I'll ring you," I said, not specifying when because I honestly didn't know. I'd made the effort I felt I'd needed to make and now I wanted my own space again to think, to reflect on the day.

When I finally got back, I called through to the main house and asked Marjorie for 'anything wholesome'.

"Sounds like you're back with us, Mr Lawson. That's good to hear because I've been worried."

I liked Marjorie. She was only really a voice on a phone, but she had the whole bossy granny vibe going for her. "Yeah, time for me to start looking after myself, so anything with a good selection of veg, except…"

"Sweetcorn. You think I don't remember? I make it my business to learn about you kids and make sure at least your nutritional needs are provided for."

"You're a superstar and an amazing cook."

"Yeah, yeah. Get off the line now, before my head doesn't fit in this kitchen anymore, and let me get to work."

After ending the call, I threw myself down on the living room sectional and stretched out, resting my head on a cushion. I noted the silence once more. The thing I loved most about the bungalow. My itinerary now was food, a film, an early night, and certainly no alcohol. Tomorrow was another day and there were two days before our return to Richstone Academy.

I picked up my phone.

Liam: Hope you had a good day. Want to come over tomorrow to talk about Richstone Academy and revenge?

Her reply didn't take long to arrive.

Phoebe: Yep. Will need to be tomorrow evening though. I have plans in the daytime.

Liam: Oh yeah...

Phoebe: All will be revealed. Also, Eddie is back tomorrow and I want to check in with him about the business.

Liam: Shall we say around eight? We can eat here.

Phoebe: I look forward to it. Eight pm it is.

I hated the satisfied smile that laid upon my lips as I put my phone down. I had to keep a distance. Had to. Needed to remember how easily people could hurt you. And my priority here in Richstone had to be in finding my ticket out of here, not Phoebe.

It had to be.

I owed it to myself and I owed it to Daniel.

If I could get the girl too, that would be a bonus. But financial independence came first.

And right now, revenge held a strong joint second place next to Phoebe Ridley.

It was just how it had to be right now.

7

Phoebe

When my mother sat down to eat her dinner on Friday evening, I noted her surprise as I walked in.

"Oh, I was hoping for a quiet dinner after a busy day at work, but it seems that's not to be the case."

I didn't know how I could ever have believed that my mother actually loved me. I'd just always thought rich people had nannies and other entourage around them and it was all normal. After all, her and my father had made a huge fuss of me and Eddie at parties and other outings. I'd never known it was all fake. That she'd had children clearly to fit in and to give my father heirs. My teenage years and young adulthood were a steep learning curve.

I pulled up a chair at the side of her. "I'm not staying. I just have a collaboration idea to run past you."

"Oh?" She raised a brow while looking completely disinterested and took another spoonful of soup.

"I'm taking Ivy Sackville down once and for all. I intend to rule the halls of Richstone Academy."

That got her attention enough that she placed down her soup spoon and wiped her mouth with a napkin.

"Why now? How? And what does that have to do with me?"

"Now because I'm sick of hiding in the shadows and I'm done with letting Ivy walk all over me. How, I'm starting with a complete makeover and Renee is going to host a party like Richstone has never seen to cement us as the elite and make Ivy look like she comes from Sharrow in comparison. I also have other tricks up my sleeve, but I'll speak to you about those nearer the time. You're still going ahead with the memorial service for Flora and Daniel on Tuesday, yes?"

"Indeed. Now you all will be back in school we shall pay our respects to them both, and of course make it clear that anyone affected by these issues can approach any member of staff for support."

"Whatever. I need the go ahead to spend money on a hair restyle and a wardrobe makeover. Your investment will be reflected in the fact I'm going to be a much higher commodity as a potential trophy wife."

"Just make sure Hector Sackville doesn't come giving me grief that you're bullying his daughter."

"Oh, he won't. Don't you worry."

"Very well. If the party will be next Saturday night,

then make yourself available for a dinner with a potential suitor on Friday."

I began to open my mouth, but she held up a hand. "Until there is evidence that our fortunes are recovered, you will continue to have these dinners. I'm bankrolling your makeover, so like you said, we'll show off your worth."

I pushed back my chair and stood up. "Great chatting with you, Daphne, as always."

"Phoebe."

I turned back around to see what she wanted.

"Good luck with Ivy. I'd like nothing finer than to watch Hector Sackville fall from grace and maybe the start of that is via his daughter."

I walked out of the room without replying.

On Saturday morning, Emily came and restyled my hair in the comfort of my own home. No longer chestnut brown, I rocked honey waves. I'd kept it long, but Emily had cut it and coloured it so that it swished and shone. I had to admit, it really suited me.

Bells arrived for lunch. I'd asked Marjorie to prepare us something light to eat first. Having been here a million times before, Bells tucked straight into the mini buffet on the dining table.

"I'm so fucking excited to get you in these clothes. We're going all out, babe. Queen Bee with a definite capital Q and B. In fact, QUEEN BEE in full on shout-it-from-the-rooftop capitals and you will so see how I am *the* best stylist in all of Richstone with my little accessories. It's sure to have the required effect on Ms Sackville. Hateful cow. She's never realised why most of the things her own stylist shows her are usually brown, black and cream."

My mouth slackened. "What? Are you serious? It's not an aesthetic?"

"No, Viola hates her with a passion and so styles her in the colours of the cow she is."

I burst out laughing. Bells always had great tales to tell.

Following lunch, we went up to my room where she showed me the most incredible wardrobe of clothes. Things that mixed and matched and were smart for school but had an edge.

"And look at this necktie." Bells revealed a cream silk tie with a delicate bee motif. "It goes with almost all of these outfits, and..." she opened up a box and showed a brooch with a matching bee.

"Oh my god, you nailed it." I clapped my hands together. "Ivy is so gone, de-throned."

"I also took the liberty of bringing two smaller versions of the brooch. They're slightly different."

I flung my arms around her and squeezed her tightly. "Bells, you are incredible."

"We already know that, but I love to keep hearing it anyway. That's not all."

"Seriously, there's more?"

Opening a small box, Bells revealed three cream

silk handkerchiefs that matched my necktie. Each had a bee motif. The same one but different to the one on my tie.

"I know you'll miss Flora incredibly. She was an amazing girl. This way you can carry the missing bee with you at all times and if you shed a tear for her, she'll be proud you let it seep into a silk hankie and not a common tissue."

I sob-laughed. I really didn't know whether to laugh or cry as I picked up one of the handkerchiefs and held it in my hand.

Finally, she handed me a small memory stick. "This contains mock-ups of all the potential outfits you have here. You can not only refer to them yourself but can send them to Renee and Lucie so you can all coordinate. And my work here is done," she announced with a flourish of her arms. "Thank you for lunch. I must scoot; only I had to squeeze you in, and my next client will be waiting."

"Thank you, Bells. You're a true friend."

"I am, and never forget that, Phoebe. If you ever need a shoulder, just call me. I know more than most how fake this place is."

She hugged me again and then I showed her out of the door.

"You are far too friendly with the paid help." My mother's voice sounded out from behind me.

"That's rich coming from someone who fucked her client," I retorted and turned to walk past her.

Crossing her arms, she looked down her nose at me.

"I like this new Phoebe. She has passion. I'm sure Friday's suitor will like it too."

"And who is the lucky guy this week?" I sighed.

She smirked. "Ulric McDowell."

Time stood still for a second as my mind ricocheted with what she'd just said.

"Not a chance in hell," I gritted out. "You are kidding me, right? He killed Flora. He killed my friend."

"Think about it. What better way to have your revenge than to marry him and make him miserable until he gives you a divorce with a decent pay off?"

I closed the space between us "You're a sick bitch. You know that?" My voice shook with anger.

"I just look for opportunities, Phoebe, and I don't let my emotions get in the way of them. You'd be wise to learn from me."

She walked away. I kept myself composed until I reached my bedroom where I punched my mattress so hard I went dizzy and breathless. At that point I let it all go; let out my tears of frustration and tears of loss. Then I once more pushed it all down deep inside and put away my new outfits and accessories and messaged my friends, talking about Monday.

As he'd anticipated, my brother arrived home around four. He popped his head around my door and said he needed to grab a quick shower and would I order him some food up to my room and he'd chat with me while he ate. His face gave nothing away, but I guessed he had nothing good to tell me. If he had, I'd have known it. I knew my brother and the way he wore good news.

He came in looking fresh. At some point since I'd last seen him, his light-brown hair had been trimmed and tidied. I got up and hugged him tight.

"Check you out," he quipped. "No disrespect but I thought you'd be dressed in black and morose. This is a pleasant surprise. The new hair suits you."

We sat on the sofa in my room, and he ate his food while I got him up to speed with my plans. Then it was his turn. "As I'm sure you've worked out by my lack of sheer joy, nothing came from the trip. I'm worried because the rumours are starting to circulate and there's the chance someone could mount a hostile takeover and grab the company out of our hands."

"Fuck."

"Indeed. And while that would free me, it means you're still in danger of Mummy Dearest showing you blowing the rat if you don't play ball."

I sighed, my shoulders slumping. "Maybe it's just time to let them do their worst, Eddie. Perhaps we should just walk away?"

"Not yet. It's not over yet. I have other people to meet, and you need to concentrate on your studies."

"I can take my exams anywhere."

"I know you can, but with whatever fallout our mother and father might cause it could affect your studies. Just carry on playing the game for a while. Something will come good. I just know it."

I blew out a breath, rattling my lips. "Yeah, okay. I'll put up with her a bit longer. I mean other than asking me to lick Flora and Daniel's blood up off the street, she's done her worst setting me up with Ulric. Surely she's nothing else to punish me with for now."

"She's deplorable and we will get away from her, from them, I promise. Hey, at least we have each other."

"True. Plus, I shall use being at Ulric's to my advantage. Try to get some good information on him that I can use to destroy him."

Eddie put his hand over mine. "Don't let your anger over what happened to your friends ruin the beautiful person that is Phoebe Louisa Ridley. There are enough bitter and twisted psychopaths in Richstone."

Angry tears came to my eyes. "But I hate him. And her. And him."

Eddie knew I meant Ulric, and my mother and father.

"We'll be rid of them one way or another and then they'll be a small echo of the past. Leaving us to live our lives how we want to live them."

"I hope so."

"So anyway, how goes it with the fancy man you have stationed in the bungalow? I never thought to ask Mother if I could keep a sex slave in there. I could kick myself for not thinking of it first."

I elbowed him, "Shut up."

He rubbed his arm and laughed.

"Liam's okay. Going through his own shit. But I'm seeing him later." For a moment, I wondered about confessing what I'd discovered about Liam and how it made me feel, but my brother had enough on his plate with the business.

"Right," he ruffled the hair on the top of my head like I was about five. "I'm going to go meet Rodrick and Harry and sink some good quality beer."

He left me to it, and I sat pondering what to wear to Liam's.

Something that comes off easily, was the answer that sprung to mind.

8

Liam

The moment she came through the door I craved being inside her beyond words. She'd had something new done to her hair and she looked even more beautiful than usual. I dragged her inside by her arm and picked her up. Her legs fixed around my waist as I walked us both into my bedroom, throwing her on top of the mattress and then kicking the door closed behind me.

It was fast and without ceremony. She kicked off her shoes and I peeled off her trousers and pants, removing my own lower clothing before sinking deep inside her. My hands fisted in her hair and hers held my arse, while I drove into her over and over. Our mouths feasted on the other's, chasing an answer to the hunger inside us both. Eventually we fell apart, our chests rising and falling with speed. My heart beat fast in my chest and I felt exhilarated.

My hand lifted up a piece of her hair. "This is new. I like it."

She smiled. "That's what I've been doing today. Re-inventing myself as the new Queen of Richstone Academy."

"Huh?"

I listened as she filled me in on how she was going to dethrone Ivy. I smiled through the makeover part though I couldn't care less about clothes and new shades of hair colour, even if it did suit her. Inside though, I felt a sense of unease. I liked Phoebe precisely because she wasn't like the majority of the Richstone residents with their superiority and smugness.

"Sounds great, but I dealt with Ivy, with the video."

Phoebe hutched up against the headboard, her face a mask of annoyance where a moment before there'd been pleasure.

"To a certain extent. However, she came and sat with us yesterday morning as we drank coffee, while she gave us her faux sympathy about Flora and sat in the fourth chair."

"Oh." I knew how that would have felt having stared at our own fourth chair after the funeral.

"Yes, oh. So she joins the list of people I'm going to destroy."

"As long as Ulric is our main target."

Her eyes narrowed on me. "I've not forgotten who's responsible for my friend's death."

As her eyes landed on mine it felt like she was talking about me and guilt consumed my being. But she didn't know I blamed myself for Daniel and Flora's deaths alongside Ulric.

"Sometimes I wish we'd never come here. They'd both still be alive," I confessed. I took her chin in mine, "but then I wouldn't have met you."

Her eyes bored into me like she was searching for something, but then she sighed. It was like a deep drag on an unlit cigarette where no satisfaction came from it. Once again, I felt a sliver of uncomfortableness.

"Phoebe. Changing your appearance and taking on this 'bad girl' persona. Is that about revenge or is it about you not wanting to be the Phoebe you were before, because that Phoebe couldn't protect her friend? Is this some kind of armour?"

"Jesus fucking Christ. I came here for a fuck, not therapy," she snapped.

I felt like she'd slapped me. I certainly wasn't lying next to the girl I'd fallen for over the past few months. Instead, I was with someone bitter and angry. Her grief had moved into somewhere between rage and resentment and as I recalled experiencing this all when my dad died, I knew that she was being like this with me because she felt she could. I was the person she could snap at; someone who would allow her to do what she needed.

Moving myself, I grabbed her chin hard and turned her face towards me. "You came here just to be fucked. Fine. Let me know when you've had enough."

I turned her over, so her face was in the pillow and pushed her knees up, parting her thighs. I knelt between them and once more thrust my dick inside her, riding her over and over. Pushing two digits into her puckered hole, I held her with my other hand via her new shiny hair. Phoebe wouldn't leave here a pampered princess. She'd leave here a well ridden mess. As her climax approached, she almost mewled, desperate to get her release, but I pulled out before it came. She turned herself back over, looking at me with the haughty expression she did so well.

"You said you came to be fucked. Didn't say you came for orgasms." I smirked. Now it was my turn to come out on top, literally. I lifted her leg up over my shoulder as I once more entered her. It excited me to watch her expression as she got close. The desperation in her features. "Eyes open and on me if you want to come, Fifi."

Those amber eyes held pleading and desperation while the rest of her face scowled. She was nothing short of adorable.

"Say please."

Another scowl. "Please."

"Please what?"

"Please can I punch you in the face?" she ground out.

I flicked her clit lightly in punishment.

"Sorry, I can't hear you."

Desperation won over her annoyance. "Please can I come? Please make me come, Liam. I can't take it."

"Oh I think you're taking it just fine," I said as I upped my pace, and pinched and rubbed her clit until she exploded around me.

But I didn't stop. I moved her from position to position until she begged me to quit.

"But you came here for a fuck." I repeated her own words.

"I'm fucked good. I'm sure I won't be able to walk."

I laughed and rode her one last time until I pulsed inside her.

"I'll go warm up the pizza," I said, withdrawing my dick and climbing off the bed. I was damned if I was doing cuddles and aftercare when she'd been such a bitch. I didn't look at her expression as I headed to the bathroom first to clean myself up, but I hoped she'd realise I'd come out on top, literally and figuratively.

The pizza was almost done by the time she came out into the kitchen/diner. She'd got back dressed and I watched as she pulled out a stool and climbed up. "Well, I've certainly got an appetite now, though sitting is more of a challenge than usual." She was avoiding eye contact with me and I was starting to feel irritated.

"Look, I know you don't want 'therapy' as you put it, but we've not talked properly since it happened, Phoebe. We need to. I can't talk to Brett and Marlon about this the same way I can with you."

"What's there to say?" She shrugged. "They're dead. Talking won't bring them back. It just hurts."

I placed the pizza on plates and slid Phoebe's across to her, before placing mine in front of my own seat. I grabbed some cans of Coke and put them on the table along with a carafe of water and a glass. Phoebe's eyebrow arched.

"We do have water in Sharrow, you know? It's not beyond my capabilities to set some out on a table."

"I'm sorry. Looks like I'm a true riches after all."

I had to do something to break what was happening between us right now. It was like a fissure on the ground that threatened to widen, and I needed to find a way to correct the fault. So I changed the subject.

"I went to see my ma yesterday."

Her eyes widened. "You did? And how was she?"

I told her about the visit, about how Ma seemed to be making an effort.

"But I just don't trust it, Phoebe. I can't. We've been here before. Something will happen and she'll reach for the alcohol more, not get to work again. It's just what she does."

"And she still has months to wait for treatment?"

"Yes, and there's nothing to say she'd stick to it anyway. At least Uncle Karl has some peace again now though."

"Yeah, I bet he's ecstatic to have his own space again."

The conversation dwindled off and I hated it, wanted it back to how it had been before the deaths of our friends.

"So how have things been with your mum?"

Phoebe took a bite of her pizza and chewed while considering her response. She swallowed. "Tense. That's the best way of describing it. We know we're stuck at an impasse and until things change to swing the power one way or the other that's how it will stay. Eddie says there's no good news about the business and so the games go on. She's already booked a dinner date for my next potential husband and she excelled herself on this occasion."

Her eyes met mine and I knew who it was without her even uttering the words.

I ground my teeth before I was able to open my mouth to speak. "Your mother will pay. For every single thing she does to you. For treating you not only like a commodity but as a chew toy. She knows how much this will hurt and she does it anyway."

But Phoebe didn't look angry herself. She actually looked empowered. "At first, I was so enraged, but then I realised that in actual fact she showed she's desperate. I mean Ulric already did the worst he could possibly do to me. My having dinner with him will surely punish him more than me? I'm seeing it as an opportunity to do some digging and to get a feel of how I can get revenge. Maybe I can even pretend to forgive him and give him a false sense of security first?"

"We speak about this and make the plans together," I insisted.

"I'll go on the dinner and we can take it from there."

"When is it?"

"Friday. Oh, and Saturday we're holding a party. Me, Lucie, and Renee. To celebrate Flora's life, we're throwing the ultimate of parties in her honour. Part of our new status as the uber elite of the school."

"I feel like your plans aren't including me, Phoebe," I warned. I was hurting too. I needed vengeance too.

She shrugged. 'The fact remains that while my mother has me playing her games, I can't be seen with you. I have a role to play. I know we said, 'one day at a time' and that we wanted to see where we went as a couple and that's not changed for me, Liam. But what has changed is that I'll do whatever it takes to bring down those who have hurt me, who've treated me like shit, and that especially includes Ulric." Her eyes landed on mine once more and they were cold as ice, calculating. In that moment there was no doubting whose daughter she was as I saw a younger Daphne staring at me.

"Just as you got Ivy to suck your dick in the name of revenge, I'll do what I need to do, and you need to know that, Liam."

My fists clenched. "What are you saying, Fifi?"

"I'm saying that if I need to suck a dick to get my revenge, I'll do it. I'll do whatever it takes. And just as I accepted it when you showed me the video of you and Ivy, I expect the same from you."

"I will want to kill them." My hands curled into tight fists at the thought of someone else with Phoebe.

She smiled, and it chilled me to the bone.

I loved the fire inside her, but I feared for her, because I'd been raised on deceit and disappointment, unlike Phoebe. She was an innocent. Yes, her parents were a pile of shit, but she had a naivety from the life she'd led. I just couldn't see this new femme fatale/Queen Bee idea being anything other than a façade, and when the real Phoebe was re-revealed, how would she fare?

However, as she said, I'd done what I'd done to Ivy and so I couldn't protest even though I wanted to. Even though it would kill me inside if she let anyone else inside her.

Because she was mine.

"I won't like it, but I accept it. As long as you remember whose bed you belong in."

"You say that, but you didn't want me here last night, Liam, and I don't need your acceptance. Now is there any pizza left? I am absolutely starving."

I nodded and went to fetch her another slice, happy to be able to turn away from her. Because I had not only a deep sense of foreboding about the months ahead, but I also once again felt I had to protect myself against Phoebe. She'd just openly declared that her vengeance came before me. Just as I'd thought the same about her.

I didn't see how we could ever make our way out of this together. Events had already changed us both, and what I wanted in my future: power and money, were what Phoebe seemed to greatly despise.

Her words came back to me once more.

One. Day. At. A. Time.

And for now, it was time to eat pizza and try to find some kind of new normal between us.

After that, the evening got a little easier. I had a couple of cans of beer and Phoebe drank a few glasses of wine. It seemed to relax her. She lost her prickliness and I wondered if she had just built up her own walls after the tragedy to try to stop from hurting so much. I had to be patient with her. Phoebe wasn't used to the darkness, whereas I could almost call it a friend. We talked about anything and everything, and by the time we went to bed it felt more like the old 'us', the boy and girl from opposite worlds who'd found common ground. We spoke of school and how we'd cope with the mention of our friends. Talked about the memorial service and more about the party. When we went to bed I pulled her into my arms.

"I'm sorry for saying I wanted to be alone the other night. When I woke in the night and you weren't there I regretted it."

"It's okay. We're back at school now. There'll be times I can't stay over, especially with the exams being so close. We're going to need to study. But it also means our exams will soon be over and hopefully we can make plans for the future." She fell asleep curled in my arms and it no longer felt that despite her closeness there was still a vast space between us. It felt more like she was back where she belonged.

On Sunday we rose leisurely and I fixed us a cooked breakfast and lots of coffee.

"What are your plans for today then?" I asked Phoebe.

"Catch up on schoolwork is unfortunately the order of the day."

"Same. I want to make sure I pass these exams and pass them with the highest marks I can," I confessed.

"Well, that will be music to Daphne's ears. Anything that makes her seem like the creator of miracles."

"If you need help with maths, we could do that tonight?"

Phoebe sighed. "I'd much rather have a repeat of last night."

"Sorry, darlin'" I drawled. "Tonight, the only figures I'll be studying are the ones that come in equations."

"We'll see," she threatened as she rose to leave. But it felt a lot more like a promise than a threat.

When she left, the bungalow seemed entirely vast, quiet and lost. It had been the strangest evening, with first Phoebe's hostility and all these revenge plans, though things felt better now. Like we would get back to how we were before.

For a moment I just stood there realising that I didn't have the first clue who I was anymore. Who was this guy who worried what a girl thought? Jesus, I'd probably grown a vagina.

I went to dig out my study books because though I might not know who I was right now, I knew who I wanted to be.

And passing my exams was my path to success.

9

Phoebe

Monday morning arrived and I woke with butterflies deep in my stomach. The kind of feeling you got when you were going on holiday, a mix of excitement about the prospects of relaxation and good food, but with an underlying unease about being on an aeroplane and in the sky for hours. I'd not gone back to Liam's last night. I'd told him I wanted to get ready from my own bedroom, which was partly true, but I also wanted to reject him like he had me. Though I hated being under the same roof as my mother, I needed to learn independence for the day when I left all this behind.

I checked in with Renee and Lucie that they were prepared and ready, and then I got myself showered and dressed. I could barely eat a slice of the toast I'd asked

Marjorie for. Even my coffee felt like it was choking me. Thank God, my mother had already gone to work.

My phone beeped and made me jump. I was so on edge.

Stefan: How are you doing?

Though we didn't talk as much since our parents had distanced themselves from each other, we still checked in from time to time and I appreciated his text that morning.

Phoebe: Okay. But it's going to be weird. I know that.

Stefan: You know where I am if you need me.

Phoebe: Thank you xoxo

Driving to school I played Lizzo's *Good as Hell* and sang along to both psych myself up and distract myself while I made my way to Richstone Academy's student car park where I pulled my car in alongside Renee and Lucie's. They stepped out of theirs as I did mine.

I took in my friends' new looks. They'd sent snaps to my mobile phone, but it wasn't the same as seeing the finished product in real life.

Renee's hair was a dark chocolate brown. Glossy, it had been cut so it hung in waves. She was wearing an emerald-green wrap dress that hugged her curves. She looked sensational. Lucie's hair was now a razor-cut mid-length bob in cherry-red. She wore a black cotton shirt-dress and green wedges.

I had on black cropped slacks and an emerald-green blouse with my bee necktie. Going into my purse, I handed my friends their handkerchief and their brooch. We placed the hankies in our bags and put on our brooches. Water threatened all our lower lashes as we became emotional.

"Time to go sting the bitch," Lucie said through a brave and smug looking grin.

"But bees die when they sting, don't they?" Renee protested and my thoughts immediately went back to Flora. Would this happen every time the word death was mentioned now?

"Not all bees," Lucie said. "Now come on. This is for Flora, looking down on us laughing that she got us made over even if she wasn't physically present."

"And also for the complete satisfaction of destroying the current King and Queen of Richstone. Why we put up with them for so long, I don't know, but enough. If that bitch can't give genuine sympathy for us losing our friend, she deserves to be ruined," I declared.

We high-fived each other and made our way into school.

It felt like a movie. Like we moved as a unit in slo-mo, looking fabulous. Other pupils gawped at us as we walked in. No doubt because they knew we were the best friends of the dead girl. I could also see the enquiring looks where some pupils raised brows at each other as they took in our outfits and the fact we were groomed to perfection.

And that we'd just strode into school like we owned it.

The usual crowd of Ivy, Ulric, The Poisons, and

Ulric's friends hung around just outside the main school entrance. The satisfaction when Ivy noticed it was us approaching fired me up inside as I watched her close her mouth and a sneer come to her face.

"Wow. Phoebe found her straighteners. Have you heard the saying about not being able to make a silk purse from a sow's ear though?" Her eyes met her friends seeking approval for her putdown. Of course they gave it, little titters erupting like the puppets they were.

I smiled at her as her narrowed eyes met mine. "Yes, Ivy, I've heard the same, frankly unoriginal retort from you a zillion times before because you never have anything new or noteworthy to say. You're just so completely... boring." I flicked my hair, smiled at my own best friends and we linked arms and strolled through the entrance hearing the low sniggers emitted by Ulric's friends behind us.

We got straight to work. As soon as anyone approached us with their condolences, they were immediately told of Saturday night's party. By that time Lucie had decided there would be a fundraising auction at the end of the party too, with money going to a charity that supported people through bereavement.

"Oh that's an amazing thing to do. It's so terrible what happened to Flora and this way not only can you celebrate your friend's life, but other people can be helped in her honour," Tamsin Wheaton droned on. She was one of The Poisons and I'd take bets was here in no other capacity but to fact find.

"I trust we can count on your support then?" I stood

tall and stared as imposingly as I could muster down at the curly-haired blonde girl. "Because if Ivy does anything to try to spoil this party and you have any involvement in it, there'll be hell to pay."

"Y- yes, of course." Tamsin clutched at her blouse. "I really am so sorry for your loss. I liked Flora a lot."

Feeling guilty about my threat, I softened my voice. "It's none of my business, but I don't know why you hang with Ivy and let her push you around so much. Your family is just as wealthy as hers, yet you let her treat you like some servant or court jester. You can do better."

"Ivy's a good friend," Tamsin protested.

"Is she? Oh, forget I mentioned it then. It must have been someone else she was saying she could get to do all her dirty work for her. Anyway," I squeezed her arm. "We look forward to seeing you on Saturday."

"Wh- what? Oh, okay, yes." Tamsin walked away looking dejected.

"Did you really hear Ivy say such a thing?" Renee asked.

"Of course not, but it's exactly what she does. I'm just making Tamsin uber-aware of that fact, because as Ivy gets increasingly agitated with our popularity, she'll be ordering her friends around more than ever."

"Is anyone else having the best fun?" Lucie announced. "Only I dreaded this day, the looks of sympathy we'd get, but it's actually okay. The best it could be under the circumstances."

"And we've only just begun." I smirked and we headed off towards our first lessons. I'd yet to see Liam or

Brett this morning and I wondered how things were going for them.

It turned out, the answer was not so well. As they walked into the canteen at lunchtime, Liam and Brett looked like they were ready to compete for some major boxing trophy. Both of them had clenched fists and wary, hostile gazes. Most people gave them a wide birth. But there were a few who seemed to have either rewritten history or heard the wrong version of events because they were shouting out things like, 'that's another one gone', that Daniel had been a murderer, and they 'weren't surprised he offed himself', and more to that effect.

Liam sat himself opposite me.

"I won't ask if you're okay."

"No, don't, because I'm far from fucking okay. Some of these cunts think Daniel was responsible for Flora's death. My fucking amazing friend Daniel. What's the point of a memorial service about him tomorrow, huh? It's Sharrow versus Richstone all over again. Flora will probably get a sainthood."

'Well, Flora didn't actually do a fucking thing wrong," I spat out.

"And Daniel did? What did he do, except fall in love with your friend?"

"Cool it, you two, people are looking, and by people, I mean Ivy Sackville, who is heading this way. I hope it's worth her efforts as it's taken her all morning to gather her strength since your last diss."

I took a deep breath as Ivy walked over like she was doing some great civic duty. I was surprised she didn't get The Poisons to put a ribbon over the school entrance each morning for her to cut before she walked inside.

"Hey, Phoebe. Just to let you know that Daddy said whatever the main prize is at the auction, he's prepared to better it." She placed a business card on the table and slid it across to me using her index finger. "Here's his direct telephone number. He passes on his regret once more for Flora's death and says he'd like to help in whatever way he can."

"That's extremely generous of him. Thank you." I looked away dismissing her, but she wasn't finished.

"His only condition is that I stand on the stage and offer the final prize. It's only fair seeing as it's coming from my family, don't you think?"

God, she never stopped. Even had to hijack a memorial party and make it all about her. Well, that worked for me.

I smiled at her as if I was giving sympathy to someone moaning over a broken false nail. "That's fine. We'll be more than happy to have you on stage for that most generous donation. I'll phone Hector to discuss before we go ahead and finalise our plans."

"Perfect." Ivy waltzed off.

"You're not really letting her steal the show Saturday, are you?" Lucie hissed.

"Some people need to be careful what they wish for."

I grinned in what I hoped was an enigmatic manner. I didn't know what I'd do yet, but I'd make sure she regretted asking for the limelight.

"I do like the new Phoebe. She has some lady balls," Lucie laughed.

As I shrugged my shoulders, feeling pleased with myself, I saw Liam watching me. Although I knew he was pissed at the day's events so far, it seemed to me that his anger was somehow directed at me too. Did he really think I was on my way to becoming one of Richstone's clone women, just because I'd had a makeover and had a plan for revenge?

You don't care what he thinks, Phoebe, I reminded myself.

"So has anyone else noticed that Ulric has kept his head down today?" Renee said. I followed her gaze to where he sat in a corner with his friends, rather than at the main table with Ivy. I'd completely ignored him, but as if he felt my eyes on his, he looked up and over, our eyes meeting. He put his head back down and that was it. I was up and out of my seat and storming over towards him.

He didn't notice me again until I was standing just feet in front of him. "Ph- Phoebe."

"Stand on your fucking chair," I demanded.

'Wh- what?"

"If you have any remorse in your body, stand on that fucking chair and tell everyone here what happened, because right now, Daniel is being blamed for my best friend's death and that is not what is going to happen here. There will be a memorial service tomorrow where both Flora and Daniel will be mourned. You fucking killed her."

"It was an accident, Phoebe." Ulric's eyes filled with tears.

"Is that what you're telling yourself so you can sleep at night, Ulric? Because it's not what I remember. Stand on the chair or I'll make you wish you were never born."

"I- I can't."

"This is some bullshit." I slammed my hands down hard on the table in front of him.

"I- I'm having therapy because—"

"Oh my fucking god, are you kidding me? Am I supposed to feel sympathy for you?" My breath stuttered as I demonstrated my incredulousness.

Liam's voice came from behind me. "Phoebe, come and sit back down. He's not worth it."

"Everyone will know exactly who you are," I ground out. "If it's the last thing I do, they will all know."

I turned and walked away. I hoped this morning had given the King and Queen some warning of what was to come, but really, they didn't have a clue.

"What have I told you about us making plans together about what we do to him?" Liam whispered to me out of the corner of his mouth as we walked back. Some eyes were on us while others pretended not to pay any attention to my recent outburst. "I could have easily ended a dozen people today, but I'm waiting for the right moment to show these bastards. I want Ulric's head on a stick, there for all to see as the murdering bastard he is."

"You're right." I whispered back. "Emotions got the better of me. I'm okay now. Let's go sit back down and eat the rest of our lunch."

"Before we do, I need to tell you something. Something important that happened last night. I've been trying to find a chance to get you on your own."

"Oh yeah?" I had no clue what he was talking about.

"Ivy had an envelope pushed through my letterbox. She offered me ten thousand pounds cash for me to delete my video."

"Wow," I shook my head in disbelief. "She's such a piece of shit. How did she react when you told her to go fuck herself?"

Hesitation flickered across Liam's face a moment before he straightened his body. "Actually, I called her on the number she'd left on the note and told her I'd be delighted. Along with the money from Ulric's father, that's fifteen thousand pounds saved for getting out of here."

I stared at him a moment before replying. "I suppose so." I didn't speak of my annoyance that the person who'd just given me shit for not making plans with him had once again gone ahead and made his own decisions. Seemed it showed on my face though.

"Don't pout, pretty girl. The video served its purpose, and she knows if she tries anything smart, I'll just organise a repeat. Only it would be ten times worse."

"You say the sweetest things." My voice was laced with heavy sarcasm.

"I don't know why you're so pissed off. It's not like

you don't have your own revenge plans organised for her."

I sighed. "You're right. I'm just frustrated that's all. I feel like they get away with everything, both of them, and enough is enough."

"They're not getting away with anything. But these things take time, Phoebe."

I nodded. "I'm going to the bathroom. Tell the girls to dispose of the rest of my lunch. I lost my appetite," I said, and I walked away.

While I wore a great disguise of someone who looked ready to take charge, inside I was hurting. Still mourning my friend, and still so worn down by the fact that the riches felt everything was solved by money and therapy. Frustrated because usually they were damn right.

But not this fucking time.

This time they would pay, and it wouldn't just be financially.

10

Liam

Lucie and Renee moved to stand up as I walked back over to the lunch table.

"Is she okay? Where's she gone?" Renee asked.

"Bathroom. Leave her to it. She's frustrated and just needs a moment. Ulric has no remorse over his actions, just sees it as an accident. It's fucked her off. She'll be fine in a few. Gone to collect herself and get ready for the afternoon. She said could you clear the rest of her lunch away. She lost her appetite."

They finished their lunch and headed off after clearing their own crap away. I heard footsteps approaching from behind me shortly after and spun around with a face full of thunder expecting some more shit about Daniel. Instead, I found myself staring at Casey, the girl from the party at Ulric's house who I'd got drunk and used so I could get my revenge on Bailey Trainor, Ulric's arsehole friend.

I stared at the petite blonde. Her baby-blue eyes were wide and I dropped my ferocious gaze. "Sorry, Casey. Been getting some hostility today about things."

Brett side-eyed me as he looked to Casey and back to me again, clearly wanting the lowdown on who the new chick was and how I knew her.

"I just wanted to offer my condolences about your friend. I only saw him briefly at the party, but he seemed like a nice guy."

"Thanks."

I turned to Brett. "Brett, Casey. Casey, Brett. I met Casey at Ulric's party the night you had a temper tantrum."

"He's winding me up, take no notice." Brett scowled at me, much to my amusement.

Casey smiled at Brett. "Liam kindly gave me some support when my so-called best friend was being a back-stabbing bitch. I apologise, Liam, for not thanking you for getting me out to my driver safely before today. I no doubt made a total fool of myself."

I waved her off. "Nah, you didn't. You were just slurry with your words. We've all been there. I don't recommend you do that at a party with sleazeballs like Ulric present though. It could have been a lot worse." She remained clueless that I was the one who'd fed her half of the alcohol in the first place while I offered her faux sympathy for not being able to land Bailey. Shame I couldn't tell her I fed Bailey dog shit shortly after tricking him that he was meeting Casey outside.

"Well, it's very gracious of you to say so. Anyway, like I said, sorry about your friend. Nice to meet you, Brett."

She walked away, back over to the table she'd come from and I noted the best friend from that night sat there, staring over at us and then looking back to her 'friend'. She was clearly Ivy version 2.0.

Brett arched a brow at me. "Okay, that was unexpected. Liam Lawson made a new friend. How do I not know about her?"

"She wasn't anyone to know. Used her to get to Bailey that night."

"Ahhh, now that sounds more like it. For a moment there I thought you'd been a knight in shining armour and I was gonna check you for alien abduction experiment scars."

I elbowed him. "Yeah, right. I created the battle and then rescued her. Means to an end to sort that arsewipe out. Shit went down," I winked.

Brett pushed the rest of his brownie away. "Thanks for that visual, dude."

I chortled.

"She actually seems nice though. Not sure I have any classes with her."

"She's from the lower sixth, not upper. Brett seen something he likes? Thought you'd be all up in Renee again after her makeover."

"Nah, after what happened with Daniel and Flora, I'm staying away from anything but a quick fuck. Renee's too close to home. Besides we already went there, and it didn't click for me." He nodded in Casey's direction. "And that one seems far too innocent for my dirty dick."

"Yeah. She needs to toughen up. Shame you can't be a nice person without being walked all over." I stared back at her friend and sent her a death stare. She quickly averted her gaze. "Right, you ready to brave the afternoon and try not to kick the absolute shit out of people for the rest of the day?"

"I suppose so," Brett replied, and we cleared our stuff and headed off for our afternoon classes.

As expected, the afternoon passed with a few more sly digs, but overall, it went better than the morning had. It was a sign that my friend's death would pass like yesterday's chip paper as it was replaced by something juicier that Richstone could sink its teeth into. I didn't realise at the time just how 'waiting around the corner' that juiciness was.

Back home at the bungalow, I heard gravel crunching under tires nearby and rising from the sofa, I strolled to the front window seeing Ivy depart her car. She caught my gaze and nodded towards the front door.

I kept her waiting on the doorstep for a minute or two longer than necessary, opening it and resting lazily against the doorframe like I had all the time in the world, which I did where making Ivy suffer was concerned.

She waved her designer holdall at me. "I'd like to conclude our business."

Stepping back from the doorway, I gestured for her to walk inside. "Let's head on out the back seeing as it's a nice day."

Ivy nodded and followed me. I knew her eyes would be taking everything in, checking out the bungalow she'd only seen once before through the eyes of terror. Sure enough as she took a seat on the outdoor patio sofa, she said, "You certainly landed on your feet here. Whereas I ended up on my knees."

Christ, she actually sounded wounded. Ivy's narcissistic tendencies were something else.

"I'd been given an opportunity to get out of Sharrow and better myself. You were trying to stop me. Therefore, I stopped you first. It's nothing personal."

"Oh please. It's always personal."

"Hmm, tell me why you hate Phoebe so much?"

"I have my reasons."

"Other than just the fact she's prettier than you and nicer than you, and people genuinely like her?" I snarked.

Her lips pursed. "You've been here for months, Liam. And you're biased towards the Ridleys because of what they've offered you, but you'd be wise to keep your guard up."

Reaching over, she opened the holdall. "I'm dealing in cash, Liam. It's better for us both, but I'm sure you can understand my reluctance to believe that you won't use either the video or the information on what you witnessed that day in the car."

That pissed me off. "Ivy, filming you with my dick in your mouth was self-protection, and if you hadn't started shit with me it wouldn't have happened. If you're going to play with the big boys, prepare for the fallout."

"Big boys? You flatter yourself. Hardly noticed it was in."

I laughed. "Shall we watch it again for old time's sake then and see where you gagged because it was so large it almost blocked your airway?"

She looked away.

"Anyway, the other thing. The fact you binge food. Not my business. We all have our demons, and I'm not about to exploit your self-harming behaviour for my entertainment. I might be a blackmailing bastard, but I'm not a total shit. My mother drinks, you use food. Not my place to judge. You have money for endless therapists at your fingertips, so I'll leave that one to you."

Ivy let out a large exhale. "Thanks."

I snorted. "God, I bet that hurt, having to thank a Sharrow boy."

She actually smiled at that. "Yeah, that's something I might have to seek therapy about. So, anyway, how will I know this video is gone?"

"I'll delete it now in front of you. It's only ever been on my phone. Like I said, if we have no beef then I've no need for it. Just let me get my education so I can get out of here and live a brand-new life somewhere I might actually fit in."

Her brows pulled in as she looked downward. "You act

like you're the one with the bad life who needs to survive, but everyone has their battles to fight, you know?" she said, actually sounding like a real person for once in her life.

"Oh yeah? Is that why you're such a bitch?"

"Like I could be anything else. I'm the only daughter of Hector Sackville. I'm heir to a billion-pound empire, set to inherit fortune and power like you couldn't begin to imagine. I can't be fat. I can't be weak. I can't show a single vulnerability. And I can't trust anyone, because wealth attracts gold diggers and jealousy. Yet I'll have to try to choose well since I'll be expected to provide heirs to continue after me."

"You're not so different from the girl you hate, you know?"

"Oh, I think I am. Because I don't apologise for being a bitch. I need it to survive. Do you know what would happen if I was kind-hearted? A do-gooder like dear little Phoebs? I'd be surrounded by hangers-on. No thanks. Phoebe will become the dutiful little wife her mother is aiming for. I will rule my empire. Phoebe Ridley and I are nothing alike. I'm Queen of that school because I was born to rule. You might want to pass on to her that cute new outfits and hairstyles don't usurp royalty. My father will get rid of Daphne Ridley once and for all soon and the Ridleys will move on. The Sackvilles rule Richstone and we're going nowhere."

I stretched out my legs lazily. "That was quite the speech, Ivy. I felt it came from the heart. Like for once you were actually being genuine. Which intrigues me.

Because why would you confess all to me, someone you don't rate?"

She fiddled with the chain around her neck. "I've not really said that much, and no one would believe anything you said about me anyway. You will always be an outsider. Always be treated largely with suspicion. At least you have the right idea, to move away. Because once your education ends, you'll be pressured to move along. Once Daphne gets whatever she wants from this debacle, and we all know she didn't do it for anyone else's greater good than her own, you'll be out on your ear."

"Why do you think your financial offer was so tempting?"

If she'd been a dog, at that point her ears would have pricked up like I'd just said the word 'treat'. "Hmmm. There's a thought to keep in mind for the future should I need some dirty work taking care of."

I ignored her, grabbing my phone and passing it over for her to delete the video.

"Next time, the offer of a drink wouldn't go amiss."

"There won't be a next time. I didn't offer hospitality because you're not actually welcome here."

"So confident. We'll see about that, Liam. Because I told you, people always follow the money."

I showed her out, noting once she'd gone that despite the fact I was ten grand richer, I didn't feel like the winner here tonight.

11

Phoebe

The bitterness ate away at me all afternoon. Ulric's victim mentality. Liam making deals with Ivy. I could trust no one. No one at all. Maybe my best friends, but even then, you could never actually fully know someone, could you? Better I just carried on with my own plans and started my fresh life somewhere new. Somewhere I could hope to meet a good, trustworthy, reliable man and have a family of my own where they knew they were loved beyond any doubt.

I cried off seeing anyone after school because I was mentally exhausted from the day. From being switched on in my role as potential new queen. From not breaking down thinking of my friend. From the headache pressing behind my eyes as hatred threatened to leak out in all its ugly truth. I wanted to stick a knife in the lot of them so they could feel like I did. I was invisibly bleeding out.

And Liam was collecting money for his fresh start. Paid to keep his mouth closed, while I, the supposed rich girl had relatively nothing of my own. Yet I did. I had designer handbags and watches. Couture. While I couldn't sell any of it right now, didn't want to draw attention to myself, I could earmark the pieces, place them somewhere safe. I spent the rest of the evening after food and homework doing that. Placing my valuable clothing in one closet all side by side. My valuable jewellery was in a safe that I changed the combination on just in case. The bags and shoes were in my closet.

Sitting in front of my dressing table, I stared in the mirror as I used cleansing wipes to take off that day's make-up and reveal my true self. I dreamed once more about walking down a beach. Being free and strolling along with the sea breeze blowing my hair.

It was the memorial in the morning and time for me to up my game. Having made my excuses to Liam about going over there once more, I crawled into bed and settled down for an early night, making sure the alarm was set early enough to give me plenty of time to get ready and to ensure I saw my mother before she left for school.

———

"And what can I do for you this morning, Phoebe?" My mother stared at me over the top of the morning's paper.

"I'd like to know what you're going to say at the

memorial. Do you have photos or something? I want to be prepared."

She folded the paper up and placed it on the table. "I spoke to both sets of parents and have what they want me to read out, and then yes, I have photos of both pupils on a memory stick. I've created a montage of first Daniel and then Flora."

"Could I see it?"

"Not now. I need to be on my way, but you can make your excuses from registration and come help me set up the equipment. We can do a trial run to make sure everything is in order and then you can stay in the wings on the stage just in case I need you should the equipment fail etc."

"Okay. I guess that will have to do."

I left the room and went to get ready and then set off for school.

When we met in the car park again like yesterday, Renee and Lucie were subdued. They had no idea what I had in store. I couldn't risk anyone stopping me. We'd agreed to don the appropriate memorial attire of dark tones and were all dressed in navy-blue. I would wear no more clothes of mourning. I had on a long wrap dress and dark sunglasses to hide my eyes.

Ivy and the gang stood at the entrance again, but this time she didn't say anything. I guessed the reprieve was only because of what would be expected of her this morning. That she'd be publicly respectful. Still, her eyes watched us all as we walked into school. The group were all dressed in black. Ulric stood there looking awkward in his suit with a grey shirt and tie. God, I hated him.

After registration, I told my form tutor I was assisting my mother and he excused me from the rest of registration. I walked down towards the hall and saw Liam and Brett in the distance. They'd arrived late. Both had their funeral clothes on again.

"Morning," I said, addressing them both.

"Yep, here we go again. In answer to your question of why we're late, we don't want to be here," Brett replied, more vocal than I'd ever heard him. "I hope your mother is going to be nice, otherwise today is the day I'll be expelled, leaving Liam the only rat in Richstone."

"You're safe. I'm off to look through it all now and help her set up. Go get signed in and let's get this ordeal over with. I might give out awards for most authentic-looking grief-stricken pupil."

I wasn't being fair really. Most pupils were upset about the deaths, but my mind had been poisoned by Ulric and Ivy.

My mother was setting up the audio-visual equipment, being helped by her secretary. "Ah, Phoebe, excellent, you're here. Lydia, you may go back to the office now. Phoebe and I will take it from here."

Lydia looked at me, clearly wanting to roll her eyes. I just smiled as I passed her.

"Okay, so here are the tributes." My mother handed me a printout. "And I've set up the montage. Lydia did it.

It's all photographs fading in and out with suitable accompanying mournful music. I'll leave you to check it all over while I grab a quick coffee. Then I'll visit the ladies and be back ready to start."

She left the room and I read the words both sets of parents had written for us. Tears threatened my eyes, but I'd already decided my crying was done. I pressed the shortcut icon Daphne had created and started the montage. Photos of Daniel I'd never seen before came up. From when he was younger up until his eighteenth birthday celebrations. I turned it off before Flora's came on screen. I couldn't watch. Not right now.

I got everything ready for my mother and then I sat on the edge of the stage and waited.

The hall filled with pupils and I watched as the upper sixth took their usual seats at the back. I wanted to sit with my friends to support them, but my mother had insisted I stay at the front. I gave a small wave to Renee and Lucie. I noted that Brett sat next to Renee with Liam at his side.

With hardly a look at me, my mother walked to the front of the stage, waiting until quiet descended on the room.

"Good morning, Richstone Academy," she said in a sombre tone. Murmurings of 'good morning' came back.

I watched Daphne in action. She'd dressed in a smart, black trouser suit and a cream blouse. Her chestnut bob

ANGEL DEVLIN

was as straight as the blade on a guillotine and just as sharp. Her make-up was neither subdued nor overdone. She took a sip of water as she waited for the replies to stop.

"This morning's assembly is not one I ever wished to have to make. As you all know, a couple of weeks ago Richstone sadly lost two of its pupils, and so this morning we shall celebrate the lives of the two students who regrettably won't ever sit in this hall again. Who won't be able to go on and benefit from their education and grow and have a family. Two pupils whose flames were extinguished far too quickly."

She took a moment to look at her audience. "There is an order of service on everyone's seat for you to follow. If you turn to the inside page, I shall now read a poem written by Helen Lowrie Marshall titled *Afterglow*.

I'd like the memory of me to be a happy one.
I'd like to leave an afterglow of smiles when life is done.
I'd like to leave an echo whispering softly down the ways,
Of happy times and laughing times and bright and sunny days.
I'd like the tears of those who grieve, to dry before the sun;
Of happy memories that I leave when life is done."

Give the woman an Oscar. As if on cue, Daphne took a tissue from her pocket and dabbed at the corner of her

110

eyes. "I chose Afterglow because I am sure that Flora and Daniel would indeed want you to remember the happy times you shared with them. I will now read out the words Mr and Mrs Preston sent me about Daniel, and then Mr and Mrs Chadwick's regarding Flora."

She did so and I was glad I'd already read the words so I was prepared, because the pride and loss within them was so evident. The noise of sobbing arose, sniffling providing an accompaniment. Some pupils dabbed at their eyes with tissues.

"Before I play the photo compilation of both Daniel and Flora, I would like to take a moment for us all to be silent. I know not everyone worships, but during this couple of minutes of silence I would like you to pray or think of a good memory about Daniel and Flora."

Silence descended once again. I watched to see which people genuinely shut their eyes and which couldn't be bothered. I saw Ivy whisper to her friends throughout the whole thing and I felt the hatred unfurling within me, filling me up.

"Okay. I hope she won't mind me doing this, but I actually think it would be of benefit for my daughter, Phoebe, to now say a couple of words before we close. Would that be okay, Phoebe?"

I looked at her, my mouth open. Why hadn't she warned me of this? I could have thought of a speech. Trust Daphne Ridley to try to wrongfoot me. I came out from the side of the stage. My mother temporarily muted the microphone. "Just press the video when you're done," she said, "and don't waste the opportunity."

I did a double-take. She'd known I was up to something and she was giving me her permission to do my worst. And I would.

I pressed the unmute button.

"Good morning, Richstone Academy. For those of you who don't know me, my name is Phoebe Ridley. Flora and Daniel were both friends of mine." I took a deep breath. "I knew Flora right from nursery school. Daniel I had only got to know when he came on placement here. They were both people whose hearts were large and I wonder if God took them because they were just so full of love and the good stuff." I looked out over the audience. Ivy had completely given up any pretence of interest now my mother had left the stage and was looking at her mobile phone.

"There has been a lot of gossip about the day in question and I would like to make clear the tragic events of that day." Ulric, who had sat with his head bowed, now looked up sharply and he shook his head from side to side. Like I was about to stop now I had a relatively captive audience.

"I'm sure Flora and Daniel would like me to tell the truth today no matter how uncomfortable that is, in order that they can indeed rest in peace and be mourned appropriately. That day, they had had a small quarrel and Flora had dramatically taken off down the street in a huff," I said, making light of the true events. "Daniel went after her, not wanting for her birthday to be ruined by a simple misunderstanding, and I accompanied him in the car." I took a sip of the water my mother had left by the stage.

"Just as we found Flora and pulled up, Ulric McDowell arrived behind us in his car and began beeping loudly for Daniel to get out of the way."

People were now looking at Ulric. He got up to try to get out of the room, but Brett and Liam rose too, along with Renee and Lucie and they blocked his path. The couple of teachers still in the room looked at each other, but because Daphne had let me take to the stage they didn't stop me.

"I asked him repeatedly to just wait a moment and he refused. Point blank refused, and then revving his engine intimidatingly, he drove his car past Daniel in such a way that Dan thought the car was going to be damaged and so he reacted. In his panic and because he wasn't used to the car, he hit the accelerator and we know what happened after that. Unable to deal with the loss of his new fiancée, because they had just got engaged before the silly misunderstanding, Daniel chose to take his own life." I left a moment of silence and then I stared directly at Ulric. "If it weren't for the questionable actions of Ulric McDowell, I have no doubt in my mind that both my friends would still be here today. So, with that cleared up and the truth out there, it's time for us to take a moment to watch the video montages of both Daniel and Flora. May our friends rest in peace."

I pressed play and this time I did see my good friend Flora as I'd seen her over the years. Always with a smile on her face.

And then as the montage stopped it went straight onto the video I'd tacked onto the end this morning while 'setting up'. The video I'd airdropped to my phone from Liam's while he was asleep. Ivy giving Liam a blow job played out on the huge screen in front of everyone.

This time the teachers did run forward, pushing me aside to get to the laptop to turn it off. But the damage was already done.

I stared out from the stage into the crowd of pupils. Ivy was screaming at Liam, who was looking at me with a mixture of disgust and confusion. But I didn't care. I'd done what I'd set out to do. Destroy Ivy. I'd like to see her get out of this one. And at the same time Liam had a taste of just what I was capable of. Not only screwing him but screwing him over.

The teachers yelled for me to get to the waiting room ready to talk about my actions. As I began to walk down off the stage and away towards the exit, Renee and Lucie caught me up. "What the fuck? Why didn't you tell us you were going to share the video so we could have averted our gazes? My eyes will never recover." Renee tugged at my arm. "Come on. Let's get you to reception. I can't wait to see how the school handles this one. Ivy Sackville's face was incredible."

"Yeah, you're only forgiven because it was. Fucking. Epically. Awesome," Lucie added. "Oh, and I heard Ivy say you were going down for this, so I asked her if she meant in the same way she had."

We all burst out laughing. Right at that moment I didn't care if it was the last step I ever took inside Richstone Academy. I'd avenged my friends and made it clear who was responsible for their deaths, had cleared Daniel's name, and had got even with Ivy to boot.

"Phoebe, please come inside," my mother said as I reached the reception. I left my friends and went into her office. She closed the door firmly behind us and lowered her voice. "Well, I knew you were up to something, but that video was quite spectacular. I'm very surprised Liam allowed you to show it."

"He's very understanding," I lied. "For the greater good and all that."

"You're aware Hector Sackville will be on the phone to me at any moment?"

"Tell him I'll meet him and we can talk about it directly," I said.

My mother laughed as if what I'd suggested was funnier than a top comedy performance.

"I'm not joking. It's about time he found out what his daughter has put me through and that she got what she deserved."

"You know as my daughter, I will have to hand this over to Peter?" Peter Marshall was the Deputy Head. "I can't be impartial with my own daughter."

"Do what you need to do. That's the philosophy I'm living by right now."

Daphne regarded me. "Indeed. Should I feel nervous that I have a similar fate waiting for me?"

"Oh definitely watch your step, Mother dear," I smirked, "because as soon as you stumble, I'll be there to knock you all the way over."

She gave me a saccharine smile. "So very confident,

but don't forget pride comes before a fall and I'm a very formidable enemy."

I let out a bored sigh. "Let me know when Peter wishes to see me. In the meantime, I'll go to class."

She nodded.

"Nice spending time with you, Mummy," I said sarcastically, and then I left her office, bursting into triumphant laughter once back out in reception.

12

Liam

I'd been happy when Phoebe stood on the stage and cleared the air about Ulric. After all, Daphne had invited her there. Judging by the slack-jawed then annoyed expression on Phoebe's face, I'd thought the matter had caught her unawares. Happy Daniel could be mourned freely, and everyone knew who really was at fault, it had settled something inside me.

When she'd finished speaking, Phoebe had begun the montage and we'd moved away from holding Ulric back, happy for him to fuck off out of the room now the truth was out there. My heart fractured a little more as Daniel's face came across the screen and once more guilt consumed me with the tragedy that I'd never see that face again in real life. As Flora's montage played out, my eyes moved to Renee and Lucie. Brett put his arm around each of them as they broke. I couldn't offer them comfort.

I just wasn't that guy. I could slash a dude for someone, but not offer a hug. Fact. I was fucked in the head for sure.

The music stopped and Flora's full name and the date of her birth and death appeared on screen before fading out. Memorial assembly over, people rose from their seats and I moved my feet ready to make my way over to Phoebe, who'd not been allowed to join us; not been allowed to be in the proximity of her friends for the memorial. I wanted to check she was okay and thank her for saying what she had about Daniel.

And then the projector screen filled with fresh images and sounds that hit me as all too familiar.

'I'm the Queen of Richstone Academy. What would this do to my status? But please, fuck me. I need it. I beg you'.

Gasps and giggles came from pupils who were now standing still looking at the projector screen onstage and then at each other. My eyes shot to Phoebe. Her expression was triumphant, even as teachers leapt on stage to try to turn off the horror playing on screen.

And then Ivy was screaming in my face.

"You utter fucking shit. You promised. You said it was gone. I'll ruin you."

I grabbed the hand she was about to slap my face with, and I thrust her up close to me. "I didn't do this, and I didn't know about it. She did it."

"I'm supposed to believe you?" A tear ran down her cheek. "What the fuck am I going to do?"

"Go home."

"I want my money back, you fucking turd."

As people began to point and stare at her, Ivy ran out of the room, pushing past people and knocking them out of the way.

"Want to get out of school for a while?" Renee looked at me, but she wasn't shocked.

"You knew about the video? Did you know she was going to show it to everyone? Because she certainly didn't tell me." My eyes narrowed with suspicion.

"No, we just knew it existed. Come on, let's cut class, and go outside for a while. Give you time to come to terms with the fact most of Richstone Academy has seen your manhood."

I nodded. "Yeah, seeing as all I've got is an appointment with Principal Ridley in my future, let's get out of here."

"I can see why Phoebe was so enamoured with you," Lucie winked.

"Same way Renee was enamoured with me," Brett waggled his brows.

"You wish. More like this bird was searching for a worm," Renee retorted.

As we moved out of the room, I expected people to come up to me with smart arsed comments, but they didn't. They gossiped to each other and stared instead. I was sure that if Ulric hadn't fled the room followed by his entourage, they'd have had something to say. But Ulric and Ivy were currently indisposed. Phoebe had achieved her aims, but she'd taken me down with them.

If I got excluded now, that was the end of my time

and opportunities at Richstone. With just fifteen grand to my name, I'd be no better off really. It wasn't enough to start a brand-new life.

In the end we went and sat near the outside picnic benches. No one came to tell us to come inside, no doubt busy trying to calm down the rest of the pupils and attempting to get them to sit and learn something after their interesting start to the day.

"So she didn't tell you she was planning to screen the video?" Renee queried.

I waved a hand over my face. "Do I look like I knew about it?"

"Sorry, daft question given your pissed off expression. So what are you going to do about it now she has? How are you going to handle things?"

"Renee, I understand that you're concerned about your friend, but this is between Phoebe and me. I've no idea yet what to do about any of it to be honest. I'm as blindsided as everyone else." I scrubbed a hand over the scruff of my shaved head. "I just hope she's not cost me my place here."

"If anyone is going to get suspended, it'll be Phoebe," Brett said. "Look at what she did today."

"There's no way Daphne's going to let that happen. Anyway," I looked as the woman herself stepped out from the shadows. "Looks like it's my time of reckoning."

I found myself walking down to the Principal's office with Daphne while the others made their way back to class.

"Am I out of here?" I asked her.

"Of course not. I need you to be a shining example of what happens when you let shit be around roses remember? Just play along and you'll come out of it just fine."

She knocked on her own door, which I found strange, but when we walked inside, Mr Marshall, the deputy head was sitting in Daphne's seat.

"Take a seat, Liam. I'll try not to keep you long," he indicated to a chair in front of him and Daphne took the one alongside it.

The guy sat up straight and cleared his throat. He was clearly in his element enjoying being in charge for a while.

"I'm leading the investigation into what happened this morning with regard to the video that ended up being played out to the school. I just need to ask you a few questions so that we can try to work out how it ended up on a school computer."

I sat back on my seat and let my legs fall apart. "Yeah, I'm interested in finding out the answer to that myself."

Mr Marshall adjusted his tie as if it was strangling him. "Indeed." After picking up a pen and shuffling his A4 notepad in front of him, he looked at Daphne. "If you could tell me the events of this morning please, Principal Ridley."

"Of course. So Lydia and I walked into the room at just after seven to set up. When everything was done, we left the room. I thought I'd locked the door behind me but it's possible I didn't."

"So you saw no one enter the room and tamper with the equipment?"

"No."

"And Phoebe?"

"Phoebe came into school with her friends and didn't join me on stage until just prior to the room filling up with staff and students. She had no idea I intended to invite her onto the stage. She had no opportunity to go near the equipment until she set the montage running, and there was clearly no opportunity there for her to set up the video. So whoever did it must have done it in the space of time between me and Lydia grabbing a quick coffee and my returning to the room ready to start the assembly."

"Okay. Now, Liam."

"Yeah?"

"Did you know about the video prior to seeing it this morning?"

"Yes. It was a private matter between me and Ivy Sackville. We had mutually agreed to record it." Thank goodness you couldn't tell where it had been videoed, the only thing evident being my cock, Ivy's mouth, and our voices.

"And this was on your phone?"

"Yes."

"How do you think it managed to be on the school computer?"

"I have no idea, but I did misplace my phone last

week," I lied. "Only for a short period of time, like ten minutes. I found it on the sports field. It must have dropped out of my pocket at lunchtime."

Peter sighed.

"So we have the opportunity that someone had time to access your phone last week, and also the opportunity for them to put the video on school equipment this morning. Do you know who might want to do that to you, Liam?"

I needed to think on my feet here and I wanted to punch the air in triumph when it came to me.

"While I don't want to accuse anyone because I have no proof, Ulric McDowall has been making life for me and my friends difficult here since we started. As you know he instigated an incident that led to my friend Marlon having to leave on the first day. I also hold him responsible for Daniel's death. It wouldn't surprise me to find he was behind this also. But again, I have no proof of this. It's just a gut feeling,"

Mr Marshall tugged on his tie once more. "I will be meeting with Ulric and his father shortly and I will make sure to raise the possibility, though I doubt very much I'll hear an admission of guilt. Is there anything further either of you would like to add before I bring this to a close?"

I shook my head and Daphne said no.

"My apologies, Liam, about this morning's unfortunate events, and my condolences about your friend. Might I suggest that maybe you password protect any future videos you might collect for your 'entertainment?'"

I nodded and the guy actually gave me a wink. Perhaps the video had given him a hard-on, something for his spank bank. Whatever. I was out of here and happily had found myself in the position of victim in all of this, plus I had managed to throw Ulric a further stint of inconvenience while I was at it. All I needed to do now was to confront Phoebe and work out what to do about Ivy.

Daphne stayed behind as I left, and I walked out of the reception and headed down the hall. It was almost lunchtime, so I'd go grab something to eat and hang around waiting for Brett to get out of class.

Only as I approached the canteen, I saw Phoebe waiting there at the entrance to the nearby girls bathroom, kicking her feet against the wall.

"Finally," she said. "You not answering your phone?"

I realised it was still on silent from the assembly, but right now I didn't give a fuck about my phone. I grabbed Phoebe by the hair and dragged her into the girls bathroom. It was empty, but I didn't give a fuck anyway. I'd have thrown out anyone found in there. I kicked open a stall door and pushed her inside.

"You have some fucking explaining to do, bitch," I ground out.

"Liam, I..." Phoebe's eyes looked pleading, like she wanted to apologise, but I wasn't in the mood for sob stories.

"You seem to have forgotten who I am, Phoebe Ridley, so I think it's time I reminded you." I went back out to the main toilet door and jammed it shut with pieces of a discarded tissue box.

Then I returned to the stall where Phoebe now sat on the closed toilet seat.

I took my knife out of my pocket and flicked it open.

13

Phoebe

Just before I was called to see Peter Marshall, I got a text from my mother.

I've squared it with Lydia and you weren't around first thing this morning. You came in just before the assembly started. Someone must have come and put the video on the computer while Lydia and I were out of the room for a short while...

It meant that when I went to speak to Peter, my interview was over in minutes and I was free to go. I wasn't in trouble for sharing the clip. I was exonerated from having had any part in it at all.

Which meant that the only person I had to face now was Liam.

Though I knew he'd be furious, I was taken off guard

when he grabbed me by the hair and dragged me into the girls bathroom.

And now he was waving that knife around at me and suddenly I didn't feel as confident as I had earlier.

"Put the knife down, Liam, and let's talk."

He scoffed. "Now you want to talk, do you? Now you've shown my cock to the entire school. You could have cost me my place here. Did you think of that?"

"How? It's just a video. You're not robbing somewhere or attacking anyone."

"Because if it hadn't been worth Daphne's while to keep me in school, I have no doubt the riches would have held me accountable for that video being shown." He stabbed the knife into the doorframe, making me jump. "You had no fucking right to share that. And how did you get it? I didn't give it to you."

"A simple airdrop," I confessed.

He shook his head. "I don't think so because my phone is accessible only via my fingerprint."

"You sleep like a dead person. It was easy as pie."

"Huh," he scoffed. "I finally let a girl stay the night and they screw me after I sleep. That's a new one."

I rolled my eyes. "There's no harm done. Ivy ran out of school. Ulric left too. They're both shame-faced and their lofty positions at school are on very shaky ground. I thought you'd be pleased."

He pulled the knife out of the wood. "Well, I'm not. Because you're sneaking around while I'm asleep, making plans without talking to me, and pulling little stunts like that one this morning. I'm trying to fit in at this school to get my education and now I'll be the talk of it."

"You've come out a hero. They're all impressed. Who says size doesn't matter?"

"My dick was legendary back in Sharrow, Phoebe," he replied, and I felt my stomach twist in jealousy of his past fucks. Stupid, betraying body. "So I don't need that infamy here."

He stalked towards me. "Take off your clothes."

I tried not to smile. I liked it when Liam 'punished' me by fucking me. I stripped off while he passed the knife from one hand to the other. He took his tie off and pulling my hands behind my back he fastened it tightly around my wrists.

I waited for his next instruction, but none was forth-coming. Instead, he brought out his phone, grabbed my hair with his other hand and he thrust his dick down my throat. I gagged as it hit the back of my throat, trying to get my breath as he rammed it in and out violently, recording it the whole time. Then he pulled out, pushed me to the side of the stall and fastened himself away. He picked up my discarded clothes and threw them in the sink switching the tap on. I watched helplessly as my clothes sank under the weight of water.

Walking back over to me, he took my phone out of my bag and held my own finger on it until it gave him access.

"Now you know how you made me feel this morning. Naked and helpless and not given a choice about being exposed. Come to the bungalow tonight if you've any remorse and decide you want us to do this together now.

Otherwise, keep the fuck out of my life." He video-called Renee, threw the phone on the seat and undid my hands before walking out of the bathroom after unjamming the door and then slamming the door behind him.

Renee appeared on screen and her eyes went wide seeing me naked with my hands over my breasts.

"Hang on." She made her way out of the room telling the teacher she had an emergency. "Where are you?"

"Womens bathrooms near the canteen. I need a towel and a change of clothes."

"I can get a towel from the gym but where the fuck will I get a change of clothes from?"

"I don't know," I sobbed.

"Look, I'll come to you with the towel, and I'll get Lucie on change of clothes duty. You're around the same size."

And that's what she did. Five minutes after getting my call, she came into the bathroom and knocked on the stall door. A few people had come in, but I'd taken a chance and grabbed my clothes out of the sink after speaking to Renee. While I'd waited, I'd been squeezing them out over the toilet.

"Who the fuck did this?"

She saw the hesitation in my face. "Oh no. You're fucking kidding me that he left you like this. I'll kill the fucker with my bare hands. That is not how you treat my best friend."

"I've hurt him."

"And this is a fair way to deal with that? He's a dick. But for now, let's concentrate on getting you dried off with this towel and then out of here and home. Lucie's bringing some clothes and then we'll go to your place. Today can suck it. And then over a nice large cocktail of some kind, you can tell us exactly what's been going on with you and Liam. No secrets. We are best friends. We're there for each other. But all that this morning, Phoebe. It threw us all for a loop. We were outside standing together wondering what the hell was going on."

"I- I'm sorry. I might need a w- warm drink before a- alcohol," I whimpered.

"Do I need to report this to anyone? Mr Marshall or your mother?"

I shook my head, and she sighed a deep sigh.

"I hope you know what you're doing, Phoebe. I don't want a repeat of what happened to Flora."

"I- it's not like that. He's just angry because he didn't know what I was going to do."

"And in return he leaves you naked in the bathroom?"

Renee was steaming with anger and ready to wring Liam's neck. I needed to calm her down as I didn't want her getting into trouble for my actions.

"I know it looks bad, but I did show the whole school his cock. He was the one who called you before he walked out, so I guess that's something."

"If you end up having hate sex then I'm going to be very jealous," she sighed. "I really can't stand Brett now, but he wasn't kidding when he said his own dick was big. Unfortunately the one on his head is even larger."

I chuckled at that and Renee smiled. "Now that's what I was looking for. My bestie's kind smile.

"Can we go to Café Renzo rather than mine? It wouldn't surprise me if my mother has my rooms bugged."

"Sure. Wherever you want, Fifi."

She'd not called me that in ages and thankfully she was looking away and didn't see when I winced. Liam had stolen that innocent childhood name from between the two of us and turned it into a name twisted in lust and hatred.

Petula asked no questions about why we were out of school. I guessed it being lunchtime helped. We ordered toasted sandwiches and drinks, and I sat in a skirt and top that Lucie had brought to the bathrooms after she'd quickly nipped to a shop. I'd managed to dry my pants and bra under the hand dryers enough to wear them and Lucie had brought her swim bag for me to put everything else in until I went home.

"Okay, now tell us everything about you and Liam and I mean *everything*," Renee warned.

"There's not really anything else to tell you from what I shared with you at the bungalow after my dad attacked me. Since Flora and Daniel died, we've been distant and our fledgling relationship has just, well, let's put it as the baby bird tried to fly off the ledge and lies splattered on the ground."

Lucie rubbed at my arm. "It was going to affect things. You've both suffered major losses, but you could be there for each other, instead of letting it distance you. If you like him, you need to fight for it."

"He just left her naked in the toilet. I say she never bothers with him again," Renee huffed. "I think we should work out how we're going to get our revenge on the rat bastard."

"No can do. Look at her face." They both stared at me. "The girl is a lost cause. She likes him even though he does the bad stuff. I bet if we saw inside her head, she's already made it into an erotic fantasy."

"Shut up!" I exclaimed blushing. But her words hit me hard. Was it true? Did I like him despite *everything*? They said there was a fine line between love and hate.

"So how do you feel about Liam now?" Renee asked.

"Sometimes I hate him," I confessed.

"But sometimes you don't?"

I threw my hands up in the air. "I don't know how I feel. I'm a mess." It was true. I might be super primped and polished on the outside, but inside I was just a jumble of conflict and confusion.

I decided to tell my friends the truth, but without revealing it was responsible for the death of our friends.

"I overheard Liam talking to Brett, Daniel, and Marlon a while ago." I took a deep breath. "They made a pact when they came here to blackmail a riches. But they didn't appear to have got far with their plans. They were pissed with Daniel because he'd genuinely fallen for Flora."

"And you didn't think to share this with us?" Lucie whisper-shouted, looking around herself afterwards.

"I would have done but then the accidents happened, and I felt we all had enough going on. It wasn't like they'd succeeded in blackmailing any of us anyway was it? But it means that I don't trust Liam. Does he genuinely like me, just as Daniel fell for Flora, or am I part of a game he's playing himself?"

"If Brett slept with me because of this bet I'm going to put his penis in a vice," Renee growled out.

"Do we tell them we know though? Plus, we had our own bets about them. That's what's made me feel so conflicted."

Plus, it led to a chain of events that killed two people.

"We didn't intend to blackmail them," Renee protested.

"No, but we did use them as our own personal puppets. We objectified them. We aren't innocent in all this."

We sat in silence for a moment, all deep in thought about what to do.

"You have to tell him you know, Phoebe. It's the only way forward." Renee sighed. "Then you listen to what he has to say, and you decide whether or not you believe him. If you decide to stick with it, then all I would say is don't completely let your guard down. With all the shit going on with your parents, and after Flora, well, you'll be pretty vulnerable right now, and I don't want you hurt anymore."

I nodded.

"These games between you. Him blackmailing Ivy, and then you showing everyone the clip today. It's a lack of communication that makes me feel you aren't right for each other," Lucie admitted. "If I'm wrong then the two of you need to start talking and get on the same page."

'Yeah. I'll talk to him later. Tell him everything." It felt right as I said it. To tell him how much I currently hated him and see what happened from there.

"So, apart from Liam, what else is circling around that pretty little head of yours? Because after I've seen what you're capable of today, I want to know how you plan to deal with the fallout from what happened. Ivy's father will be gunning for you."

"Yeah, I'm waiting for him to make a move," I confessed. "And I'm hoping I can turn a meet with him to my advantage."

I told them what I hoped to achieve.

"That's either fucking genius or the craziest shit you've ever come out with," Lucie stated.

Shrugging, I finished my drink.

14

Liam

After storming out of the ladies bathroom, I legged it out of Richstone Academy. I was done with school for today. I messaged Marlon and asked him to skip the rest of his classes and to meet me in the pub. I needed alcohol. Needed to block the day out. Fucking Phoebe Ridley. I hated her and loved her in equal measure.

Loved her?

Fuck that. My dick loved her more like. No way was my mind thinking of this shit. It needed alcohol to close it down fast.

Twenty minutes or so later I was sat in The Crown nursing my first pint. I'd already knocked back a whisky chaser. Marlon walked in, nodded at me and went to get his own pint. He came back over with two bags of crisps.

"Ordered us steak pie. Got us these in case you're already hungry."

"Not sure I have an appetite."

"Brett messaged me..."

"Of course he did," I huffed out.

"He wanted to warn me after you failed to turn up to classes. Figured you might head back to Sharrow."

"I headed back here to talk to my mate, not to come back 'home' or some shit."

"You can say what you like, but it is home. It's what you've known. And while it might have been a tough life here, Richstone has certainly not shown itself to be the amazing place we all thought it would be. Not by a fucking long shot."

"I wish I could rewind time. I'd never go there," I admitted.

'Yeah, well seeing as magic doesn't exist, or time-travel, you'd better find your bollocks and man up to the fucking shit show that is life and just try to make the best of it."

I took a sip of my pint.

"Do you blame me? For Daniel's death?" I blamed myself. I knew that. Couldn't help it. It felt like a weight around my neck that could drag me under at any time. He'd only been in Richstone because of me. Only met Flora because of me.

"No. It was an accident. Our friend was in love. Fuck knows what had made Flora go running out of the restaurant, but given she was preggers, her hormones would have been all over the place. I remember what my mum was like when she had Cadence." Marlon had a five-year-old sister. His mum and dad were divorced, and his mum had remarried and had another child.

"Well, I blame myself. I brought everyone to Richstone."

"Man, what good is that going to do anyone, never mind yourself? You only had everyone's best interests at heart when you came up with your crazy scheme and we all thought it would be an adventure. My mother says when your time is up, it's up, so there's nothing to say Daniel wouldn't have blinked out of existence another way. I mean we didn't exactly live saintly lives here, did we?"

"I suppose not."

"He wouldn't want you like this, pal. In fact, he'd be majorly pissed off with you for not living life to the max."

"I fucking miss him so bad," I confessed. "Just as much as I miss my dad."

Marlon's chin dipped slightly. "I know. I fucking miss him bad too. We have to rely on time to help us deal. It's the only thing. One day..."

"at a time." It made me think of Phoebe. I'd given her an ultimatum, and right now I didn't know if she'd turn up tonight or not. She'd never been what I'd assumed she'd be, the spoiled little rich girl, but now, more than ever, I couldn't predict a single move she'd make.

Phoebe was fighting for her own survival against parents who were happy for her to sacrifice the rest of her life to some rich fuck, no matter who. Let's face it, if your own daddy beats the shit out of you, he's hardly going to

care what your new rich husband does, as long as the
riches keep flowing. And Friday she was to go to meet
Ulric. Daphne had gone too far this time.

I pictured Phoebe how I'd left her, naked in the bathroom. I'd fucked up. Yes, I'd been angry, but it was abuse.
I'd been no better than her father. Okay, I'd not touched
her, but I'd bullied her, left her vulnerable. She must
have been questioning what I'd intended to do after she
realised it wasn't to seduce her.

I slammed my pint glass on the table, making Marlon
startle.

"You could just ask for another, rather than give me a
fucking heart attack."

"I fucked up again. With Phoebe."

Marlon sighed. "What did you do?"

I told him about the bathroom incident.

He shook his head from side to side. "You're beyond
screwed. Look what she did to Ivy Sackville. She's going
to destroy you."

"And I deserve it."

"So apologise. Get there first. Send her a text."

"Fuck off."

He shrugged. "It's that or your gonna find horse shit
in your bed."

"What the fuck is happening to me?" I got up ready
to get another pint, but Marlon wasn't finished talking.

"You went to Richstone in search of fortune and
instead you're finding yourself."

"You're fucking sounding more and more like your
mother with every passing day. You know that right?"

The barmaid came over with our pies.

"I'm going to get us two more pints and then you can tell me about life in Sharrow and how you are. I'm done thinking about my crap for a bit."

I headed off for the bar, thinking of how Sharrow would always be part of me, deep in my marrow, even if I went on to better myself. The first thing I'd done today was to head back to what I knew. It was a sobering thought, so I grabbed another whisky chaser and drank it straight down again. Trev gave me a quizzical gaze, but I ignored it and carried the pints back to the table.

"Thanks, mate," Marlon said as I set the pints down on the table and retook my seat.

"So, tell me what's been happening in your life," I prompted.

"School's the same as ever, though it's weird without the rest of you. I talk to Skye quite a bit because our ordeals kind of bonded us."

"You have my permission to tap that," I told him.

Marlon pulled a face. "That's gross. I ain't putting my dick where yours has been. Though that rules out quite a few women."

"Lucie still would if you get stuck, I'm sure. Oh, by the way, there's a party Saturday night that the girls are throwing. It's in Flora's memory and a fundraiser. You'll be there."

"Will Ulric be there?"

"Not sure, but let's face it, he's not going to be so cocky now he's in the frame for having killed our friend."

"I'll think about it."

"Nah, you're coming. We need to stick together, and you need to show Richstone that just because you returned to Sharrow doesn't mean Ulric managed to drive you away from there."

"Know that I won't be encouraging Lucie. She's not my type."

"Rich and pretty isn't your type?"

"No," he said, and I felt like he wanted to say more, but he didn't.

"So poor and ugly?" I pushed.

He rolled his eyes at me. "I have an on again, off again thing here. But I don't want to talk about it. It's complicated."

I pushed again. "Complicated by wedding rings, or are you scared to come out of the closet? Because we're here for you, my man. No prejudice here. Bring him along on Saturday."

"I'm not gay. But, yeah, there's another person involved. Actually, there's been other people involved. It's a mess I need to walk away from."

"But you can't?"

He nodded.

"I'm here whenever you want to talk."

He laughed.

"What are you laughing at?"

"You. Declaring you're here if I want to talk. The man currently about to be force-fed his own cock after the stunt he's pulled today."

"Fuck you," I said, tucking into my now cool enough to eat pie.

"I'm glad you came to meet me," I told him as I got up to leave. I swayed a little to the side.

"Alcohol has never made you all lovey-dovey before so please don't start now."

It must have been the daytime drinking because I didn't usually feel the effects, but I had downed four pints in quite quick succession plus a couple more whisky chasers I'd consumed at the bar. I'd done it behind Marlon's back given he was trying to be sensible about our alcohol consumption because he 'had to go home and revise'. Such a bloody goody goody.

And then she walked in, Lisette bloody Handley. One of Sharrow Manor's teachers—Science I think—though she taught the younger kids and had only been there a couple of years. I'd caught her in my house via a dogcam shagging Vin, my mother's ex. She'd proven helpful when I'd needed her to assist us to get into Rich-stone. Blackmail was good like that.

She looked from Marlon to me and her face went from one of shock to repulsion. I looked behind her and saw a tall, thin, pale-faced man who looked a good ten years older than her.

"Reid, go find us a table and I'll be over in a moment," she said.

She looked at us both. "I'm here with my husband so I'd appreciate it if you'd just leave us in peace."

"You mean you don't want me to confront you about shagging Vin again then?" I sneered.

She moved closer and hissed, "Keep your voice down. I paid my dues for you to keep quiet about that already."

"What do you mean?" Marlon said, looking confused.

"She made sure to weed out surplus applications for us when we applied to Richstone." I smiled.

"Oh, right."

"I am genuinely sorry about Daniel," she said. "The teachers spoke of his aptitude for science. He could have been an asset."

I nodded over at where her husband sat sorting out cutlery. "You got over looking for excitement then, or have you found another lover to help you get through Sharrow life?"

Marlon grabbed me by the collar and pulled me into his side. "Liam, cool it now. You might be at Richstone, but I'm still here and Mrs Handley is one of the teachers at my school. Have some damned respect."

I shrugged out of his hold and straightened myself. "Thanks for your condolences," I said to her. "We'll let you get back to your husband, and don't worry, I'm out of here, so my mouth will be firmly shut."

She nodded and scurried away.

"That was unnecessary," Marlon chastised me.

"Whatever. I'm done drinking now. Going to get myself home and leave you to your revision."

I got up and walked out of the pub and as the fresh air hit me, I was suddenly five times drunker.

"Fucking hell, Liam. All this because Phoebe screwed you over? It's nothing at the side of the other shit you've had to handle."

"Women fuck with you. I mean look at Mrs Handley, acting like the good little wife here tonight. I bet shagging her is like dropping a party sausage in a well. She's a tramp."

His fist came out of nowhere. Straight in my mouth. I felt my lip slice open from my teeth. Wiping my hand on my mouth I stared at the blood incredulously.

"You hit me!" I said astonished.

"Someone had to shut your mouth. It was running away with you, and I told you already. I still live here."

I realised then that what I wanted now was a good old punch up. I regretted what I'd done to Phoebe and needed to feel punished for my actions. Marlon had turned to look back in the direction of the pub for witnesses to what he'd just done.

My right fist connected with his kidneys.

"Motherfucker." He doubled over and my next punch came under his chin.

He quickly recovered and rained his own fists down on me. Marlon had done boxing for a while as a kid and so I soon found myself coming unstuck, but I welcomed it.

Lying on the ground, pain shooting around my body from several different places, Marlon staggered back just as people came running out of the pub.

Lisette stood there. "What happened? Are you both okay? Do we need to call for an ambulance?"

I started laughing from my position on the ground and Marlon dropped to my side laughing too. He pulled me up and we hugged.

Staring at Lisette's bewildered face and that of Trev who was looking pissed off at the side of her, we both shook our heads.

"We're fine," Marlon said. "Just needed an outlet for our grief. We'll be on our way now."

Marlon and I walked down the street. Well... hobbled and staggered might have been a better description.

"You're a fucking idiot, you know that?" Marlon rubbed his red, swollen cheekbone.

"Yeah, but I'm your fucking idiot," I said in a girly voice and we started laughing all over again.

I washed my face and drank some strong coffee at Marlon's where we received a lecture from his mother, and then with a wave and a thank you, I made my way back to the bungalow.

It took me a while. The punches I'd taken were making me a little sore, but it also made me feel alive. And then it made me realise something. I understood how sometimes Phoebe could let me 'punish' her and be okay with it, and yet not accept it of her father. Because when I did it, she knew it was safe. That I ultimately wouldn't genuinely hurt her. Just the same way as I knew I could fight Marlon and we'd know where to draw the line.

Now I just had to hope she did come to the bungalow tonight so we could talk about the future. I had to hope I hadn't completely screwed this up.

Taking some deep breaths as I dropped onto the sofa in the living room, a few for the pain and one for what I was about to do, I picked up my mobile phone.

Liam: I am so very sorry for what I did earlier. It was wrong. No matter your actions, mine were inexcusable. I hope you give me the chance to apologise in person.

Then I put my phone in my pocket and stripping out of my clothes, I headed to the patio because I needed the soothing warmth of the Jacuzzi pretty damn quickly.

15

Phoebe

Arriving home, I smirked while imagining how Ivy's day had gone. She would have had to tell her father, surely?

Though it was tempting to message Hector Sackville, I knew I needed to wait until I'd spoken to Liam. No matter what happened between the two of us, I couldn't make any more decisions solo. I had to let him in.

I hovered around the sitting room until my mother got home.

"I thought you'd be around here somewhere, waiting to see what had happened this afternoon."

"And?"

"And not a lot. No call from Hector. Ivy didn't return to school. You and your friends went missing. Liam went AWOL. Only Brett remained in classes."

"Liam skipped class?"

My mother looked bemused. "You mean you didn't know? Is your little love affair on the skids after this morning's activities?"

I ignored her, though her remark stung.

"And Mr McDowell had nothing to say?"

"Didn't hear from him, but what could he say? A student had an emotional outburst due to the loss of one of their closest friends and they spoke the truth. Not really anything Richard could complain about. I'm sure come Friday he'll want to fund a memorial bench or something for the school. I'd take a wager."

"Huh, I wouldn't wager a bet on that. The moment you said it, I know it's going to happen. It's exactly how he operates."

"So, you're free at the moment, Phoebe. Nothing has come yet from what you did. But it will. You didn't cause a ripple in a puddle of water today; you dropped a bomb in the sea."

"I'll be ready for whatever comes."

My mother looked bemused. "Just make sure you look good and you stay polite on Friday. I shall expect you to apologise for your outburst to Richard, Margot, and Ulric."

Once more she made me react by pushing my buttons. "Are you kidding me? I will not apologise to that bastard."

I was rewarded with a smirk. "You will because I said so, and our agreement is you make nice with the rich boys. You can go to your room and make a voodoo doll of him for all I care. Put it alongside mine, but Friday night you'll be my on-her-best-behaviour daughter."

"As if Ulric wants me as a wife."

"Why would he not? You're beautiful. You'd bear him great children. It's not like love is involved in any of this." She laughed at that as if the thought was the funniest thing she'd ever heard.

I watched her retreating back and imagined the daggers I was hoping to throw in it.

You're getting what you deserve soon, Daphne Ridley, I thought and with a satisfied smile I went up to my room.

I was so happy to get out of my skanky bra and pants that had remained a little damp and the borrowed clothes. I showered and changed into some charcoal-grey yoga pants, and a pink-cropped sports top with a hip-length, grey vest overlay. With my hair dried and tied up in a ponytail, I finally felt cleansed of the day as I laid back on my bed and stared at the ceiling.

Imagining counting down the days until I could leave this place, I decided I'd put a ring around my final exam day on my wall calendar and to put large crosses through every day in Sharpie. It was a job for another day though. Right now, I was enjoying the softness of my mattress and the peace and quiet, but a countdown to freedom was definitely in my future.

My phone buzzed with a text notification disturbing my peace and quiet. Sighing, I reached to my bedside table where I'd thrown my phone down, and then I read Liam's text.

I then re-read it another approximately thirty-three times. Liam Lawson was sorry? He was apologising for his actions? Clearly either Hell had frozen over, or this was a lie to make me vulnerable to another revenge attack.

Or maybe he really is sorry?

There was only one way to find out. My fingers flew across the keypad.

Phoebe: I'll be there tonight to discuss things. Order dinner from The Aegean.

The dots appeared on the screen.

Liam: I'll order now because I'm bloody starving.

Phoebe: I'll be there shortly.

I jumped off the bed to grab my bag and slip on my trainers.

The nearer I got to the bungalow, the more my heart beat faster with nerves. This was stupid. It was Liam. I'd been here a ton of times before, yet this time it was different. His actions in the bathroom, coupled with my confronting him about what I'd heard meant this could be the night we went our own separate ways.

He opened the door and stepped to one side. "I've got the menu on my computer screen in the dining room. You just need to decide what you want."

I walked in and heard him close the door behind me, but instead of heading into the dining room, I turned into the living room.

"No, the dining room," he said.

I turned around. "We need to talk first, Liam. Hopefully, I'll have more of an appetite after."

"Well, I just appear to have lost mine," he grumbled, but he gestured for me to lead the way.

Sitting on the sectional, I folded my arms across my chest and sucked in my top lip while I waited for him to get settled opposite me.

I gave him his due, he made direct eye contact.

"What happened to your lip?" There was a scabbed over cut.

"I met Marlon and needed to expend some energy."

"You fought Marlon?"

"We fought each other. It's cheaper and quicker than therapists."

I shook my head in disbelief.

"Do you want to start, or shall I apologise?" he asked.

"I'll start."

"Okay."

"When Flora ran out of the restaurant it was because she had heard you talking in the men's bathroom."

"Huh?" Liam's eyes crinkled with confusion before being replaced with a look of foreboding.

"My friend was a romantic idiot and she decided to put a bug in Daniel's shirt, so she could hear him give you his news."

Liam's mouth dropped open, but he quickly recovered himself. "Bullshit. You mean she wanted to see how genuine his reaction was." His jaw set. "If you're telling me what I think you're telling me, then don't put some fantasy angle on your dead friend's personality. I'm done with lies. The truth comes out now. All of it."

I sighed. "Fine. Flora put a spy cam in Daniel's tie because she wanted to hear his true feelings. But she was just anxious, that's all. There was no malice to it."

"I know. Flora was a good person. As was Daniel."

"I know that too. But we heard a conversation."

"Who's we?"

"Flora and I."

He nodded.

"We heard Brett say something was 'fucking mental' and then Daniel asking why when the whole plan had been to get a riches pregnant or to blackmail one it was a problem he had. We heard him say Brett had fucked Renee with a spiked condom."

Liam sat forward with his elbows on his knees, head resting on his hands. He looked like if he had enough hair, he'd be pulling it out by the roots, "and that's why she ran?"

"Yes. When I saw Daniel, I told him, and he said how they'd both been careless, and I knew anyway he loved her. And Flora knew that too. She was just in shock at what she'd heard. And then I saw her on the street while I was in the car. We pulled up and I shouted to her that everything was okay and she looked so hopeful. Everything would have been fine..." my voice trailed off.

"If not for Ulric, and then Daniel pressing the accelerator because he was in a state about everything." I didn't realise Liam was crying until a tear dropped off his chin onto the carpet. "I knew his death was my fault. I knew it. I thought it was because I brought him to Richstone and that had led to that fateful day, but it was the actual stupid fucking plan I'd made that did it." Still leaning forward he covered his eyes with his hands. "You must hate me, Phoebe. I basically killed your friend. I'll go back to Sharrow if that's what you want. You only have to say the word."

"I do hate you," I confessed. "It's why I showed the video today. I wanted to hurt you. To ruin you. And then you did that to me in the bathroom. Made me see how you treat your enemies. I wanted you to suffer for what you started. You set out to use us for your own profit, to blackmail me or get me pregnant. I wasn't a person to you. I was a means to an end."

He opened his mouth to say something, but I held my hand up.

"But I also don't hate you and that's where I come unstuck. Because you already told me before in front of my mother that you'd seen me as a potential opportunity to exploit, but then said you found me worth more."

"You are worth more." His eyes implored me to believe him. "So much more. What I did in the bathroom. It was wrong, so very wrong, but it was my automatic reaction because the very person I'd started to put my trust in... The one person who I'd begun to show my true self to, betrayed me in front of everyone. I was angry, hurt, and I retaliated. I was sorry as soon as I left the bathroom, even before that when I dialled Renee. I don't know how to be around you, Phoebe, because I've never done this before, but I know I fucked up, and because of what it led to... well, I understand if you can't even look at me now."

I sighed and just sat there for a moment. It felt like my hatred had cut my skin and leeched out into the rug. Pooled there, ready to be re-absorbed or to stain.

He'd said truth and now it was time for mine.

"We had our own bets. The four of us girls. Not as major as yours. I wanted you to take down Ivy. Flora was to give Daniel a makeover. Renee wanted to fuck a rat. Yours were worse, but you were coming from a need for survival. We were coming at it from an angle of rich girls with new playthings. I'm not saying that excuses your actions, but I do understand them. And like you've said. You didn't know us then. We weren't real to you."

"Have you talked to the others about this?

I nodded. "About the pact, yes."

"What did they say about it?" He looked up at me again now. His eyes were red-rimmed.

"They don't know about the spy cam and they don't know about Flora's overhearing things and what it led to, and that's how it needs to stay. Nothing good can come from the truth there, Liam. If Renee finds out Brett spiked condoms, she'll report him to the police."

"And she'd have every right."

"She would. But then Brett's life would also be

ruined and where does that lead? Renee didn't get pregnant, or a disease, so whether it's the right decision or not, I want your silence on this."

He nodded, "Okay. But if Brett ever decides to confess..."

"That would be up to him. But he'll never know about the spy cam because you'll never tell him. Promise me."

He huffed. "The fact you think my promises are worth something has me doubting your sanity."

"I'm here for the truth, Liam. That's why I'm here now. I mean, you know my family don't have vast amounts of money and you also know the last thing they'd ever do is let you near it. Yet you stayed. You offered me comfort when shit went down and you stayed with me."

Liam cleared his throat. "The night of Ulric's party, I called the whole bet off. It's why Brett didn't make the party and I ended up there with just Daniel. Brett took off in a huff at me moving the goalposts, although shortly afterwards he agreed it was the right choice. He felt guilty about what he'd done."

He'd called it off? Stopped the bet.

My voice trembled as I spoke. "Y- you called it off? Why?"

"Because I'd fallen for you, Phoebe. Despite wanting to come here to try to guarantee a future with prospects, and using blackmail to do so, I'd decided that I wanted both things. Wealth and you. And I'd decided the way I'd get both would be to pass my exams and gain wealth the honourable way."

He rubbed his right temple as if in pain and his eyes welled up. "But I fucked everything up. Daniel and Flora are dead. How can I allow myself any happiness when my stupid cunt of a brain led to the death of my friend? I don't deserve anything but to be punished and rot in hell and torment for what I've done."

Tears ran down his cheeks now, though he made no sounds of sobbing. "You can go, Phoebe. I thank you for coming to challenge me about all this and I am so sorry." He huff-laughed. "God, I've been gearing up to apologise for what I did in the girls bathrooms, but that doesn't hold a candle to the real destruction I caused."

This was the moment I had to make a decision. To get up, leave. Tell him I'd hate him for the rest of my life. That I wanted nothing else to do with him and would always hold him responsible for the deaths. That his behaviour today had shown me just how cruel he could be.

But I couldn't do it. Because underneath the anger I'd seen the real Liam. The man that hurt others was hurting inside himself. Lashing out to make people leave him so he could go back to being wrapped in barbed wire and left the fuck alone.

But he'd let me in. He'd stopped the bet for me.

I moved so I was sitting next to his knees and I looked up at him. "Liam. The plans you made came from love for your friends. For wanting more for them. They chose to come here of their own free will. You didn't blackmail them... right?" I double-checked because with Liam Lawson you never knew.

"It was their choice to come here. Although Dan would have agreed with anything I said I'd do, even if it was coating himself with jam and running through a wasp's nest."

I half-smiled. "Because he had your back, like you had his. When he got together with my friend, you supported him. We were all happy that they were happy. They showed us what was possible in life. For love to win out. Do you not see that, Liam?"

"All I see is that they had their whole lives ahead of them and now they don't."

I spoke more firmly. "We can't rewrite the past, but the truth is the accident was a culmination of circum-stances: Flora's spying, the bet, Ulric, the accelerator."

"I will blame myself every day until I die," Liam said.

"Daniel wouldn't want that," I said tersely. "He and Flora were all about fairy tale style happy-ever-afters, so if you want to make reparation for your past mistakes, then find your own happy-ever-after and live it for Daniel. Pass your exams and do something with your life. Make having come to Richstone worth it. My guess is that if he saw you loved up and pussy whipped he'd be chuckling in his grave."

"He would," a small smile tilted Liam's lips. "He'd be fucking hysterical."

"Go wash your face and then let's order that food," I said. "Then we can talk more if you want or watch a movie or something. Or if you want to be alone, I can head home."

"I don't want to be alone, Phoebe," Liam said, his voice edged with a vulnerability I didn't even think he was capable of. My heart threatened to fracture hearing it. "Not ever again."

16

Liam

Surprisingly, I managed to eat a decent amount of food. The fact it was from the best restaurant in Richstone might have had a lot to do with it. The food was exquisite, but I mainly put it down to the fact I felt better for telling Phoebe the truth. Now she'd confessed about what she'd overheard everything felt lighter, even though she could yet tell me she didn't want to spend time with me anymore. It was all out there now. Aired between us. I knew why she'd been acting how she had and that it hadn't only come from a place of grief, but one of anger. That she hated me. Hated me and didn't hate me. I had to hope the latter would win out. Because otherwise Sharrow Manor would win, would have poisoned me like it did most who lived there. Wrapped its suffocating tendrils around me and pulled me back in. To a life of misery.

I stared across the dining table at her. "How come you stayed over here every night, given you hated me? Were you hoping for an opportunity to smother me with a pillow?"

A curl came to her upper lip. "I needed you for comfort, and I hated that I needed you, so that's why I never spoke, just came and went."

There were a few minutes of silence while we ate. It turned uncomfortable. Empty.

I broke the silence. "What happens now?"

"You load the dishwasher," she joked.

"Fifi..."

She looked at me imploringly. Like I needed to not ask questions of the future. It showed how we walked on a tightrope right now. Our chances slim, fighting with our feet clinging on, while the rope kept moving. "How about we relax on the sofa and I tell you my plans to hopefully ruin my parents' lives? And then you can tell me how we're going to get away from here and how you're going to be a rich, successful man."

When she said *we're*, I felt just that bit more secure on the rope.

"You're going to try to make a deal with Hector Sackville, given he'll want to bury you alive right now? I don't know, Phoebe, that sounds like a big risk."

Her mouth formed a petulant pout. "I need to take

risks or I'm just going to be stuck in Richstone for the rest of my days. A financed birth canal."

I began to laugh.

"What's so amusing?"

"You just have a way with words. A financed birth canal. You should train as an advertising executive."

"Oh go fuck yourself."

"I'd rather fuck you," I said.

The air seemed to charge around us. The last time we'd fucked it had been an outlet for grief, Phoebe letting me lose myself in her. I knew that this couldn't be a simple fuck though. Phoebe was torn between hating me and seeking reassurance that what we had was real. I wanted to lose myself in her and not come up for air.

I closed the gap between us and let my lips brush across hers, waiting for any hint of resistance or reluctance; any sign she didn't want this.

"I hate that I want you," she said, moving closer, pushing her lips further into mine. I winced slightly at the pressure on my lip, hoping it didn't split back open.

"I know," I replied. I pressed her backwards on the wide sectional sofa, moving so I was beside her, her back up against the back of the sofa. Wrapping her leg around me, I pushed my hardening cock into her core, grinding against her until she moaned. She moved herself, the seam of my jeans working against the soft material of her leggings. Her breath hitched.

Opening my eyes to look at her, I took in the gentle flush on her cheeks, her engorged lips. Her arousal was evident, and my cock ached to spill inside her. But I wanted to take my time; to savour each moment.

I ran my hand down her cheek, then a fingertip across her plump lips. Those rosy-pink lips parted and she accepted my finger into her mouth, sucking on it. Opening her eyes, Phoebe gazed intently at me with mischief and taunting.

I knew I was a goner. No matter how hard I tried to resist making myself vulnerable to anyone, giving them a piece of my heart, it was just too late. Phoebe hadn't waited for a piece of my heart, she'd just ploughed right in and stolen a chunk.

Withdrawing my now wet finger, I trailed it down from the edge of her bottom lip, down her chin, her neck and teased it across her collarbone.

She arched her hips up towards me again, seeking the friction she needed to get off.

"Liam," she pleaded.

"I'm taking my time and enjoying watching you desperate for me," I admitted.

Her cheeks bloomed a little more scarlet.

"Don't get embarrassed, it's cute." I pushed her top off one shoulder to find another layer underneath it.

"Okay, help a guy out here. You've got a double layered top on and a bra. I'd like to look like I can handle taking all these off you in style, but if you help we can get to the good stuff quicker."

"I thought you were taking your time?" Phoebe retorted, shuffling up and lifting up her top.

"I am, but just on the good stuff, not the logistics."

"You're such a romantic."

Her tops off and bra undone and slipped off, I silenced her with my mouth before breaking off to remove my t-shirt and then moving my body against hers again, warm skin to warm skin. Her breasts squished against my chest and I enjoyed the sensation for a while as we carried on kissing. Next, I broke the kiss off and teased trails of kisses down her throat and all the way to her breasts, pausing to take a nipple in my mouth.

Fuck The Aegean. This was the perfect morsel to savour. I cupped her breast in my hand while I teased her rosy bud with my teeth, biting enough to make her gasp and wriggle under my touch.

I paid my respects to her other breast too. By now this slow burn was tormenting me as much as it was Phoebe. My dick was so hard it was being strangled in my jeans.

Standing up, I undid my top button and lowered my zip, shrugging off my jeans and then my remaining clothing. I knelt down beside the sofa.

"Lift up your hips so I can get these clothes off you," I demanded. She did and I pulled her grey leggings down her thighs and off, throwing them beside me on the floor. Grabbing her behind the knees, I shuffled her to the end of the sofa, lowering my mouth to her pussy. My tongue circled her clit with slow, lazy licks, coaxing out the orgasm I was sure she was on the cusp of.

Phoebe cried out, "Liam, please. I can't wait any longer, please," as I carried on lapping at her clit and letting my tongue dart in her pussy. As she thrust wildly against my face, riding me to get herself all the way there, my lazy licks became a desperate search as I feasted on her until with a loud, "Ohhhhhh fuuccckkkk," she exploded against my mouth. I kept my mouth on her until I'd swallowed every last tremor.

Sitting back, I raked my eyes over Phoebe's naked body. Breasts pert, her back arched. They rose and fell with her heady breaths. I wouldn't mention it, but she'd allowed herself to put a little weight on lately, just enough that those curves were even more pleasing on the eye, her breasts fuller. Since becoming estranged from her mother, Phoebe had recently cast off the expectations of Richstone females to look like they needed a good meal, and I was pleased that grief hadn't reversed that. She would need her strength in the coming months to go up against her parents.

Opening her eyes to look at me, Phoebe looked drowsy and satiated, and I considered leaving her to relax and claiming my own release later.

But Phoebe had other ideas.

Sitting up on the sofa, she demanded that I sat down on it and then she straddled me, adjusting my cock so it slipped straight into her warm heat.

I groaned as her cunt consumed my cock.

Her hand came between us and she fisted my shaft.

"I'd stop doing that unless you want this over in about three seconds," I challenged.

"Doesn't matter. We've got all night," she said, though she did let go, resting her hands on my shoulders instead, using me to push against as she rode me.

Her hips circled and once more her stamina from

horse riding came into its own as she expertly rotated her hips, lifting and falling on my cock.

And then she increased her speed and made small mewls and loud moans. Whether they were real or faked to get me going, I didn't give a fuck, her noises spoke straight to my cock. I held firmly onto her hips and yanked her down on me as I pushed up with all my might. My balls tightened and I came hard, my vision going black for a second or two while Phoebe milked my cock. With a flick of a finger on her clit she pulsed around me again, and then we fell back onto the sofa. My hands played in her hair while I listened to her breathing and felt her heart thudding against my chest.

And I felt my own heart beating hard. The heart that was letting me know it wasn't locked away any more for its own protection, but instead, what Phoebe hadn't already claimed was hanging on an imaginary white picket fence, waiting to be collected.

I was fucked. Literally and figuratively.

We went to my bedroom and curled up together under the covers. Where before there had been silence, this time we talked.

"It's okay if you still hate me, Phoebe." I stated. "Just promise me while you also don't hate me too, you'll stick around."

"I don't have a choice. I also don't hate you too much," she confessed, and I kissed her hard and deep.

After that I asked Phoebe to tell me about her dream place that she wanted to escape to.

A smile pulled at her lips as she settled in to tell me about it. "I don't know what's out there and how much it costs, but I imagine a little cottage. Not very large at all but detached. Maybe just two bedrooms even. There's a wooden gate, painted in cornflower-blue, but worn off in places with age. The garden is full of large blooms of all different colours at the front, at either side of the path that leads to the front door. At the back there are flower beds, a lawned area, and a swing seat on a patio where I can read and relax." She smiled. I don't think she even realised, but I could see she'd thought about this many, many times. Maybe escaped to this place mentally when things had got bad with her father? I wouldn't ask. I didn't want to pull her from the thoughts that had made her smile.

"So is this in the countryside?"

"It's near the beach. If it's near country walks too then that's my ideal dream home, but if I'm not able to look at the sea, I want it to be within a close walk. And I want a dog. A gorgeous rescue dog that I can take on walks while I enjoy the scenery."

"Sounds lovely."

She happy sighed. "Yeah. But most of all, I want to be free. Even if my home doesn't end up more than a space where I hang a photo of a beach and have a vase of freshly cut flowers, I just want to be able to breathe freely. To let my breath flow in and out without anxiety that someone is on the cusp of ruining my day or telling me how to live my life."

"Let's do it," I said, my words surprising my own ears. "We can't know what the future holds, but we can aim to escape. Pool our resources and search for that dream."

Her eyes widened and she pushed out of my arms slightly to look up at me. "Are you serious? You'd come with me?" she said.

I scoffed at myself. Who was I these days? "Yeah, I believe I am."

She smiled but then it tightened. "What about your mum though?" she asked. "You wouldn't want to be too far away from her I'm guessing?"

I leaned in, my lips brushing over Phoebe's. I couldn't stop touching her. "My mother is a work-in-progress at any time. She has my uncle nearby and I'd keep in touch, but I can't make my life choices based around her."

Her eyes opened slightly wider, became more alert. "We should go see her together. I only met her the one time when she was drunk and naked. If she's doing better, we could call there later on Sunday afternoon. What do you think? After we've had time to get over the hangovers we'll no doubt have from Saturday's party. I'd like to meet her, find out more about Liam Lawson from Sharrow Manor."

"Yeah?" I ran my fingertips up and down Phoebe's arm, eliciting goosebumps. "I reckon she'd like that. I'll call her in the morning."

Phoebe tried and failed to fight a yawn. "Sorry."

"Okay that's enough talking. You close your eyes and drift off back to your dream cottage."

She smiled, pressed one last kiss against my mouth and turned over, curving herself so her back was to my front. I wrapped my arms around her, but it took me time to fall asleep.

Because I couldn't help but worry I'd made a promise I couldn't keep about trying to leave and live the dream. I was still a schoolboy from Sharrow Manor, with fifteen grand to my name and nothing else.

17

Phoebe

W hen I woke curled up in Liam's arms, this time I didn't steal away from his bed without a word, but instead, I woke him up in an entirely, much better way. After a quick shower, I headed up to the main house to get ready for school.

Once more I met my friends at the main entrance, and we walked in together. More heads turned to look at us than usual. Some whispered and so many more said 'good morning' to us. The younger ones looked at us like we were some sort of goddesses and I guessed this was why Ivy loved her role as Queen Bee. She loved the admiration. It made her feel important and accepted. Whereas I knew this was a façade; as fake as one of Ivy's smiles.

When I heard whoops and hollers, I turned around to see Liam walking in with Brett. He did a mock bow as others from our year wolf-whistled like he was a rock star of some kind. A group of boys caught up with him and started talking, no doubt wanting the lowdown on what had happened between Ivy and the scholarship kid.

"What a difference a day makes," Lucie quipped. "The boys all want his advice, and the girls will all want his goods." She stared at me. "So, spill. What happened when you talked?"

My cheeks heated.

"Ooooh," she teased. "Did you actually talk at all or was your mouth full?"

"Lucie. Leave her alone," Renee protested, and then she elbowed me. "I'm lying. Tell us everything."

I gave them a rundown on how Liam seemed genuinely remorseful and that even though I still felt on my guard a little, for now it looked like we were back being a secret couple while Richstone thought he'd rocked Ivy's world.

"So he's gonna make out like they had something going on, while all the time she was pretending to hate him?" Lucie checked.

"Yup. It serves to distract people away from what's really going on."

"That he's boning you instead," Renee explained helpfully.

"Okay, let's get on with the day, let Liam have his fifteen minutes of fame and then during breaks and lunch we need to finalise these party plans," Renee said. "It's going to be the best party Richstone has seen in years. The amount of local companies who have offered freebies either for the party, the auction, or for both has been overwhelming."

Renee had secured the main function room at the country club for the party. It had been booked for a sixtieth birthday, but the guy in question had donated his booking to Renee, telling her that secretly he was more than happy to do so because he preferred to celebrate at home with a nice port, some cheese, and none of his wife's family. Renee had arranged for an extra special selection of both port and cheese to be delivered to him as a surprise on his big day.

I was halfway through the morning and walking between classes, when Sarah, another of The Poisons sidled up beside me. Ivy was officially 'off sick with a virus'.

"Ivy wanted me to pass a message on that you should watch your back," she said.

I got up in the girl's space, "Or what?"

She flinched and stepped back. "I d- don't know. It's just a message."

"Well, if you don't want crap from me in return, I suggest you tell her to contact me directly to deliver her empty threats," I warned. "I'd hate to have to put you on my shit list."

She scurried away and I laughed. It would be so easy to get sucked into a power trip with Ivy's minions. Hopefully with time away from her they might develop their own personalities, but I wouldn't hold my breath.

The boost from scaring away The Poison meant that when I saw Ulric approaching me from the opposite direction, I stopped him, grabbing his arm. He'd still looked subdued and like he was trying not to be noticed. It was very un-Ulric like.

"Can I have a word?"

"Haven't you already had enough?" Bailey Trainor snarled from Ulric's side.

"Eat shit and die, Bailey," I quickly retorted, and once again I saw a personality deflate right before my eyes.

"Yes, a quick one, because I don't want to be late to class. I'm already in enough trouble," Ulric replied. Bailey walked away, giving me side-eye as he went.

Ulric and I stood off to one side.

"You understand why I did what I did yesterday?" I asked.

"Does it matter?" he replied. I ignored his snark.

"Have your parents told you that I'm coming for dinner on Friday?"

"Yes. What an absolute joke." He sneered. "I told them to cancel, but they won't listen. Especially my father. He says he understands your anger, but he's not happy with what you did. So he's probably letting it go ahead so he can have a word with you."

"My mother is going to force me to apologise anyway. Just know in reality I'm not the slightest bit sorry."

He rolled his eyes. "Don't worry, I'll know it's insincere."

"Look, Ulric. I know you didn't mean for your actions to lead to my friend's death. I do know that. But you still hated my friends for that split-second. It was in your eyes as you refused to wait, as you moved your car forward. Your hatred took over all common sense. And then you were letting Daniel take the shit for it. I couldn't let that happen. You made a shitty decision and you have to own it."

He just stood there, waiting for me to be done.

"I've repeated what I did in my head hundreds of thousands of times," he admitted. "I've prayed to wake up and it all have been a nightmare. I've tried alcohol, I've tried therapy, but every time I close my eyes, I revisit speeding past and then looking in my rear-view and seeing the Porsche mount the kerb."

My eyes widened in horror. Ulric had driven away, hadn't he? Hadn't know what he had caused. The boy in front of me read my mind.

"I just thought he'd banged the car and I laughed thinking that he'd get shit from your father. I didn't know he'd killed Flora. Didn't know he'd then kill himself. Not until my mother came rushing home from the country club having heard it from a friend."

I stayed silent because Ulric was no longer seeing me even though his eyes were still on me. He was in his memories.

"I told the police it had been a tragic accident. That I'd just been tormenting him as I went past, but you're right, in that moment I'd hated Daniel. I'd hated that these kids had come from Sharrow and were eating in our restaurants and driving our cars and acting like they belonged here. Because I really did think that I was King

175

of Richstone Academy. Untouchable. Worshipped. Precious." He looked at his feet. "And now I know I'm a piece of shit who had ideas of grandeur and who took every fucking thing he had for granted."

His eyes were flat and lifeless as he looked at me. "I might still have a fortune to inherit, but I've lost my mind."

Resting my hand on his arm, I dropped my voice to a gentle tone. "We're all suffering, Ulric, and I'm sure in time you'll be fine. But you'll be a different person to the one sat behind the wheel that day. Hopefully it will make you a better person. Because if not, if I see any evidence of King Ulric again, I'll encourage you to wrap yourself in rocks and throw yourself in the river."

He blanched at that, like I'd slapped him.

"If you want forgiveness from me. Redemption. You're not going to get it. Not right now. But if something good comes from this and you become a better person, then maybe one day I'll be able to find it in me. You do have a fortune to inherit, and you can make sure to use it for good. Be better."

Ulric nodded. "I'd better get to class," he added.

Then he walked away.

Walking up to my car after school, I found it had been blocked in by a Rolls Royce that was idling behind it.

I strode over to the rear of the car and waited for the window to roll down and reveal Hector Sackville.

"Could I persuade you to come share tea and a scone or something with me, Miss Ridley? I've asked your mother and she has no problem with it."

I squeezed both Lucie and Renee's arms in reassurance, as they had immediately moved in at either side of me.

"I'd be more than happy to do that, Hector," I said, enjoying my use of his first name as if he were my equal. It would annoy him. Hector Sackville felt he was below no one. I said goodbye to my friends. Renee whispered that she'd check where I was via tracking me on my phone and that I was to contact her immediately if there was a problem.

I walked around to the other side of the car and just stood there until Hector requested the driver get out and open the car door for me. I wouldn't be disrespected. While deep down inside I was nervous about trying to deal with an astute businessman who didn't get to his position in the world of media by being a nice guy, I reminded myself that he was exactly that. A businessman. And I wanted to negotiate. All I could do was hope that he'd agree to my terms.

Hector had us driven out of Richstone to an almost equally wealthy neighbourhood that bordered us called Heathfield. There, the driver pulled up outside a luxury hotel, opening my door for me.

During the car journey, Hector hadn't said a word to

me, spending the whole journey on a business call. I
didn't care. It felt like a tactic to make me feel small and
unimportant and bringing me here felt the same. I was a
decent drive away from home, and clearly, as the hostess
greeted us, Hector was a frequent visitor to the hotel.

We were taken through to the bar area, with its rich-
orange leather seating and background piano music. The
room was dark and had some circular booths where
people could hold a private conversation, and it was to
such a booth Hector steered me towards. He took one
side and indicated for me to slide in at the other.

Menus were offered, water set on the table and then
we were left to decide on our food and drink choices.

"How does an afternoon tea sound? Feel free to order
a gin or whatever it is you young ones drink these days."

"Coffee and water will be fine, thank you. I'd like to
keep a clear head."

His eyes perused me with calculated interest. Not in
a lustful way, but rather like a snake would eye up its
prey while lying in wait.

I sat back and crossed one leg over the other while I
waited for the waitress to return. "I'm glad you turned up
today, although a phone call in advance would have been
nice. I was going to contact you myself over the next day
or so."

He looked bemused.

"Hopefully that was about my donation to the
upcoming fundraiser? However, today I'm simply here as
a father to appeal to your good nature with regards to the
unfortunate event that occurred with my daughter. I

don't think for a moment that someone snuck in and put it on that computer. I think your mother is protecting the fact that you did it." He paused to pour himself a glass of water and then nodded towards another glass.

"Yes, please," I replied, waiting until he'd handed me my glass. I took a sip, my mouth dry through nerves while I made sure to keep my hand steady in front of him.

"I need that video gone and for us to invent some story as to how it was all a cruel hoax and a joke between two silly schoolgirls always trying to one-up each other."

His comment fucked me off and I felt my nostrils flare. "Oh I'm far from a silly schoolgirl, Hector, and you'd be as well to not underestimate your daughter either. We might still be at the Academy, but I can assure you that I'm a woman, not a girl." I leaned closer over the table. "I didn't want to meet you regarding the fundraiser or talk about your daughter. I couldn't give two fucks about Ivy. She's reaped what she sowed. I'm here because I know you hate my mother, and I want to know how far you're willing to go to help me destroy her."

I saw Hector swallow and fidget, wrongfooted for a brief second, before his mask returned.

"Well, Phoebe, it seems I may have underestimated you." He smiled like I'd imagine a serial killer would if you tried to negotiate for your life, and my heart thudded in my chest, but I would brazen this out. I had to. Because it was better to be destroyed by Hector Sackville while trying for a better life, than letting Daphne and Maxwell Ridley kill me slowly in my current one.

Hector beckoned over a waiter. "I do believe we

might be in need of a bottle of champagne. Can you have one on ice just in case?" He carried on and ordered the afternoon teas.

And as the waiter left, he gestured to me as if giving me permission to speak. "What are you proposing, my dear Phoebe? I am intrigued."

18

Phoebe

This was it. My one and only shot I believed, at convincing Hector Sackville to get on board with my idea. The one that could save my brother and I and get rid of our parents.

"I want to ask you something first, and you don't have to answer, but... why do you hate my mother so much? Why are you always looking for ways to get her out of Richstone?"

He let out a bemused snort. "It's quite simple really. Your mother took the job my brother was lined up for. Drummond had been deputy head here at Heathfield High for years, waiting in anticipation of the retirement of the old fool who pre-dated your mother's employment. And yet, out of apparent nowhere, Daphne Ridley was appointed. I'll probably never know what she did to get that job for sure, but I could hazard a guess that old Moorhouse had secrets and your mother knew them."

"So what happened when he didn't get the job? Did he just stay at Heathfield?"

"No. He moved to the other side of the country where he's now a headteacher at a small country school. He seems happy enough, but that's not the point. He should have been here in Richstone."

"Where having him would have given you more power over the place?"

"You learn fast, Miss Ridley."

At that point our afternoon tea was delivered. I waited for the waitress to move away from the table.

"So, is it too late, or would your brother welcome the opportunity to return?" I asked.

"Drummond could be persuaded to return. But how do you propose we remove your mother?"

Here went nothing. I was digging now and whether it was my own grave or a tunnel of escape I'd not know for a while yet.

"I know you've heard the rumours that my father's publishing company is struggling. My brother is frantically trying to keep it afloat. My father's recent business decisions have apparently been questionable. I want Eddie and I to be free of them both."

"I put your question back at you, Phoebe. Why don't you like your mother... and your father for that matter?"

My body tensed as I thought of the bastards. "My father beats me up and my mother lets him. All she's interested in is that I make a good marriage match and

182

send her enough money to keep her in the life to which she's accustomed. I'm a puppet to her, not a daughter."

"He does what?" Hector's voice remained calm and controlled but the skin on his face mottled.

"He abuses me. Kicks me. Stands on my fingers. He's supposedly having treatment for it. You know," I did finger quotes, "while he's away on business."

A grim twist settled on Hector's lips before he spoke. "I had my money on him being in The Priory for alcoholism with the amount he puts away. I'd never have thought he'd do that. Your mother's behaviour on the other hand doesn't surprise me at all." He sat back in his seat. "So, what do you want me to do?"

I felt my shoulders drop a little. He was actually open to hearing my suggestions. "I can get Eddie to fuck up something that means the shareholders lose faith in my father's capabilities completely and make the company's fortunes dip further, meaning you could then mount a hostile takeover. Butter them up and buy the company. Remove my father from it."

"But your father is the major shareholder is he not?"

"By fifty-one to forty-nine percent. But faced with a revolt from the rest of the shareholders, that acquisition would look a lot more tempting. Plus, you can challenge him. Find out what clinic he's in and tell him you know everything. Just do whatever you need to do to get the entire group to sell up."

"And then what shall I do with an on its arse publishing company? I'm a businessman, not a charity."

"You make my brother the CEO, with an amazing

financial package, and let him do what he does best. With your contacts and the name Sackville Publishing in place and my brother in charge, that company will fly. All I ask is that if Eddie ever wants to leave, you let him do so. I don't think he will. He loves the business and he's good at what he does. He's just not let free to modernise it. To do what he needs. But I want him to be free to make his own life choices."

Hector tapped against the side of his glass. "And what do I get for this? I mean it's going to take some time and investment."

"My father will be in disgrace. I'm sure my mother will play the victim and leave him, but all the money they will have left, their assets, will be tied up in the house and with what the company sells for. I don't see that they'd have any choice but to leave Richstone, especially when you also discover my mother was my father's therapist and married an abusive man, breaking all her oaths. I mean should such a person run a school?"

Hector actually gasped and then his upper lip twitched.

"I could do all this anyway, you know? You've given me enough that I could destroy your parents and take the company and what could you do about it?" The way he looked at me was like I was being interviewed for a job and he'd given me a scenario I had to talk him through while he considered my application. I guessed in a way that was exactly what this was.

"I'd sedate Ivy, place her in a bath, slit her wrists and make it look like a tragic suicide," I said calmly. I looked at the trays of food and selected a sandwich. "All this talk of sweet revenge has given me quite an appetite," I declared. "So what's it to be, Hector? Do we have a deal, or do I need to go sharpen my knife?" I bit into a cucumber filled triangle.

"I've held meetings with some power crazy, desperate people, Phoebe, and Ivy has been threatened many, many times in order to blackmail me."

I kept my cool while inside I felt sick. He was going to tell me to fuck off and play with my doll's house and not try to play with the big boys. Then he'd take my parents down and Eddie would suffer too. I didn't care about myself, but my brother deserved the world.

"And yet none of them have made me feel the unease you just have. I love my daughter beyond words. Yes, she's a spoiled princess, but I'd never harm a hair on her head, and I certainly wouldn't let anyone else touch her. So, you tell me that video won't see the light of day again, and let the school know it was all a hoax, and we have a deal. I'd be delighted to know you weren't keeping company with an abusive man and I will dance when your mother has to leave Richstone."

He held out a hand.

Liam was not going to be happy about Ivy once again getting away with things.

But my need to be rid of my parents was greater than revenge on Ivy; greater than Liam being hailed a hero for having a big dick.

So I took Hector's hand and shook it.

"I'll talk to Eddie this evening and pass your number

onto him and you can liaise about how that side of things goes down."

"And Liam? Will you deal with him?"

"Yes, I'll go to the bungalow and speak to Liam too. By the end of the week, the video will be said to be fake and Ivy will be able to return from her sick leave."

"She can stay home the rest of the week and attend the party on Friday. Can announce our auction prize as originally agreed. Now what shall it be?"

"I don't care. A holiday? A mentorship with you? Just let me know in time for the auction, so, say by Thursday evening? And make sure Ivy knows that the focus on Friday is on Flora, not her. Because deal or not, if she tries to steal the thunder from my friend's memory, I'll drag her off the stage in front of everyone by her extensions."

"That won't be necessary. Ivy will be learning some lessons from all this, mainly to show a professionalism and eloquence at all times, and not to put herself in positions of making enemies. Lord only knows she'll have enough people try to cut her down once she takes over the business."

I put a hand over my chest. "For a brief moment there I actually thought I felt a little sympathy for your daughter, but I'm sure it was just a bite of sandwich going down the wrong way."

He laughed and we carried on eating for a while.

"What will you do then, Phoebe, once your parents are out of the picture? And what of Liam? If your parents leave Richstone then there's no home for you and no bungalow for Liam."

I shrugged. "I figured I'd stay with one of my friends until I've completed my studies at Richstone Academy. Liam would have to return to Sharrow and walk over here daily like his friend Brett does."

"And after your studies?"

"I'm leaving, Hector. I have no wish to stay in Richstone whatsoever, and if I have to go with only the clothes on my back, so be it. It would only be until I was twenty-one. Then I'm due to receive some inheritance from my grandmother. Nothing huge at the side of Richstone riches, but enough that I can live a simple life."

We finished our food and Hector asked for the bottle of champagne that had been placed on ice and handed it to me.

"Keep it for the night you're free of your parents and celebrate. Now let me get you back to Richstone."

And that's what he did. He took another business call on the way back and then dropped me off at the school entrance.

"I'll be in touch, Phoebe," were his final words as I stepped out of the car.

Walking back to the student car park and around to my driver's door, I climbed inside. Sitting back in my seat, I breathed out a huge sigh of relief. For a minute or two I just stayed sitting there, my music on playing the latest Taylor Swift release and then I noticed the sunlight dipped into shadows for a split-second before a knock on my window made me jump a foot.

Turning, I sighed and wound down my window. My mother leaned in, arms folded. "Do you want to tell me what Hector Sackville had to say that meant you were gone for two-and-a-half hours."

Shit. I needed to think of an explanation. Fast.

I mustered my best disinterested look. "He insisted on taking me to some fancy hotel where he tried to intimidate me into letting Ivy off the hook. I told him I'd say the video was fake if he gave me a massive donation for the fundraiser."

She tutted. "You have no backbone. For one glorious moment, Phoebe, I thought you might have taken after me a little. Seen how to take opportunities in life; but no, Saint Phoebe strikes again. May I remind you that your friend is dead, but you are still alive. You might want to start thinking about the family for a change. We had an opportunity to destroy the Sackville's reputation and you bottled out. I shouldn't be surprised you've disappointed me once again."

Her words stung hard, but I wouldn't let her see.

"Sorry, Mother."

"Well, there's still Friday evening. You'd better be just as amenable to the McDowells as you've been to the Sackvilles," she snarled and then she walked away.

I thought of the bottle of champagne in my school bag. I would certainly celebrate the day I ruined her.

19

Liam

The day had certainly proved different. I'd also discovered just how many people were delighted to see Ivy Sackville knocked off her throne.

"I'm going to flash everyone at the party on Friday, so I get the same amount of attention as you. I want all these offers of fresh pussy you're getting. It's not fair when you're already balls deep in Phoebe's kitty," Brett complained.

Leaving school a little later as Brett's class had run behind, I noticed that Phoebe's car was still parked in the car park. I took my phone from my pocket and sent her a text.

Liam: Everything okay? I can see your car's still here?

But there was no reply.

"Are you calling for a driver?" Brett asked.

"Nah, I'll walk with you until you turn off to Sharrow and I'll enjoy a meander back to the bungalow."

"Might take you a while if you have to manage that big dick..."

I patted the front of my trousers.

"I meant the one on your head."

I pushed him, "Fuck off."

After saying goodbye to Brett, I took my phone back out of my pocket and called Phoebe.

The number you require is switched off. Please try again later.

I had a sense of unease but could do nothing but wait.

It was almost three hours later that I got a response back.

Phoebe: Hector wanted a meeting. You at the bungalow? I'm just about to start driving back now.

Liam: Where else would I be?

Phoebe: The other day, Sharrow, getting in a fight.

Liam: Fair point. Yeah, I'm home.

Home. Jesus, did I consider this my home now? I had to remember that I was a temporary resident here and with the way the game kept changing, who knew how long this would last.

Phoebe: Be there soon.

For some reason I felt like ants were crawling all over

my skin. I knew Phoebe had intended to make a deal with Hector, but he was a cunning businessman, a mogul at the top of his game. She was a schoolkid.

My skin feeling like it was crawling didn't ease when I let Phoebe into the bungalow and her eyes danced with satisfaction, a grin splitting her face from ear-to-ear. She dug a bottle of champagne from her bag. "Let's go out the back, stick the patio heaters on and enjoy this. It might be a little early to celebrate, but I don't care. We'll get another bottle for when the deed is actually done." She waggled the bottle.

"So, it went well then?" The sarcasm was thick in my tone.

"Yes, so come on. The quicker this is poured, and we're sat outside, the faster I can tell you everything."

We went out the back and Phoebe shook the bottle and popped the cork. The champagne went everywhere. I was surprised she didn't ask to be doused in it like the Formula One winners. I couldn't help but think she was headed for a fall. The story of her meeting spilled out as fast as the champagne and then she sat back, sipping her drink and grinning again. I saw the moment the grin slipped off her face, leaving that haughty pout.

"Why do I get the feeling you're not as excited about this as I am?"

I fiddled with the friendship bracelets at my wrist for a moment. "Well, let me think. For a start you've agreed that I will declare this video a hoax without asking me. So much for us doing this together. Then there's the fact that he's Hector Sackville, a man known to be as powerful as

Sir Alan Sugar, and you're Phoebe Ridley, known for... being a sixth former at Richstone Academy. You're fooling yourself if you think he's going to stick to his side of the bargain."

"He will, because if he doesn't, I've threatened to kill Ivy and make it look like a suicide."

I guffawed then. I couldn't help it. She'd taken me completely unawares.

"Of course, he'll totally believe you're capable of doing that. Wake up, Phoebe. You're not going to hurt Ivy. You're not a murderer. You've no clue about how hard it is to sit with a knife and cut someone to get them to give you the money they owe you. Never mind take a life. Hurting someone carves at your own soul. And then there's DNA etc. You're living in fantasyland." It made me realise just how much Phoebe had been living a life so far removed from my own reality.

She huffed, looking petulant. "He believed me, and that was enough. Anyway, he'll destroy my parents one way or another and that's enough for me."

"Well, that's okay then. As long as you're all right. And what about when Drummond Sackville takes over as principal and he finds a way to end the scholarships? Says how I treated his niece means I can fuck off back to Sharrow with my tail between my legs?"

"It's not going to be like that, Liam. God, I thought you'd be pleased. Yes, you have to let Ivy off the hook, but I'll be rid of my parents and free to leave."

"You don't know that. Do you think your mother

won't have another plan? Do you think she'll just leave Richstone in the dead of night, quiet as a mouse?"

Phoebe stood up.

"Where are you going?" My voice was raised on a par with my level of annoyance.

"Back up to the main house where I'm going to drink the rest of my champagne and celebrate by myself. I was so fucking happy, Liam, because I had hope. Maybe it won't turn out exactly how I planned, but at least Hector agreed with my proposals. It's a start. Yes, Ivy gets away with things, but it's for the greater good. For us to get out of here."

"Ivy getting away with it is annoying, but I can deal with that. I'll just gloat about my having pulled the stunt. You're the one with deep-seated Ivy issues. She only pisses me off the same way any of the privileged riches who look down their nose at me do." I sighed. "I'm sorry, Phoebe. It's just I can't bank on fantasies, so we have to make sure that Hector does what's asked, and that means that if it comes to it, you live up to your threats and you put Ivy in a situation where Hector feels he has to give you what you want." I took my blade from my pocket and handed it to Phoebe and then I stripped my top off and offered her my shoulder.

"L- Liam, what are you doing?"

"I'm going to teach you how to cut for maximum pain, but minimum damage." I grabbed the champagne bottle. "I'm going to need some of this."

"There is not a chance in hell I'm going to cut you with a knife. I like you."

"Exactly. So if you like me and can cut me, then you'll definitely be able to slice the skin of an enemy. But you don't want a murder charge. So just as you taught me how to ride a horse, I'm going to teach you how to cut someone for blackmail purposes etc." I raised a brow. "How come both end up with me in pain?"

"Liam, I'm not sure," her voice trailed off and I could see the point where she realised she had no choice.

"So this here is the safety mechanism." I pointed to the relevant part of the knife. "Move that up to take it off and then press that button to release the blade. Always make sure the safety is on, or you'll end up stabbing your-self in the leg."

Phoebe took a deep breath and then did as asked. Following that, I showed her how to safely close it.

"Great. Now show me again."

She did.

I stood up. "I'm just going to get some things. I'll be back in a minute."

I returned a few minutes later with alcohol wipes, cotton wool, Savlon cream, a plaster, and a bandage.

"Do I *have* to cut you?" Phoebe whined, "only since you took your shirt off, I have other things in mind."

I smirked. "I'm sure you do. But you'll have to get in the queue now. Plenty of women want a piece of this fine arse now, you know?"

She flicked out the blade, "And suddenly I'm finding it easier to want to cut you."

I took the switchblade from her and wiped it down with alcohol wipes to sanitise it and then after handing it back, I turned to her once more offering the top of my arm.

"Now, put the blade next to my skin."

'Liam, this is crazy."

"It's not crazy. I'm teaching you how to defend yourself. What's crazy is threatening Hector Sackville," I snapped.

She ran the blade down my arm, now pissed off with me. It nicked my skin in a couple of places but barely did anything. "A little more pressure, Phoebe. Press and drag. For about an inch maybe."

I felt the coolness of the tip of the blade against my skin and then she tilted it slightly. I watched her swallow and then she applied pressure, pressing down and dragging the blade an inch. Beads of blood bloomed and she sat back and gasped. "Fuck, I did it. I cut you."

The sting of pain bloomed, but it wasn't my first experience of being cut by a knife and I was sure it wouldn't be my last.

"You did. It stings like a bitch." Picking up another alcohol wipe and tearing open the packet, I wiped it across, hissing with the sting as alcohol hit the cut.

"Now see how alcohol can make that tiny cut give even more pain?"

She nodded.

I picked up some cotton wool and held it onto the cut.

"Can I do anything?" Phoebe bit her bottom lip.

"Yeah, get a wipe and clean my blood off the blade."
She did so and then waited. Once the blood on my arm

had started to clot, I added a little Savlon and then covered my skin with a plaster.

"There, see, it wasn't so hard, was it?"

"I could definitely cut Ivy Sackville. Without a doubt," she replied.

"Let's hope it doesn't come to that."

"What's the bandage for?"

"Well, that was in case you got a bit carried away and a plaster wasn't enough. But now I think I'll use it for something else."

"Like what?"

"Like a blindfold, and maybe to secure your wrists."

"Huh." She pouted again. "I don't think so. This time, you can be blindfolded, and I'll secure your wrists."

I handed the bandage to her. "Sounds good to me. I'm your willing sex slave. Do what you will."

And she did.

Afterwards she left me to go back to the house to get changed and to do some studying. I went online and found a business email contact for Hector.

To: HectorSackvilleGlobal@industries.com

From: LiamLawson@gmail.com

Date: 4 May

Subject: Meeting Request

. . .

I would be very grateful if we could arrange to meet to discuss recent events with Ivy at your earliest convenience.

My telephone number is: 07985 245231
Regards
Liam.

I had my own price for playing a part in this charade.

—————

It was the following morning before my phone rang. I answered it quietly from my place at the rear of the classroom. "Mr Lawson, this is Hector Sackville."

"Just a moment," I said, excusing myself from class, saying it was my mother and was urgent.

When I got outside the door, I checked the corridors making sure I could speak freely.

"Thank you for calling me back, Hector. Only, I spoke with Phoebe last night and while it all sounds tickety-boo for yourself and for her, I'm not sure what advantage there is for me in all this. Because from where I'm standing, I can first look like a lying fool, and then your brother comes in and throws me out of school."

"What do you want, Liam? Bearing in mind I know you already have ten thousand pounds of mine. Make it quick because I'm currently between paying you off or paying for someone else to deal with you."

"I want another ten thousand pounds, and your

agreement I can stay in school until I've finished my exams. Otherwise, the principal's office isn't far from here and I'll just tell her everything."

A mocking laugh came from the other end of the line. "If you try anything else, I'll come for your friends and family, Liam. You already know what it's like to lose someone. I'd hate for anyone else to suffer because of your foolish actions. You can keep the ten thousand you already have and stay in the school. That's it. Nice doing business with you, Mr Lawson."

He ended the call.

I kicked at the wall. "Fuck." I'd hoped to add to my funds, but at least I got to keep the original amount and my place at Richstone.

This education better lead me onto bigger and better things, because all it had done so far was cost me.

On Friday lunchtime, I stood on a table in the dining room and banged a spoon on the top of a mug. "Hey folks. Can I have your attention?"

Canteen staff came to try to get me down, but I shook my head, telling them I'd just be a minute.

"It's been a laugh this week, but I need to tell you that the whole video thing with Ivy was a hoax I set up." People in canteen groaned simultaneously, some people yelled, and others started throwing bits of food and wrappers. I held up my hands. "Don't be too pissed with me. It's just Daniel was always a bit of a joker and I just wanted to do something as a tribute, you know, a prank. But..." I paused for dramatic effect and then swung out my hips. "The size of my dick in the video was however totally genuine, and I wouldn't be surprised if Ivy doesn't ask for me to put it in her mouth when she's well again and back at school."

Some laughed at that, and I jumped off the table and returned to sit with the others.

"I can't believe she's got away with it," Renee said. "She'll be a nightmare on Monday."

"She'll still get teased regardless," Lucie added. "They'll think no smoke without fire, and those who hate her will still delight in it. I just hope backing down proves worth it."

Phoebe and I exchanged a glance. Lucie wasn't the only one hoping.

20

Phoebe

"Are you ready, Phoebe?" My mother had knocked before opening my door and now hovered in the doorway.

She was dressed in a long, tunic-style dress that cinched at the waist with a belt. Over the top she wore a white cardigan because she hated her 'scrawny arms'. She liked to dress as Daphne, not Principal Ridley, whereas I couldn't have been less enthusiastic to get ready for the evening. Still, I'd made every effort. I wouldn't let my mother tell me I wasn't doing my bit for the family. So I wore a black wrap dress, my black high heels, and had my hair twisted into an elegant chignon with some wispy tendrils at the front. Simple eye make-up and a sophisticated red lip completed the look.

"As ready as I'll ever be, so let's do this," I replied, grabbing a black leather jacket and my bag.

It didn't take long to get there. The car journey was silent as George drove us, apart from the occasional comment from my mother about someone having a new car on their driveway or having had their garden landscaped. I so wanted to yell at her that I didn't give a fuck. I just had to be patient. The time to do just that would be coming sooner rather than later now.

The usual fake greetings happened the moment we arrived. Air kisses to the cheeks and the sharing of compliments about clothes and how well everyone looked. Ulric and I shared a blank look, not daring to roll an eye or raise a brow.

"Come straight through to the dining room," Margot said after our coats had been collected and taken to the cloakroom.

We walked into an elegant room with white marble flooring and floor-to-ceiling windows. The table was gilt and glass and I would have hated to be the one who had to keep it fingerprint and dirt free. Someone must need to be employed to keep the furniture in this room clean alone. There was a matching sideboard and large mirrors on the walls.

"Oh this room is just wonderful," my mother simpered.

"Thank you. I just had it redecorated a couple of months ago. Have to keep things fresh, don't we? Keeping the place maintained is a job in itself, isn't it?"

My mother nodded, but her smile didn't reach her eyes given she worked hard. People like Margot

McDowell who spent money all day and pretended it was some kind of work had a special place in hell reserved for them by my mother. Though these days I wondered if she actually liked anyone at all.

Wine was poured, and the meal got underway. At first it was all surface conversation and then right in the middle of the main course, my mother dropped her first bomb.

"So, Ulric, I know I'm not here this evening as Principal Ridley, but it would be remiss if I didn't ask how this week has been since Phoebe's outburst on stage. Phoebe actually has something she wants to say to you; don't you, Phoebe?"

I put down my knife and fork, holding up a finger while I finished the morsel of food I was chewing. I then took a drink of water and after placing that down, I reached for a table napkin and wiped my mouth.

"Yes. Ulric, while I don't regret asking you to take responsibility for your actions, I do regret how I delivered them. It wasn't becoming of the principal's daughter. For that, I apologise."

"Thanks, Phoebe. I actually don't have a problem with what happened. I was allowing people to believe it was all on Daniel and it's that, really, that's unforgivable. I was a coward, and for that, I'm also sorry."

His words surprised me. I'd just thought he'd take my apology, but he'd actually made his own.

I looked away to find Margot staring at her husband. She caught me and smiled before saying, "Well, that's all sorted then now, isn't it? Time to put the past behind us and look towards the future. Don't you think, Daphne?"

"I agree," my mother said. "It was a shame they had the falling out because Phoebe has admired Ulric from afar for a long time. You used to put little love hearts with arrows and your names in your diaries didn't you, darling? It was so sweet."

I tittered along. To say this was awkward was an understatement.

"I was thinking that now the two of them are friends again, they might like to go out. Not necessarily dating, although I know Phoebe would like that, but if they just hung out and gave the impression they were, then everyone at school would know Ulric was forgiven for his involvement in Flora and Daniel's deaths and could get his good reputation back again."

I could see that Richard McDowell was about to protest, but Ulric cleared his throat. "I'd love to hang around with Phoebe sometime. I had a secret crush on her all through senior school, though I didn't have a diary to draw love hearts in."

That makes two of us, I thought.

"Perfect. We'll leave you two to make the arrangements. They don't want us old ones interfering, do they?" Daphne said, and I wondered if she was actually becoming unhinged because this behaviour was far from normal even for her.

After the meal had finished, Ulric asked if I wanted a house tour. I'd not been here before and welcomed the chance to escape to be nosy and to get away from my mother.

"That wasn't the slightest bit awkward," Ulric noted.

"Confession time. I almost died of embarrassment," I told him.

"I might ask if I can look at those diaries sometime," he joked.

"She'd have a task producing them from her imagination."

"Yeah, I didn't think it was real."

"Thanks for saying you crushed on me too though. Stopped me cringing as hard."

"Yeah, I wasn't lying, Phoebe."

"Oh."

"Don't worry. I realised it was a waste of time and moved onto Tabitha Saint. When she left at the beginning of term, I was devastated."

"You never wanted to date Ivy?" It was something I'd always wondered. Why the King and Queen had never united.

He snorted at that. "Are you joking? She tried when she first claimed the so-called title of Queen Bee, but I wouldn't trust her to post me a letter. She'd steam the fucker open to search for blackmail fodder before throwing it in a hedge."

"Yeah, she would," I agreed.

"I have to admit to being disappointed when I discovered Liam's video was a hoax. It was a bloody good fake. Unless of course he was paid to say that, given I know how much Hector would want this to go away and how lacking in funds Liam would be."

"You called him Liam, not rat," I said.

"Guess I have to grow up sometime."

"I don't know the truth about the video," I lied. "Liam wouldn't let me be privy to something like that."

"No? I thought you'd become friends."

"We have. I mean I didn't really have any choice with my mother heading up the whole project, but he's nice, and so is Brett. It's not their fault they were born in a different postcode."

"I guess I'm guilty of being a complete arsehole full stop. I'd better apologise to Liam and Brett."

"That's up to you. I'm not sure how Liam would respond to that."

I brought up the party to change the subject because while I was trying to be tolerant of Ulric, given the collection of circumstances that led to the accident, I still held a grudge somewhere deep down that I didn't think would ever leave me.

"I'm coming with Bailey and Richie. My dad's offered a week's stay in our Barbados holiday home, so I'm hoping that raises some good money for your charity."

"I'm hoping we raise a lot for charity and that we can use our tragedy to help others. It should be a bit of a release for everyone to let their hair down a little after the sombreness of the week, given the memorial service and everything."

We returned back to our parents. Margot and

Richard looked delighted to see me and I figured they'd had as much of Daphne Ridley as they could stand.

"Thank you for a lovely evening," I said, first to Ulric and then to his parents.

"It's been lovely to see you, Phoebe. Daphne, please give our regards to Maxwell and let him know he was missed," Richard said.

"Of course. Hopefully he won't be so busy next time."

"Pass on my regards to Liam, Phoebe," he added. "Only without him this daft idiot would have drowned at his last party."

"Dad! I've apologised several million times for that now." Ulric looked thunderous.

"There's always something with children, isn't there?" My mother said. "Makes you wonder if having them was worth the hassle sometimes." She let out a little snigger, "but of course it is. Come on, Phoebe darling, let's leave the McDowells to enjoy the rest of their evening."

As soon as we were outside, she grilled me. "What was Richard talking about regarding Liam?"

"Ulric got drunk at his last party and almost drowned. Liam rescued him."

"Surprised you didn't mention his heroic act." She rolled her eyes.

"I was too busy recovering from being beaten by my own father that night."

"Must you always bring everything back to that? He's

having treatment. You'll be fine from now on. You managed to forgive Ulric for what he did to your friend."

"I have not f—"

George got out of the car then to open the doors for us. It was good that he did because I was recollecting the feel of the switchblade as it travelled down Liam's arm, imagining it going down my mother's neck. She was continually pushing my buttons and I just didn't get why she couldn't leave me alone. I was doing what she asked.

As we walked into the house, she paused in the doorway. "I do believe things happen for a reason. If you hadn't given Liam that blow job and got caught, then we'd still be trying to match you with Stefan Barratt. Ulric McDowell is a much better match for you."

"You mean he's richer and that suits your purposes? I'm still living in hope, Mother, that the company's fortunes turn around and I can go to university."

"If you need a few years to get your independence out of your system and go to university I'm sure Ulric would be fine with that. He's no doubt going to university himself. You could even attend the same one."

I put my hands on my hips. "What are you talking about? Our deal is if the company is financially sound and you and Maxwell are no longer in need of pressuring your own children, that I can go to university and make my own life." My voice was rising with every word.

"Don't be ridiculous, Phoebe. I said you could go to university. Then you come home and marry into a good family as expected."

"Why are you like this?" I challenged. "I thought you loved me. How could I have been so damn stupid?"

She smirked. "The same way your father was. Everyone wants to believe in love, Phoebe. I convinced your father that I was his saviour and he married me, meaning I no longer had to worry about money. Power is addictive. I understood where my clients came from when they spoke of addictions and bad behaviour, because when people don't want to say no to you, or you give them no option, it's exhilarating. And you, my darling, you and Eddie, are two people I birthed especially so I had insurance against becoming poor again. The heirs to their father's wealth. If Maxwell had kicked me out, he'd have still needed to part with a large chunk of change to cover the vast childcare expenses I would have claimed for."

"So that's it. We were a safety blanket?"

"You were power and leverage. By the way, your father is returning tomorrow evening. He's more or less completed his treatment and there are business matters to attend to at the company. It's probably best if you two try to stay out of each other's way until you decide to let bygones be bygones."

She walked away from me then and all the fight left me. I dragged myself up the stairs to my room. I'd told Liam I would go round to the bungalow, but I just didn't have the energy. I texted that the evening had been so awkward I'd returned home with a foul headache and was going straight to bed.

Liam: Feel better soon, but damn it, I've

told Marlon and Brett they can stay over here tomorrow night after the party, so that will be two nights without you in my bed.

I replied that it was fine, and we could catch up properly on Sunday when we went to visit his mother.

Then I removed my make-up and got ready for bed, climbed under the covers and let sleep take me and block my current reality out.

21

Liam

B rett, Marlon, and I were dressed in smart trousers and shirts. Marlon wore a tie, but Brett and I had ours open by a couple of buttons at the top. It was a far cry from a party at Sharrow, where jeans and a t-shirt were the uniform for guys, and girls turned up dressed anywhere between looking like they couldn't care less in onesies to resembling hookers.

"I am going to get completely and utterly wasted," Marlon declared. "So look after me tonight. That's why I wanted to stay at yours."

"You might want to rethink that plan, mate," Brett said. "Wouldn't look good in respectable Richstone."

Marlon sneered. "I don't give a fuck about Richstone. In fact, I don't give much of a fuck about anything right now."

"What on earth has got into you?" Brett nudged his shoulder.

"It's what he hasn't got into, I'm guessing," I stated. "Love life giving you trouble?"

"I don't have a love life. Just keep messing around with a stupid bitch. I'm over it. Might give Lucie one after all."

"No, you absolutely won't, and in any case, the only thing you'll be receiving from Lucie will be dirty looks. Your rejection hurt."

"I'll apologise for that. Now I know how it feels," he sulked.

I squinted my eyes while I appraised him. "You've already been drinking, haven't you?"

He nodded. "Since last night. Had a few hours' sleep and a couple of coffees. Though they had whisky in them."

I clapped him on the back. "Let's just remember the girls have organised this to celebrate Flora and raise money for charity, and it's supposed to be a happier occasion than the funerals, so cheer the fuck up."

"Yes, sir. I'd hate to piss your girlfriend off so she won't put out."

"She's already not putting out because you're staying at mine." I gestured to the door. "Cars here, let's move it."

Brett talked for most of the car journey, no doubt so that Marlon couldn't whine. But when we pulled up outside the country club, all of us found ourselves speechless. Outside were men on stilts, women with beards, people performing magic, and there were outside stalls. It was circus and fairground themed, and no doubt held a nod to *The Greatest Showman* and American teenage movies like *The Kissing Booth*. I knew all the girls liked those movies. They talked about them at lunch sometimes.

The themes continued inside with an acrobat whirling herself around in swathes of material in one corner. There was indeed a kissing booth and Brett and I groaned simultaneously while Marlon asked if he could borrow some money for it.

I spotted Phoebe chatting to someone. As if she could feel my eyes on her, she turned towards me and then after excusing herself, she dashed over towards us all, throwing her arms around Marlon.

"Marlon Rowe, you stink of scotch. You'd better behave yourself tonight," she warned.

"I will, I promise," he said, squeezing her tightly. And I felt jealous. Because here in public he felt free to do that. No one would think twice about her greeting the boy she'd not seen since the funeral, whereas I couldn't touch her in public at all. Unless... suddenly the kissing booth seemed the most amazing idea ever and I was glad I'd brought some of my Richstone 'earnings' with me tonight.

"This all looks incredible," Brett told Phoebe. "The three of you have done a brilliant job."

Phoebe grinned. "It was Renee and Lucie mainly. I just did as I was told." She looked over my shoulder and rolled her eyes. "Here comes the queen. It doesn't look like her recent fall from grace has affected her."

I turned to look as Ivy sauntered in, head held high, and snooty look upon her face. "It'll have affected her, but like everyone else here, she'll have been brought up not to show it."

"She's coming straight over," Brett stated.

Ivy grabbed a glass of champagne from a tray as she walked past and carried on until she was in front of us. She'd gone all out, dressed in a clingy, shimmering gold dress. She even wore a headband with a little crown in the centre of it.

She threw the drink in her hand straight in my face and said loudly, "That's for making me look like a slut, you fucking dickhead." Passing the glass to Brett, I heard her mumble. "Tell him I'm sorry, but I have an image to maintain."

Phoebe beckoned over a server and took the towel from over his shoulder, passing it me to wipe myself down.

"She was bound to d—"

"Don't." I held up my hand cutting Phoebe off while I towelled my hair and shoulders. "Once more she's making me look like the fool." It came out bitter, my resentment at not having agreed it clear in my tone.

"Then don't let her. Laugh and shrug it off. People forget worse things," she said cuttingly, and I heard what she didn't say. *Like bets that led to friend's deaths.* But right there she'd shown she hadn't forgotten at all. It showed that we still had issues with each other and the air between us turned thick as the conversation froze.

"Right, I need to get back to my hostess duties. Good

to see you, Marlon. I might drag you onto the dance floor later."

She walked away and Marlon fixed me with a stare, "What the fuck was all that about?"

"She's probably due a period," I sneered, trying my best to appear like the Liam of old, the one who didn't let a girl affect him. 'Anyway, fuck it," I replied. "I'm with you. Let's get drunk."

"Great," Brett groaned. "Now I have two of you to babysit."

"Or you can join in?" I rolled my eyes.

"No can do. Someone has to make sure we keep our places at Richstone. I've always had to be the fucking sensible one. One day, I'm going to do something reckless and you'll be the one who has to be fucking level-headed." He held out his hand. "Shake on it. One day, sometime in the future, because of Brett's sacrifice to take care of you both no matter what, you will have to take care of him."

"Why? What are you planning? Sounds exciting," Marlon asked.

"Nothing. But I guess at some point a girl will piss me off and I'll end up like the sad fuckers you two currently are and I'm just making you remember that on this night, Saturday 11 May, I sacrificed a good time to look after my friends, and I'll be calling in the debt."

"You're such a dickhead." I shook his hand and Marlon followed.

"Come on, Marlon, let's get to the bar. Free champagne sucks. I want a real drink."

Agreeing, he followed me and Brett followed him.

When the dancing started, Marlon and I were already merry, and we headed down to the dance floor and cut some moves.

Casey joined the dance floor with her bitch of a friend. They started dancing near us and Casey waved and said, "Hi."

"I think you've got a little admirer there," Brett shouted in my ear over the music.

"Nah, man. She's just thankful that I put her in her car that night. She knows how badly it could have ended."

"If you say so," he replied, going back to dancing.

When I turned back around, Casey was chatting in Marlon's ear and dancing near him, and her friend was looking murderous at being left out. She saw Brett and I had finished talking and moved closer to us, shimmying her hips and raising her hands above her head.

"Desperate," I whispered to Brett.

"What's your name?" he shouted to her.

The brunette looked at him from under her lashes. I think she was going for coy, but it just didn't ring true for the woman who'd just almost had her tits pop out of her bustier as she raised her hands up.

"Sasha," she shouted back. "Sasha Templeton."

I looked around the dance floor and saw that Bailey Trainor was looking daggers over at us. Seemed like he was still laying claim to the bitch. He could fucking have her. After we'd played with her a little first that was.

"Trainor's watching, so flirt up a fucking storm," I told Brett.

"You got it," he said, moving in nearer, grabbing Sasha's hips and dancing close. I moved over to Marlon and Casey and lost myself in the music until thirst hit me and I decided to go get something else to drink. I made a drink sign to Brett and Marlon and all five of us moved off the floor and went to the bar. I bought everyone a drink, because Bailey was still looking over on occasion and pissing him off made me feel good.

Then Renee came to join us. "Hey, boys, how goes it?" she said. "You look like you're enjoying yourselves," her eyes bored into mine pointedly. "You gonna introduce me? I've seen these ladies around school, but I don't know them."

"This is Casey and this is her friend Tasha," I said deliberately.

"Sasha," she replied annoyed.

Casey moved closer. "Hi, Renee isn't it? I'm Casey. I'm in the lower sixth. My sister Sarah is in your year."

"Sarah? The Poison?" Renee blurted out and then she put a hand over her mouth. "Fuck, I'm so sorry. I shouldn't have said that."

But Casey was laughing. "Oh my god. Do you call them that because they hang out with Ivy? Even though I'm dying to use it myself I promise I won't tell her. We'd have to talk to each other for that to happen anyway. I can't stand her either."

"I think they know anyway so feel free to call it her. I was just scared I'd slagged off your sister, but if you don't like her anyway..."

Casey's mouth downturned. "She changed when she started hanging around with Ivy, but anyway, I want to say thank you for organising this great party. Richstone teens needed this."

"That's exactly what we thought. So how do you know the boys?"

"I met Liam at Ulric's last party. I'd got ridiculously drunk and he helped make sure I was put in my car and sent home safely. I'm thankful as I dread to think what would have happened otherwise."

I noticed Sasha didn't pick up on the dig. Clearly, it wasn't obvious enough and needed handing to her via a huge spade.

"Well, as far as I knew friends agreed to come to parties together and leave together, or at least make sure everyone had a way of getting back safely," I said, turning to Sasha, who suddenly found the floor fascinating.

Renee stared at me for what felt like a few seconds longer than necessary before looking back at the girls. "It's great to have met you both. I've got to get back now as we're about to do the kissing booth and then the auction. Enjoy the rest of the night." She leaned in to Sasha and then Casey and I heard her whisper, "anyone you have your eye on for the booth?"

Sasha said Bailey, quelle surprise. Casey whispered in her ear and Renee grinned and said, "I think that sounds great, and of course, it's all in a good cause."

"Gonna tell me who?" I winked when Renee had gone, but as Casey's eyes flickered over to Marlon, I already knew the answer. I just hoped she wasn't heading for a fall, given Marlon's 'complicated' private life.

Lucie took to the stage and after a little introductory speech thanking people for attending, she announced the start of the kissing booth.

"I'm going to firstly ask for six male volunteers to come to the stage," she said, gesturing to the six stands that had been erected, three to each side. "And then the ladies amongst us, plus Ivy, can bid for a kiss," she said, before looking over the crowd to catch Ivy's eye. "Only joking, Ivy, we know the clip was a hoax. So, men, please volunteer as tribute. How about you start us off Bailey? And Marlon, you up for it?" After that we'll be asking for three female volunteers because Lucie, Phoebe, and I will be taking to the stage of course."

I turned looking for Phoebe and she caught my eye and then looked away, clearly still pissed with me about earlier. Yeah, well, she'd have to get over that pretty damn quick because I was bidding for this kiss and I was going to make it worth every damn penny.

22

Phoebe

While I understood that an unexpected champagne shower was unwelcome when you'd just arrived dressed up for a party, it was hardly anything major. With his short hair, Liam was dry in seconds given most of it had been aimed at his face. His shirt was only slightly damp. His annoyance at me because of it had just really irked me. Maybe he didn't accept that letting Ivy off the hook was the best thing for our future after all? Or was he still annoyed I'd not discussed it? Whatever. Right now, I had a party and fundraiser to ensure was a success.

I'd been busy working the crowd when Renee and Lucie had come up to either side of me. "You seen Liam lately?" Lucie asked.

"No, and right now I don't care," I said like a two-year-old throwing a tantrum.

"Oh, lovers tiff," Renee said. "That explains it."

"Explains what?" I frowned.

"Why he's on the dance floor with Brett, Marlon, and two girls from the lower sixth."

I moved myself so that I could see them on the dance floor. Liam wasn't doing anything other than dancing and I watched as he whispered something to Brett, but I still felt irritated.

Annoyingly, I recognised the emotion. Jealousy. I wanted to drag him off the dance floor. My shoulders slumped. We couldn't go public, so other girls would think he was available.

"They're moving from the dance floor," Renee updated us like she was on a spy mission.

My eyes followed them as they moved to the bar. Liam didn't search me out once.

"I'm going to find out who they are," Renee said, disappearing through the crowds before I could stop her.

"Liam wouldn't do anything stupid," Lucie tried to placate me.

"No, the man who showed me a recording of himself being given a blow job by my arch-enemy probably thinks he can do what he likes."

"*Phoebe!*"

I huffed. "He's had a lot to drink, and he's pissed off with me."

"He's probably trying to make you jealous... and it's clearly working. So, let Renee go fact find and report back. We can go set up the kissing booth."

We'd just finished when Renee returned.

"All is fine. Casey is just a girl who Liam helped at a party. She was drunk and he made sure she got safely home by taking her to her driver. He's acting like her big brother."

"First I've heard of this act of heroics," I snapped.

"This shade of green does not suit you, Fifi."

"Huh. Fuck him. He's an arsehole. Come on, tonight's not about him. It's about fundraising and celebrating our friend. Let's start the kissing booth after we have another glass of champagne each."

We held our glasses together. "Flora, we love you," we shouted into the air and then we drank the champers before Lucie made her way to the stage.

"Thank you, gentlemen," Lucie announced as the guys stood behind their stands. "So, for purchase this evening are kisses from Stefan Barratt, Bailey Trainor, Marlon Rowe..."

Large wolf whistles came from the audience. I couldn't see but it was clearly Liam and Brett.

"Richie Asquith, Nelson Valentine, and Sam Dorsey. It's one kiss from each boy, so you need to bid high ladies to win. We'll start with Stefan Barratt at twenty pounds."

The bidding started and was an all-out frenzy as the girls bid high for each guy. Stefan received a kiss from a girl in our year and he looked pretty happy with the situation. The two lower sixth formers still stood beside Liam and Brett and I watched as the dark-haired one bid for Bailey like she'd die if she didn't win. Every competing bid received an evil stare. Just as she thought she had it, Ivy bid a thousand pounds.

"What the actual fuck?' I said.

"Just a Queen Bee swatting down a Wanna Bee," Renee giggled.

"Good for our charity, so on this occasion I'm happy for Ivy to be a complete bitch." We high-fived each other.

Ivy made a big show of kissing Bailey and Sasha stormed out of the room, leaving her friend looking between the stage and in the direction of her friend. She was just about to go when Liam grabbed her arm and pulled her back to his side, whispering to her.

What. The. Actual. Fuck?

I felt the bitterness of jealousy invade me again. *Do not react, Phoebe. He's done nothing wrong yet. Just see what happens and keep your stiff, British upper lip.*

The bidding started for a kiss with Marlon. I thought the riches would deliberately not bid for him, but it wasn't the case at all, and the person trying to bid amongst them? The girl standing at Liam's side. Casey. Suddenly I felt a whole lot better.

The bidding went higher and I saw when Casey's head dropped forward having been outbid. Lucie announced, "Going once," and then I saw Liam whisper to Casey, who shook her head. "Going twice," was announced and Liam brought out his wallet. He grabbed Casey's arm and held it high in the air.

Lucie looked over bemused. "Is that a further bid, Casey?

Liam nodded at her and she said, "Y- yes. I'd like to bid two hundred pounds."

Her rival dropped out and Casey was invited to the stage.

Marlon, who by this time was completely wasted, pulled Casey back in a dramatic pose and kissed her like in the movies. He had no idea of how the girl looked when it ended. First shellshocked and then like he'd hung the moon.

And then he went up to Lucie and tried the same thing.

Casey ran off the stage and went in the direction of where her friend had disappeared to while Brett leapt on stage and removed Marlon from where he was trying and failing to plant a kiss on Lucie.

Brett leaned over the microphone. "Marlon will donate fifty pounds when he's sober, for the kiss to your cheek, Lucie."

Then it was our turn. Stefan had agreed to host the women's section and he took to the stage, announcing us all.

"Welcome to the kissing booth... Lucie Wentworth, Renee Anderson, Phoebe Ridley, Ramona Ramirez, Neelam Singh, and Mallory Cork."

My heart started beating fast. The thought of kissing some of the guys from my class made me feel ill. However, I had a feeling that there was only going to be one winner.

The bidding started and Liam didn't take part—at all.

I felt a lump in my throat and didn't know if it was threatening tears or complete stress and awkwardness.

"Going once," Stefan looked around the room. "Going twice." My stomach plummeted through my boots as the gavel lowered for the third time. But with about an inch to go, Liam bid five hundred pounds for a kiss.

I could see the incredulous looks while the people in the audience wondered where a rat had managed to acquire so much money to bid on a kiss. But then my eyes met Liam's and I didn't care. In front of everyone he got to kiss me.

He took to the stage and asked Stefan if he could take over the mike.

"I figured if I was going to bid on kissing anyone after my little hoax this last week, I should go right for the principal's daughter." He turned to face me. "Hey, goody-two-shoes, ready for me to naughty you up?"

Handing the mic back to Stefan, he stalked towards me and pushed me to the wall just at the back of my stand. There his right hand fisted in my hair, while his left tipped my chin up.

"Kiss me like we're showing everyone exactly what we are," he said. 'Let's show them the truth."

And I did. I forgot our petty argument, I forgot my ridiculous envy, I just smashed my lips against his and amongst our tangled tongues and the clashing of teeth, I kissed him like my very life depended on it and he met me with every touch.

The crowd whooped and hollered, 'Go, Phoebe, go."

Having never seen me act like this before in their lives they were all for it.

As we broke off, Liam grabbed my hand and took me to the front of the stage, indicating for us to bow at the end of our 'performance'.

I looked over at Liam and grinned because despite what the audience thought, it had been so very real, and as he grinned back, I realised I was falling in love with him despite everything that meant I shouldn't.

But my realisation and shock had to give way to getting back into the swing of the auction as I began moving the stands off the stage while Stefan announced it was time to get drinks and visit the bathroom because the auction was due to start in fifteen minutes.

"That was one hell of a kiss," Renee sighed. "I hope one day a guy kisses me like that."

"One will," I said.

"Look at your face, it's all dreamy." She laughed. "Come on, we've too much to do for you to moon around."

Exactly fifteen minutes later, Renee started the auction. Tears welled in my eyes as people bid on all the generous items donated. Ivy hovered near the stage holding a golden envelope like she was at the Oscars. I sincerely hoped Hector had indeed spoken to her about how to conduct herself, because on the occasions when I had seen her tonight, she'd not seemed any different to the Ivy

I'd known pre-blow job clip. Lucie and I hugged each other's arms tightly as we mentally calculated how much money we were raising for charity. It was in the hundreds of thousands. Beyond our wildest expectations.

"Oh God, I just realised something," Lucie said.

"What?" I panicked.

"I'm hosting a fundraiser and enjoying it. I've turned into my mother."

I burst out laughing. "Looks like we're true Richstone women whether we like it or not."

"Well, I blame Flora. If she hadn't died this would never have happened."

We were a mix of noisy sobs and giggles when Renee walked off the stage to join us, having handed the microphone to Ivy. She hugged us both tightly as we watched the stage, ready to pounce should we need to.

Ivy stood on stage and she flicked her hair off her shoulder. "I'd like to announce the final prize of the night to bid on," she began. "As you all know my father is a very generous man who when I approached him about a donation said that whatever prize was out there, he would donate something grander. He wanted to help raise as much money as possible for our dear Flora's memory, given that it makes all father's think of the loss of a daughter."

Lucie fake puked behind our backs and some people behind sniggered.

But Ivy carried on, lost in her own self-worth.

She opened the envelope and put her hands on the card inside, "and so tonight, and this is as much as a surprise for me as it is you, my father has donated..." She pulled out the card and began reading.

"A studio for a week. Everything your heart desires included for you to shoot your own mini movie, with top Oscar director, Antony Stanhope at your service."

"Sure you don't want it, Ivy, for a redo of your blow job vid?" Wayne Staunton heckled. People laughed, but I'll give Ivy her due, she stood there like the show must go on until she brought down the gavel on the winning bid. With a regal wave and smile, she turned to us, "that concludes tonight's auction. I will now hand you back over to your hosts for this evening: Lucie, Phoebe, and Renee."

She left the stage and I saw her stand and gather herself, her mask slipping for a moment. Then she pasted her smile back on and walked over to her friends. Hector Sackville had given Ivy a test tonight. To see if she could handle public humiliation. She'd passed, but at what cost? Did Hector see Ivy as a daughter, or as an heir to his company, a successor? Someone he had to harden up so she could take the reins.

It was the first time I'd truly felt sorry for Ivy Sackville. Another victim of Richstone.

23

Liam

"Fucking hell, mate. You sure planted one on Phoebe there. Surprised you didn't stab her to the wall with your dick you must be that hard," Marlon said.

"At least he's not trying to kiss everybody in sight," Brett had hold of Marlon's arm. "Can we go now, before we're thrown out?"

"Yeah. I'm happy. I got to kiss my girl in front of everyone," I said and the other two's heads whirled around to me like I'd just announced I was a Martian.

"He did say that, right?" Marlon asked Brett. "Cos I have drunk *a lot* tonight."

"Marlon, he said it. Liam Lawson, you big softy."

Brett leaned over to rub my head and Marlon joined in.

"Get the fuck off me, idiots."

We said goodbye to Phoebe and the others, but they

couldn't spare much more than a quick reply as they began to pack things away and encourage the others to make their way home.

I called for the driver who dropped me, Marlon, and Brett off at the bungalow.

After opening the front door, they piled in after me heading straight for the living room where Marlon fell onto the sofa.

"He's not going to make it to an actual bedroom, is he?" I said to Brett.

"Nope."

"You get your head down in the guest room and I'll bring some blankets in here and take the other sofa."

"You sober enough to deal with him?"

"Yeah, the kiss from Phoebe sobered me up."

If I was drunk on anything right now it was lust. Why had I agreed to let these two stay over?

Reminding myself about bros before hos, I asked Brett if he wanted a coffee. Marlon had fallen asleep. I covered him in a blanket, propped his head on a cushion, placed a bucket at the side of him, and made my way into the kitchen, Brett following me.

"So, you and Phoebe. Is it getting serious?" Brett sat at the dining table.

"I'm not about to propose, but she's more than a friends-with-benefits. I really like her," I admitted.

"This place has been good for you," Brett remarked. "I know we've had tragedy, but in terms of who you are and how closed off you were from your emotions since your dad... you're better for being here in that way."

"What about you?" I countered. "Other than what happened to Daniel, are you glad you came here?" I handed him a coffee.

"In terms of my education, yes. There's no doubt about it that I'm getting access to things we didn't have at Sharrow and to have attended Richstone is fantastic for my CV, but other than that, I feel a bit lost. I go home to Sharrow, but I feel like I don't fit there anymore."

"I get you. Phoebe wants to go and see my mother tomorrow and I'm hoping that this time Ma's sober enough to speak to her. I can't work out how a new life could fit in around my old one."

"Guess we just stick it out and see where it takes us?"

"Yup."

A groan came from the living room followed by an, "I don't feel well."

I didn't realise I could move so fast. All I knew was that Marlon needed to aim into that bucket.

***

"I'm sorry, man." Marlon walked into the kitchen like a sloth while clutching his head. "I shouldn't have got so drunk. It wasn't fair on you."

"Look, I'm good. All your puke managed to hit the bucket and the inside of the toilet. I'm concerned about you though, Marl. What's going on?"

"Can I have some water, coffee, and painkillers please?"

"Coming right up." I went to the bathroom, noting he'd deflected my question.

When I walked back in, he swallowed the tablets down with the water and then looked a little green. "Might want to wait a minute before you start on the coffee," I suggested.

"Yeah, good idea." He sat staring at his mug for a moment. "Liam, if someone kept a secret from you for months because they'd sworn they wouldn't say a word, but then they really wanted to talk about it. Would you a) not get pissed off, and b) promise not to breathe a word of it even to your other best friend and your girlfriend? I'm asking for a friend."

Brett was still asleep at the moment and given he'd spent until the early hours of the morning helping me deal with Marlon, I was letting him enjoy a lie-in.

"I would do my best not to get pissed off because they were my friend, and if they needed me to keep a secret then I would."

"Cross your heart?"

"Fucking hell, Marlon, do you want the agreement in blood?"

He rolled his eyes and then groaned. "Fucking hell, my head."

"So is your friend going to confess what's going on with him?" I said as he took a sip of coffee.

Placing his cup down he took a deep breath.

"I've been sleeping with Lisette Handley."

"You've been *what*?" I yelled.

"Ssh, you'll wake Brett. You said you'd try not to get pissed off."

"Sorry, it's just I thought for a minute you'd told me you were sleeping with Lisette Handley. I mean, I clearly got that wrong, because for one thing she's married, for another she fucked Vin, and then finally *she's a teacher at your school.*"

"I did tell you it was complicated," he replied.

He wouldn't tell me anymore. Just that it had happened and now it was over and that it had started after she'd slept with Vin.

"You know where I am if you need to talk, and Brett would be there for you too, mate."

"I know and I'll probably tell him soon, but I just felt like I wanted to tell one person. Just to make it real. Acknowledge it happened and I'd thought it was something good."

"Is this why you didn't bother with Lucie?"

"Yes and no. I don't think I could take on one of the riches. I know Phoebe is different to a lot of them, but this place makes me feel uncomfortable. It makes me feel inferior."

"Think you'll always be a Sharrow boy?"

He shrugged. "Who knows? But right now, my life is there. I want to be around my little sister while she's still cute."

"Well, if you change your mind there was a girl very into you last night. Seems lovely too."

He groaned again. "What did I do?"

"You remember the huge, swoony kiss for charity?"

"No. Who did that? Did the kissing booth happen?"

I put a hand to my temple. "Oh, Marlon, we have some catching up to do."

———

Brett walked in about an hour later and proceeded to wind Marlon up even more about the kissing booth and him trying to kiss every female in his vicinity afterwards while shouting out that Brett would pay them on his behalf.

"I didn't. You lie."

"You're lucky we went home, or you'd be in serious debt today."

I made everyone a cooked brunch and then they left at midday. There was thirty minutes before Phoebe was due to arrive. I'd texted her as soon as I woke up and she'd got back to me mid-morning saying everything was still on for going to visit Ma. It gave me time to double-check with my ma and then have a quick shower.

It was good to hear my ma sound so chirpy down the other end of the line.

"Yes, everything is fine. I'm looking forward to seeing you and to meeting Phoebe."

She either didn't remember that she'd seen Phoebe before, or she didn't want to admit she remembered. It was fine by me.

"Okay, we'll be there around one."

"I've got a quiche, salad, and a few bits, so no need to bring anything."

"Sounds lovely. See you shortly."

I tried not to let hope run through me that she was finally sorting herself out, but it was hard, as she was my mother and it was the thing I wished for probably more than anything.

Phoebe and I grinned at each other like idiots as soon as we came face-to-face.

"What are you grinning at?" I teased.

"No, you first, what are you grinning at?"

I dragged her through my doorway for a few minutes. We had time.

"I'm grinning because I got to kiss you in front of everyone."

"And I'm grinning that you kissed me in front of everyone." She sighed.

I kissed her again then. Private kisses where I could also stroke my hands over her body.

I groaned. "We'd better go before I refuse to leave and carry you to bed." Reluctantly, I locked up the house and we began to walk over to Sharrow.

"Not heard anything from Hector then yet?" I asked her.

"No, but Eddie has already made sure one deal my dad pushed him to try has failed. There's a major one my father was holding out for set to be discussed Tuesday. He'll be present at the meeting, but Eddie's going to try to upset things behind the scenes and send the clients in a different direction."

"But this won't look bad on Eddie?"

"No, Eddie has been setting up some new business and met two customers on Friday. He's just holding back on further discussions until the business becomes Hector's."

I slapped my hand over my mouth. "Oh fuck, Phoebe. I forgot to ask you about your dad being back. How did it go? He'd better be leaving you alone. It's bloody Marlon putting me off. First drunk, then sick, then just a general pain in my arse."

"Don't worry. I've not even seen him. He wasn't around when I got home, and I got Marjorie to bring breakfast up to my room today. I'm hoping that I can largely try to avoid him until these things with the business come to a head. Then when he loses the business and Daphne is held to ransom, I can only hope that they do what I'm wishing and leave."

"Brett says I can stay with him if necessary. My mother said she could apply for new accommodation for the two of us if I ever returned to Sharrow, but I don't want to go back to living with her. I can't live with an alcoholic anymore, even if it's my ma. Does that make me a bad person?"

'No." Phoebe squeezed my hand before letting go. "We can't always be expected to put ourselves last. I can stay with Renee. It will suck not being able to stay overnight with you, but it's only until we get more money together. Then we can leave."

Once more I saw the hope in Phoebe's eyes. It twinned with the desperation there too.

"We ought to start selling some of your stuff. Just a couple of things. How do you fancy a trip to Brighton on Saturday? I'll scope out somewhere you can sell things and then we could do one of those walks on the beach you keep going on about?"

Phoebe let out a small squeal. "Oh my god, yes. Please. That would be amazing. Oh, but we shouldn't really. We should study."

"We can study every other night and Sunday. It will do us good to have a rest from swotting. And we can test each other while we walk on the beach if you like?"

"No, that's not part of my dreams," she giggled. "I agree. For one day a break from studies might do us good. We could even walk down some residential streets and I could dream about buying them."

I wished I could bottle the happiness on Phoebe's face. I also wished I could share in it. But it still seemed to me like we were talking about fairy tales.

However, I could take her to the beach and at least make one of her dreams come true.

And that was a start.

24

Phoebe

I refused to let thoughts that I might see my father later ruin my day. My focus was on meeting Liam's mum, who he'd said would actually be sober this time. I'd felt sad when he'd said she didn't remember meeting me last time at first. Until he pointed out that his mum could be lying because of embarrassment and either way it was better to count this as the first time we'd met each other.

Once again, the greenery and colours of Richstone faded away into the greys and blacks of Sharrow. The only things colourful in Sharrow were the graffiti on the walls and the language uttered by some of the people walking past us. The streets narrowed and we passed the main rows of shops before heading out of the main town, out towards a more derelict looking area that Liam explained was an old industrial estate.

Finally, we reached the door and Liam pressed the doorbell.

Julie Lawson answered the door with a smile which quickly fell when Liam's first response was. "Ma, what did I tell you about asking who it is before you open the door?"

"But I was expecting you, so I knew it'd be you," she said, rolling her eyes at me.

I giggled. "Hey, Mrs Lawson."

"Come in won't you, Phoebe? And please call me Julie. Liam, take her coat and put it on my bed, would you? Now would you like a cup of tea or anything?" she asked me.

"A black coffee would be lovely if you have it?" Liam was shaking his head at me, but I didn't understand why at first. Then I remembered how he'd said it was awful. It was too late now. I'd accepted a cup and I'd drink it out of politeness.

I looked around at the small space. People really lived like this? In one room with just a separate bathroom.

Though Julie was making us drinks, she watched me and fidgeted with her earring. "It's not much, I know, but I'm grateful for anything after our home burned down."

"I think it's lovely," I said.

"Oh, Phoebe. You don't have to lie just to make me feel better. You'll live in a mansion I bet. This must seem like a prison cell in comparison."

I noticed that Liam didn't say anything, letting me and his mother hold a conversation.

"Actually, my large home is a prison cell, and if I can

get away one day, I'll be happy to have a home like this one. If it means I'm free."

Julie looked at me curiously. "I'm happy here. Fresh start and all that. Right, you and William sit on the sofa and I'll bring over a chair."

"You take the sofa with Phoebe, Ma. I'll sort the chair," Liam said.

"Always fussing after me that one." Julie cocked her head towards Liam. "I'm supposed to be the parent, but half the time he acts like it's the other way around."

Liam came and sat near us.

"How are those studies going, William? You'd better be getting your head down and not getting distracted. No disrespect, Phoebe, but he went to Richstone to pass his exams, not get a girlfriend."

"None taken, and yes, our exams are the priority of us both."

"What do you hope to do when you've passed, Phoebe?"

"I'd like to go to university, but I'm not sure if I'll be allowed. I've sent in my application to study to become a vet to a few universities," I said. Liam looked surprised because I'd never mentioned this to him.

Which shows how little you still know each other, my inner voice chided.

"Liam wants to do accountancy. He has a place at a university near here in principle, but I worry about student loans and him being in debt. Still, my William has always been savvy with money. "Did you have to give up that warehouse job though to go to Richstone, son? I meant to ask."

"Don't you worry about me, Ma. I'll be fine." His eyes warned me not to ask about this warehouse job which was clearly a cover story for his drug dealing.

If he can lie to his mother, he can certainly lie to you.

There it went again. I hated the doubt, the questioning of my decisions. My apprehension of everything going wrong.

"Do you fancy a spot of lunch now? I bought some quiche, salad, and some tortilla chips and dips. Then I got a carrot cake for afters."

"That would be lovely," I replied.

"Fab, I'll just get it all out of the fridge. It won't take me long. William, can you help set the table?"

"Is there anything I can do, Julie?" I checked.

"You just carry on making sure my son's okay in Richstone. That's all I ask," she said. She looked at him with such fondness, and my heart broke a little more thinking about my own mother. Though Liam's mother was no angel, deep down she did love him. You could clearly see it while she was sober.

We all sat around the small dining table she had and Julie chattered on about how she'd found some nice items at a local charity store. Every time she spoke of anything that indicated a lack of wealth her eyes seemed to dim before me.

"You know, I never even thought about the fact you could get so many beautiful things, and also it's recycling.

When I get my own house, I want to do that. Maybe we could visit some places together to look one day?"

"That would be lovely." Her eyes sparkled with hope and it warmed me up inside. Perhaps the money I could get together would be enough after all if I spent it wisely. What I thought of as nothing at all for a handbag would buy Julie Lawson a week's food. And when I sold mine, it would buy me some food, and help pay bills. I began to feel the same flicker of hope inside myself.

"So, is everything still going on okay with your drinking?" Liam blurted.

"Liam! That's rather personal to be mentioning in front of me. I do apologise for his manners," I told her.

She sighed. "It's fine, Phoebe. Let's face it, it's my fault he has to ask." She moved her head to face him. "I'm doing so much better. I'm down to a couple of cans of cider a night. The trick is to barely go out. Having this place to do up means my mind is focused and if I feel the urge to drink, instead I'm grabbing a can of paint and concentrating on a task."

"That's wonderful, Julie," I acknowledged.

She smiled a half-smile. "Just have to hope that when the place is done, I can find something else to occupy my time."

"You could renovate furniture?" I suggested. "Get something from those second-hand shops, do it up, and then sell it on. There's lots of desire for shabby chic and vintage style still."

She nodded her head slowly, clearly mulling the idea

over. "Maybe." This time her smile was genuine. "I think I'd enjoy that."

Visit over, Liam and I walked back to Richstone.

"I enjoyed meeting your Ma. She's lovely. And she sounds very positive about the future."

Liam scoffed. "Yeah, she's Mum of the Year when she's not drunk."

"It does seem like she's really trying this time."

"Phoebe, I know you mean well, but I've seen this all before. The hobbies to distract her from drinking. It's all okay until she gets bored, or a friend calls around with a bottle of vodka because they've not seen her for a while. Then it all starts again."

"Oh," my face dropped in disappointment.

"Look, I'm sorry. Maybe this will be the time she proves me wrong. Let's hope so. I'll buy her enough second-hand furniture to last her the year if she can keep her drinking under control."

When we got back to the bungalow, Liam whisked me inside for a few hours of getting re-acquainted after our couple of nights apart, then I reluctantly made my way back up to the main house as I had homework to complete before school tomorrow.

As I walked into the house, I saw my luck at avoiding my father had run out as he was walking down the lower part of the staircase.

"Phoebe. Might I have a word?" he asked.

"You can have two, but I don't think you'll appreciate them," I replied, stepping to the right side of the stairs out of his way, presuming he was heading to his right and the sitting room.

"Now, Phoebe. I know we have had our differences of late, but as your father I would appreciate some respect."

My lips curled back in disgust. "You lost my respect when you started abusing me."

He sighed and wafted a hand over his face like I was an annoying fly. "And this is precisely what I want to talk to you about. I wish to apologise."

Though my teeth ground together, and I wanted to run in the opposite direction, I realised that in order to keep myself safely under this roof until I blew it off, I'd be wise to play along.

"Fine," I huffed.

"Thank you."

I followed him into the sitting room to find my mother already there reading a book about the craft of writing. Looked like her dreams of fame and imaginary Nobel prizes were alive and well.

"Oh you're back. Been associating with the vermin again?"

"I've been to see Liam's mother. She's an alcoholic and yet she still manages to be a better parent than you."

"Phoebe," my dad chastised me. "What have I just said to you about respect?"

It was time to put on an act worthy of a BAFTA.

Taking a seat on the sofa, I sighed. "I'm sorry. It's just I had dreams of being like Mum and having a career. Like

Eddie's been allowed to. And you pushed me into trying to get a rich suitor and I hated it, so I deliberately set out to seduce Liam," I lied.

"I knew she didn't really want him," my father said to my mother.

"I'm not convinced. She's always very happy to go down there, and today she's visited his mother."

"It just fascinates me that's all," I told her. "How the poor live. Do you know that one of my handbags could pay for his mum's rent and food for a week? And she lives in the tiniest little studio apartment. The whole thing would fit into this room."

"How very generous of you to begin to appreciate the kind of background I came from," my mother snapped. "My own family had nothing. It's why I've worked so hard to get where I am and why I want you to marry for money."

"I'd never thought of it that way, because you rarely discuss your own past, Mother."

"The whole point of this experiment, apart from getting one over on that dreadful Barratt woman, was to show you just how good you have it, Phoebe. I might not be maternal, but at least you have every other need met."

"Did your mother love you?" I asked her, and I saw her flinch.

"My past is exactly that. In the past. I have no wish to consider it. Right now, we're here to discuss the future. Your father is home, and he wishes to apologise for his actions; don't you, Maxwell?"

"Indeed. I'm sorry, Phoebe, for what I did. Your

mother helped me with a similar bad habit years ago and the stress of the business caused a relapse."

A bad habit? Beating me up and physically abusing me was a bad habit? I had to count to twenty and breathe in and out slowly so as not to pick up the candlestick on the coffee table and bring it down onto his skull.

"I've undergone an intensive treatment process and can categorically state that it won't happen again."

"And is the business doing better?"

"You don't have to worry about that. I just want to reassure you that you are safe under this roof."

"We're not worrying so much about the business now," my mother said. "Eddie reassures us that things are looking up and he has some 'irons in the fire' so to speak, and your father and I are agreed that Ulric McDowall is a perfect match for you. We want you to set up a date, stop your contraception, and force his hand into marriage."

My eyes bulged and I took an audible intake of breath.

"Ulric's careless behaviour with Flora actually did us a favour because he feels indebted to you. Plus, he openly admitted to liking you physically. You will tie our families together as soon as possible."

"Or what?"

"Or I'll throw Liam out of the bungalow and accuse him of theft." Mother smirked. "Who are the police going to believe? The principal of Richstone Academy or a Sharrow rat?"

I stood up. "I'll arrange a date with Ulric when I see him at school tomorrow."

"Excellent. I'm so pleased we've all been able to come to an understanding."

Leaving the room, I was filled with so much hatred that my own breath sounded loud in my ears. I would destroy these people, even if I went down with them.

25

Liam

Visiting my mother couldn't have gone better. I was pleased that she was doing well and that Phoebe had got to see the mother I'd had in my early childhood. But I wouldn't let myself believe this time could be different; not until there had been a much longer period of my ma being stable.

When my phone rang in the early evening, I had a hunch who it would be. I grabbed my phone and walked away from the large pile of study materials, unlocked the back door and stepped out into the fresh evening air. I'd have a break while I spoke to Uncle Karl.

"Your mum's been on the phone to me tonight, full of excitement about what a nice girl Phoebe is."

"Yeah, they really seemed to hit it off."

"How are you doing? I know your exams must be

coming up soon. Dave at work was saying Jordan won't study for his GCSE's."

Jordan Bates was two years younger than me at Sharrow Manor. I knew him from hanging around the garage and talking to Dave, my uncle's other mechanic, but not well.

"Yeah, my first is a week on Wednesday, the 19th."

"All your other grades were fantastic so there's no reason to believe these won't follow."

"I'm hoping they'll be better, but I'll feel relieved when they're done. End of June it will all be over. I'm just studying now. I'm glad you called because it's made me take a break."

"I don't intend to keep you long. Just wanted to say that your mother was talking about doing up second-hand furniture and how well you looked. I know we don't take anything with your ma for granted, but today was a good day."

"Yeah, we enjoyed it too."

"So this thing with Phoebe. Is it getting serious?"

"I like her and we're okay, but we don't look to the future. There are too many hurdles to jump."

"You're only young yet anyway, Liam. Got your whole life ahead of you. If you get those results you want, you need to be free to go get the life of your dreams."

"I know. Right now, I'm just concentrating on getting these exams passed." It was only a partial lie. I was revising. It's just I was also studying Phoebe's body alongside my other subjects.

"Okay, good to know. I'll let you go, and next time,

come and bloody see your uncle when you're in Sharrow. That's twice I've heard you've visited now and not come to see me. It's not good enough."

"Twice?"

"Yeah, Trev at The Crown thought I should know about your fist fight with Marlon outside his pub."

I groaned. "We were just letting off steam. He's such a gossip. Wasn't like it was inside the place. But, yeah, you're right. I'll come see you soon."

"Smashing. Right, you get back to those studies and take care."

Ending the call, I put my phone on the patio table in front of me and stretched my legs out before putting my arms behind my head. The night was quiet and I could see every star in the sky. There were so many streetlights in Sharrow that seeing the stars was rare. Plus no one had time to look up, we were always too busy watching out for ourselves. But right now, I gazed at the stars as if the night sky could give me the answers to the universe.

Ten minutes later I reluctantly went back inside and back to my books.

Back at school on Monday, any piss-taking of Ivy on her return was few and far between as the close proximity of our exams weighed down on us all. No one in the upper sixth was interested in who ruled at Richstone anymore as our journey's here approached their end. Teachers gave us past papers to study, and hints as to what they thought might come up on the exams. Richstone students were deadly serious about their exams and the attitudes were of getting your head down and passing with flying colours. For most of the students, exclusive university places were dependent on their results, and parents ready to bring their beloved child into the fold of their business expected their son or daughter's absolute best.

Whereas I was treading my own path. Or so I thought.

After my first class, Ulric McDowell pulled me to one side. I disliked him intensely to start with and the fact he had to fake date Phoebe was not helping things.

"My father wondered if you could ring him," Ulric said, passing me a business card.

"What for?"

"He's wondering what you have in mind for when the exams are over. You've really impressed him since you saved my life. I'm not supposed to tell you this, but he contacted the head at Sharrow to find out your results from your first year of sixth form. She had such good things to say about you that he wants to talk about opportunities at his business. I'm starting to think he wished you were his kid instead of me. I just disappoint him."

I took the card, intrigued.

"I'm sure if you pass your exams and settle into your place as heir to the family business, you'll be absolutely fine," I fake-smiled.

"That's just it though. Investment banking holds no appeal for me at all and he knows it. I want to study art. So, you see, it's actually in my best interests if you and my father come to some kind of arrangement. Become his protegee, and I'll make sure it's worth your while."

"I don't need a handout. I'll go listen to what he has to say and make my decision based on its merit. I'm no one's bitch."

Ulric scoffed. "We're all someone's bitch. I don't know anyone free to do what they want. Are you saying you're entirely free to choose your own path in life?"

I thought of my mother and of a life with Phoebe and I let out a heavy sigh.

"Thought so. By all means see what he has to say, but if you need an extra incentive, I got you covered."

Ulric walked away and I felt like I wanted to punch the wall. One day I would be free of all this game playing and would live my life how I wanted to live it.

———

"You should call him, meet him and see what he has to say. Richard McDowell is a renowned investment banker."

Though Phoebe encouraged me, she forgot that a lot of the time her face told her feelings, and right now she was wondering how a career with the McDowells would factor into our 'Escape from Richstone' plans. Richard McDowell's empire was based in all the main spots: London, New York, Paris, and Tokyo. How could I turn down the opportunity if it was amazing, given that was why I'd gone to Richstone in the first place?

Phoebe was right. I needed to go to see him for myself

and see what he had in mind. For all I know he could have found out I organised for his son to be in the swimming pool and just want his five-grand back.

"Okay. I'll text him now and arrange to go and meet him," I said. I was sending a message just as the doorbell rang with our Chinese takeaway delivery.

"I'll get that and sort the food. You carry on," Phoebe said.

We were partway through our food when my phone beeped. I wiped my hands on a napkin and finger swiped my phone.

"He wants me to go to see him tomorrow after school and to hitch a ride with Ulric. Does he not see how insensitive that is? Do you think he's hoping Ulric kills another one of us off?"

"They don't get it. He's a father and he's decided Ulric made a stupid mistake. You can say no and get the driver to take you instead."

"I'll see how I feel about it after a good night's sleep. Please tell me you're staying over tonight."

"I am," Phoebe put her mouth around a spring roll and pretended to suck it. Then she shrieked as I picked her up, food flying from her hands and ran with her to my bedroom.

In the end I decided to travel to the McDowell's house with Ulric. I'd not spoken to him about the day of Daniel's accident and I felt it was overdue.

"What happened that day, Ulric?" I said, a few minutes after we'd been in the car, interrupting the awkward silence.

"Does it matter?" he asked. "It won't change anything."

"I want to know."

Ulric sighed. "Daniel was blocking off part of the road. Phoebe leapt out of the car, and at that point I had no idea what was happening, I thought he was just dropping her off, so I beeped the horn. I was in the car with Bailey and Richie, and Bailey was riding me, telling me to get past, that we didn't wait in line behind rats. When Phoebe asked me to give Daniel and Flora a minute, I refused, wound up about Bailey's words because that's what was happening. I was being asked to wait behind someone I perceived as inferior. I'm not making excuses about any of it. I'm partly responsible, I know that. Fully responsible, I guess, if you say that without my actions Daniel probably wouldn't have pressed the accelerator."

He paused for a moment. "I don't talk about it, but it's had a profound effect on me. I'm in therapy. I expect I will be for a long time. It's also made me want to do more with my life. It's why I want to pursue my art. I've been told I could go far with it and yet I always just said yes to following in my father's footsteps. Now I intend to see if I can make a success of it and I will atone for what I did, Liam. I'll sell pieces for charity or something. It won't make it right, I know that, but it will do something."

"I appreciate you telling me."

"You must miss him a lot. Stupid question, I know,

but I just can't imagine losing my best friend. Even if they are an idiot like Bailey. I'm not sure what his beef with you is, but he really doesn't like you."

"Some shit went down in the past," I said, smirking inwardly when I thought about it, until I realised that could have been why Bailey had been pushing Ulric to drive past. Because of what I'd done to him. Because Daniel was driving my car. So at the time Bailey could have thought it was me. They wouldn't have known any different until Phoebe went to the window to plead.

The circumstances of the accident became increasingly complex. But I knew deep down I'd always hold myself mainly responsible.

Soon we were pulling up outside Ulric's house. As I got out Richard himself came to greet us. After asking his son about his day, he gestured for me to walk around the side of the house. "I have an office out there where we can speak freely. My wife is home and she just purchased a fourth Pomeranian. I'd welcome the break."

Richard was a shortish man, maybe five foot eight in height, with mid-brown spiky hair, and a pleasant demeanour. His confidence made you take note of him, but where Hector Sackville wore a constant look of smelling something bad, Richard looked like he'd just finished a day's fishing and got a prize catch.

The irony of his brick-built office being double the size of my old burned down home wasn't lost on me. I guessed the place doubled as a man cave, because he had a liquor cabinet in there, a huge television, and a leather sofa. Bookcases lined the walls, filled with business books and old looking tomes that I wondered if he'd just bought for show.

"Do you want a drink? Whisky?"

"No thanks. It's a little early for me and I need to study when I get home."

"And how's that going?'

"Good, I think. I've done all I can. Just have to hope I can bring it out of the bag on the exam days."

He gestured for me to sit on the sofa and sat at the other end and then he poured himself a shot of Jack Daniel's. Seemed it wasn't too early for him.

"I'll get straight to the point, Liam. Ulric told me how good you are with maths and I'm always looking for new blood. I'm not sure what universities you've applied to, but I want you to consider becoming an intern at my London offices. You'd be released for university classes but would also learn some aspects of the firm outside of those hours." He passed me a folder. "All the information is in there. It means you'd have a salary. Not a huge one at first, but it increases year by year and at the end of it, if we're both happy, you become an employee of McDowell Investments."

I stared at the folder in my hand and then looked over at Richard. "Wow. I don't know what to say."

"You don't have to say anything right now. Just look it over and let me know." He took a sip of his drink. "I thought you were astute and mature when I met you at the party. Then when I asked Ric who was doing well in maths and your name came up, it seemed fortuitous."

"I'll certainly look over it all. When do you need a response by?"

"A couple of weeks? I know you've exams, so fit this reading in where you can."

"Thanks again, Mr McDowall. I really appreciate this." The truth was, I didn't know what to do. I would read it, but I could do with a bloody fortune teller to advise me of my future.

"Not a problem. I was sorry to hear of your friend's death. I didn't realise at first that it was the boy you'd been with that evening."

"Yeah, Daniel. Thank you. It's hard. I can't get my head around the fact he's gone."

Richard didn't bring up his son's involvement in it and neither did I.

"And how's living with the Ridleys?"

"Good. I love it at the bungalow. Not sure how I'll ever return to normality," I joked, and Richard laughed along with me.

"Don't feel you have to answer this, but what do you think about Phoebe's parents?" He raised a brow.

I sat up straighter and tilted my head. "I'm not sure what you're getting at?"

He scratched at his chin. "I like Phoebe. Ulric has a date with her coming up. I'm just not sure what I think of her mother, and her father hasn't been around for a while."

"He's back home now," I stated.

"Ah, is he? That's good then. It's just that they were all over the Barratts for years and then there was a falling out of some kind and all of a sudden Daphne is wanting to bring Phoebe here and match her with my son. Something doesn't add up, and though I take risks with my business, I don't take them with my son."

I found myself fighting for Phoebe's honour, which was crazy given I didn't want Ulric anywhere near her. "Phoebe still gets on fantastically with Stefan Barratt, so any fallings out were most definitely between the parents. She's a great girl and seems to have a heart of gold. She was certainly the first person to treat me like a human being. So if she wants to date your son, then he'd be lucky to have her. Better than the Ivy Sackville's of the world."

Richard nodded slowly. "Thank you, Liam. That's encouraging. I'll let Ric know he can go ahead and arrange a date with her."

"No problem." I was ready to get out of here now. I didn't want to talk about Phoebe and Ulric dating.

We walked back to the house and Richard shouted Ulric.

"Can you drop Liam back off at the Ridley's bungalow, and then you could maybe go on up to the main house and arrange a date with Phoebe?"

"I already did. We're going out tomorrow night," he replied. "I can still drop Liam off though."

'Actually, it's a nice night for a walk. I could do with clearing my head. Stress of upcoming exams and lots to think about," I waved the folder given to me.

"You're sure?" Richard double-checked.

261

"Yeah, positive. Thanks once again for the offer. I'll see you at school tomorrow, Ulric."

With that I left to start my long walk back. But for the first time I was in no rush to return to the bungalow. Right now, my head felt all over the place. I had come to Richstone to gain my qualifications and prospects. I'd lost one of my dearest friends, was close to having finished my exams and having to leave Richstone, and had fallen for a girl. But I had absolutely no idea of what came next. For a boy who'd always felt he had to fight to carve a place in the world for himself, I now felt cut adrift. I honestly didn't know what came next.

And I didn't like that feeling at all.

26

Phoebe

I had a blinding headache but wasn't surprised in the slightest. The pressure of exams was upon me, and every time my phone rang or beeped, I wondered if this would be Eddie or Hector with news of what was happening with the business.

Liam had called and told me about what Richard had said to him and that gave my head even more thoughts to swirl and hurt my brain. This would tie Liam to London, and I wasn't sure I wanted to be tied anywhere. He said he was making no decisions yet, but I didn't see how he could turn down a great opportunity. Not only that, but no matter how much I liked Liam, had had that moment where I felt I was falling in love with him, I still barely knew him. Not really. And Ulric's story about following his dreams had made my shoulders tighten even further.

It didn't seem fair that he got to do that while my friend's body decayed in Richstone cemetery.

It all just left me knowing that ultimately, I still had to make my own plans and see what happened when the exams were over. Right now, I needed to be revising wherever possible.

And tomorrow I had a dinner date with Ulric. I didn't want to have to spend time with him. No matter what he said, I would always picture in my mind the way he sneered at me just before he drove his car towards the Porsche.

I slept, praying that tomorrow would be the day my parents got what was coming to them.

When I met Renee and Lucie the next day, we were all subdued given our upcoming examinations.

"I might have to go to the gym and let Jake give me a thorough workout again," Lucie winked. "You know, to ease my exam stress."

We laughed at her.

"So, you ready for your date with Ulric? What if he decides he wants to kiss you?" she asked me.

"He can't. I'd rather eat my own vomit."

"What's Liam's opinion of all this?"

"He hates it all, but what do we do? I am so sick of all this. Pretending, lying. Wondering who's telling the truth and who has a game plan."

"I gather you've heard nothing about your dad's business then?"

"Nope."

"Well, if you need an 'emergency' tonight to get you out of the date, just text me from the ladies room." Renee said. "And how do you fancy coming to mine tomorrow from school for a couple of hours?"

"Sounds good."

"Is anyone else struggling with revision?" I asked them. "My head's just not been in the game."

"No, it's been in Liam's trouser area," Lucie winked, and Renee and I groaned.

Classes passed quickly while I concentrated on exam stuff and soon it was lunchtime. As I walked down the hall towards the dining hall, I saw Ulric with his friends. He waved over at me. "I'd better go say hi and act interested," I told the others and I headed towards where they stood at the edge of the corridor before it turned towards the dining hall.

"Hey, Ulric," I said.

He smiled at me.

I felt eyes on me and turned to see Bailey looking at me with a smirk on his face. "You got that pussy shaved nice ready for later?"

I felt my face heat.

"Bailey!" Ulric spat out. "Where the hell are your manners?"

"Sorry, Phoebe," Bailey said, "I'd not realised you were a virgin. I mean that's why you've gone so red surely?"

"Fuck off, Bailey. Right now," Ulric yelled.

"God, so fucking serious all the time," Bailey huffed walking away towards the male bathrooms. I was incensed. There were few Richstone boys brought up without respectful manners, but it seemed Bailey had skipped the queue.

Ulric put his fingers to his forehead. "I'm sorry. That was entirely uncalled for. You still okay for meeting later? Because I'd understand if not after that."

"Yeah, it's fine. It's not your fault he's a jerk," I said and then I walked away.

I didn't know what it was. I'd call it a hunch. But as soon as I turned around the corner, I stopped, re-traced my steps, and hung around at the edge of the wall.

Peering around, Ulric and Richie were still standing there.

"...fucked everything up," Ulric said, pushing his glasses up his face.

"It'll be fine. Look at how red she went. She's going to be so easy to fool. The girl's naïve. Just use your charm and she'll be putty in your hands."

"She has to be. My father's ordered it. He said he'd take care of the rat by signing him up to a contract and basing him in some poky corner of the business somewhere and I needed to keep Phoebe sweet just until I had my university place and was out of here. Like I'm going to use my amazing art skills to raise money to benefit people like Daniel. As far as I'm concerned it just cleared some shit off the street. I should be knighted. Less of them to breed. I mean they'd already fucking started."

"Yep, did the world a favour really," Richie added.

Ulric pulled a puppy-eyed expression. "Do I look remorseful enough?"

Richie laughed.

"Bailey's on his way back. Let's go get some lunch. God, I hope she doesn't want to come sit with me. My dad reckons her mother has a game plan; probably thinks I'll marry the frigid little cow. As if."

I turned on my heel and ran down the hall and into the girls' bathrooms. Thankfully there was an empty cubicle, and I closed the door and sat down on the toilet seat while I tried to catch my breath.

It was all lies. All lies. I'd known Ulric was entitled, but I had genuinely believed he had remorse for his actions. What a fool I had been. When would I learn that most humans were out for themselves, especially the ones who lived here; the ones with so much money they felt they were gods and could control people and outcomes?

As I sat there, a large wave of grief hit me hard. It had only been weeks since my friend had died and I'd tried to do the best I could without her, but I missed her so damn much. She would have been here now, chatting away about loving Daniel. It struck me again then. She'd jumped in with both feet and hadn't regretted it for a moment. My friend had lived for love. The love of her family, her best friends, and Daniel. She'd been the most caring person who would help anyone with anything. She'd gone all in, and now so would I.

Just not all in a caring, loving manner.

267

I would go all in for revenge, so that I could then hopefully go all out for my life, and with any luck, love.

Lunch passed as usual and to be annoying I did keep looking over at Ulric giving him smiles and looking every bit like the stupid bitch he had me down as being.

"Liam, stop making it so obvious that you're jealous and want to punch Ulric in the face," Renee huffed.

"But I do want to punch him in the face."

Looking at Liam, I laughed. He looked so jealous, and I loved it.

The afternoon brought no further drama until I got home where my mother laid in wait.

"Have you thought about what you're wearing for your date this evening?"

"Of course. My most exclusive dress and accessories. Must look as rich as possible. Topped off by bring preened within an inch of my life so I look entirely irresistible. And then I have a diamond encrusted gold 'For Sale' sign for around my neck."

"Surliness doesn't become you. Come show me how you look before you go out."

"Fine, Mother. I'd hate to make a decision all by myself. I'm actually surprised you've not ordered me an outfit. Stepford Wife attire out of stock?"

She spoke matter-of-factly. "Someone has to take the family finances and future seriously. You need to convince Ulric that you are serious about dating him and that you'd be the perfect match. I know you have this silly crush on Liam, Phoebe, but that boy will never be your future. You wouldn't survive without money, no matter what ridiculous notions you carry in your head, because you've never had to. Take it from me, if Liam was given the choice between money or you, he'd take the money. It's why he came here in the first place. He told me precisely that at his interview."

My features tightened. "I'm doing what you said, Mother, so spare me the ongoing lectures."

She looked bored and raised a hand, dismissing me. "Run along, Phoebe, and I'll see you just before you leave."

"Yes, Moth-er," I said in a deliberate robotic tone and then I walked away.

Ulric had chosen The Aegean, which as a venue was beyond boring for a first date between two young people, though entirely fitting for a Richstone young adult wanting to show off. But I did love their amazing food so it wasn't all bad.

He'd wanted to pick me up from the house, but I'd insisted on meeting him at the restaurant. I couldn't face my parents greeting him at the door for ten minutes of polite, fake conversation. It was bad enough I had to waste study time on this crap.

"You look wonderful, Phoebe," he said, rising to take my hand and kiss the back of it while the waiter tucked in my chair. I wanted to curl up my fist and punch it straight into his eyeball.

My mother had approved the long, black lacy skirt, and red pussy-bow blouse. My hair was up in an elegant chignon that I had pinned firmly in place and my mother had re-pinned shortly afterward. I had my black Louboutin's on and a smoky eye and red lip. Tiffany jewellery hugged my ears, neck, and wrists.

"Thank you," I replied, making sure not to return the compliment, even though he'd made an effort with his attire. Every time I laid eyes on him the conversation from earlier replayed in my mind and my ears. God, I hated him. I wanted to lunge at him and let my finger-nails tear into his face. How could someone be so shallow as to not value a life because the person had been born poorer?

The whole meal was an unbearable drag where Ulric talked non-stop either about himself or what he and his family had or planned to do. I knew what holidays they had arranged, and which rare car Richard planned to buy next to add to his collection. And his self-congratulation about his university placement at the prestigious and hard to get into University of the Arts London as if he was going to be the next Picasso had me internally screaming. Yet Ulric thought this all impressed me. That I would be in awe of his father's wealth and his own incredible talent.

Just as we were waiting for coffees at the end of the meal, Ulric went into his inner jacket pocket and pulled out a rolled-up paper with a pink bow wrapped around it.

"I did this for you earlier in the week. You know how I can draw? I thought you'd like it."

'You know how I can draw?' Yes, you might have mentioned it a few times.

I wanted to roll my eyes so hard I was sure to have a brain bleed through resisting.

He passed me the paper and I pulled the bow apart and unrolled it, revealing a pencil sketch of Flora and Daniel with a baby. I'd not expected it and felt winded. He'd taken their likenesses from the memorial order of service. If a friend had done this, I would have found it touching, but this was the boy who hated the rats. Who regretted nothing and who now had used them to make me forgive him and leave him alone. I would avenge them and he would suffer for the rest of his damn days. My teeth ground in my mouth and I fought the lump in my throat.

"Thank you. It's beautiful," I managed to scrape out, trying my best to not look at it too much. He would not break me.

"I'm glad you like it. I didn't know if I'd truly captured their essence..."

Oh my god, he was seeking approval and compliments from the tragedy.

"I know how much they meant to you. It was hard sketching them. I kept breaking down thinking about the unfairness of it all. Daniel seemed such a gentle loving soul, and he and Flora would have been happy I'm sure. Anyway, I just wanted to do something I hoped you'd appreciate."

"Thank you," I rolled it back up and placed it in my handbag. As much as I loved my friends, I would burn this the first chance I got.

All I wanted to do was crush him. Break every bone in his body slowly and hear his shrieks and his begging cries for release and reprieve. Then I realised I probably could. An idea bloomed in my mind from a tight bud to an all-out display of colourful glory.

"Would you like to come back to mine and meet my horses?" I asked as they brought the coffees to the table. For a moment Ulric looked like he might make an excuse, so I quickly added, "it would mean so much to me. You don't have to stay long, and we can go straight to the stables and avoid meeting my parents."

Ulric chewed on the side of his lower lip. "Okay, just for half an hour or so. I need to get back to do some revision."

"Great, I won't keep you much longer. I need to revise too. It's just my horses are a big part of my life, I guess like your mother's dogs are to her, so it would mean a lot if you came to meet them."

"I hope you don't mind me asking but why did you stay on into the sixth form anyway? You don't need exams to become a wife and mother. I know your mum said you're not going to university."

"Pardon?" I was sure I must have misheard him.

"My mother told me after you left dinner the other night. She asked your mother about what you were doing after your exams and Daphne told her you'd be taking on some of her charity commitments. I'm genuinely interested why you stayed on at school under the circumstances. Wouldn't you have been better off going to Switzerland to one of their finishing schools?"

I wanted to get on my feet and scream out to the whole restaurant about who I really was. Stand on the table and shout at the top of my lungs that this place was the bowels of hell and all the fake bitches and arseholes could suck it. Instead, I had to sit demurely and be as fake as they were.

"I like studying and I still want to pass my exams no matter what I do in the future. It's good to have an education. I'm sure my future husband would benefit from a wife with intelligence and ideas, just as much as them knowing how to arrange flowers."

"Wives' mouths need to be open to satisfy their husbands sexually, not to try to be their equals." He guffawed. "I'm only joking, Phoebe. Oh my god, your face. Sorry, I couldn't resist."

Ulric beckoned over the waiter and asked for the bill. He insisted on settling it, even though it wasn't actually him who was paying, it was all going on his father's tab, and then he drove us back to mine.

I was relieved my parents didn't notice us arrive and come running outside. Judging by Ulric's pensive features I guessed he was equally as pleased.

We walked around to the stables and I introduced him to Alto and Bonny.

"Maybe you didn't think this through given you might struggle to ride in those heels, Phoebe," Ulric laughed, looking at my feet.

"I have riding clothes and boots here," I said, pulling open a cupboard and pulling out some jodhpurs and a top.

I shuffled the jodhpurs up my legs underneath my skirt and then I undid the zip at the back of my skirt, so the material fell to the floor. Next, I pulled off my blouse in front of him revealing my black lacy bra before swiftly putting on the top. His eyes raked over my chest hungrily and I saw him swallow.

"Okay, let's go and get the horses ready."

"You want to ride? I thought I was just meeting them?" Ulric stated.

"No, I want you to come meet them properly. You'll like Alto. Do you know that I got Liam on him? He looked so pathetic trying to ride a horse."

"Well of course he did. He'll only be used to riding motorbikes." Ulric scoffed. "Of course I'll come ride. It'll be good for you to be alongside a man who knows what to do," he said, his eyes suggestive of him talking about something else entirely.

I ignored his innuendo.

"No staff here to help this evening?" he enquired.

"No. Though I can call someone if you need some help. I just thought you said you were experienced...?"

That had the desired effect on Ulric. He bristled. "I was just making an observation. I'd rather it was just the two of us. I'm thinking when we get back from the ride, we could go check out the bales of hay..."

"Ooh, there's an idea," I replied, raising my brows, as if I could think of nothing more exciting. I turned in the direction of the horses, making sure he got a good view of my butt in the tight trousers, rather than of the scowl on my face. "You know, I never did it in the stables before."

Ulric's reply came from behind me. "Phoebe. I am seeing a whole different side to you." He caught me up and I felt his hand come onto my butt cheek. He smoothed his palm over the material. "I seriously thought you were just wanting to show me your horses. I see now you had a whole other idea for a ride in mind."

Turning towards him so we were stood closely, I trailed my hand down his cheek.

"People always underestimate me, Ulric. It's their biggest mistake."

He leaned in, his mouth coming closer to mine.

I placed a finger across his lips. "A proper ride first. I need some fresh air after that meal. The restaurant was so dark, it's made me feel sleepy. Fifteen minutes on a horse will get my endorphins going. Give me lots of energy."

"Then let's get to it," Ulric grinned.

After getting the horses ready for riding, Ulric mounted Alto, and I climbed onto Bonny and we started a gentle trot around the field.

"I forgot how much I actually like riding," Ulric said coming up to my side. "My mother got rid of our horses and swapped them for the Pomeranians."

We trotted for around ten minutes. Ulric made many comments about my firm thighs and my bouncing around in the saddle. He thought he was being seductive, but he just came across like a dirty old pervert. All he needed was a mac.

After a comment about my being a fine filly myself, it was time to bring this evening to a close.

"Shall we have a race to the end of the field where the woodland starts? Then we can ride back and put the horses away?" I suggested.

"That sounds like a very good idea, especially while my balls still work," Ulric adjusted himself in front of me. "Want to keep the goods in fine working order for when we get back." I wanted to puke as he then ran his hand over his dick.

"Okay. On your marks. Get set. Go," I shouted, deliberately letting Ulric lead.

He whooped as he raced off ahead and as we got to the edge of the field he waited there gloating and laughing. "I thought this was a race?" he taunted. "I'll give you a head start on the return leg."

I raised a hand. "No need. I was just getting Bonny warmed up. I'm going to whoop your arse this time around. You do the countdown this time."

I would hate what I did next, but I needed Ulric to come crashing back down to earth, literally. As we set off, I lifted my right leg further up so Bonny knew we were cantering, and pressed my heel in more firmly, increasing our speed until we were alongside Alto. Then I stuck the hair pin I'd removed from my hair into Alto's thigh, causing him to spook.

The horse jumped in the air and I saw the panic on Ulric's face as Alto span around in a 360 and he came out of the saddle. But I'd not expected this to affect Bonny. My own horse jumped to the side and I just saw Ulric land heavily on the ground and Alto begin to run, as I also slipped from my saddle despite my best efforts to settle my filly.

I landed hard on my left side, my head hitting the bumpy earth and then my vision dulled.

Phoebe

My eyes opened and for a moment I couldn't remember what had happened until the pain started to hit my body. Slowly sitting up, I clutched at my left forehead, feeling a lump. Then I heard whimpering and saw Ulric laid there shaking with pain.

"Ph- Phoebe. I can't reach my phone to..." he paused for a moment taking a deep breath, "g-get help."

I dragged myself towards him and reached into his pocket, extracting his phone and calling for an ambulance. How could I have been so stupid? In my desire to get revenge I'd never thought I could get hurt myself. Checking myself over, I didn't think anything was broken. My poor horses were together at the end of the field. Remorse over hurting Alto and the come down from the adrenaline meant that when the ambulance arrived, I was in tears.

Because I didn't have my own phone, having left my belongings back at the stables, it meant I couldn't text Liam and ask him to come. Instead, I rang the house and let my mother know an ambulance was on its way.

———

Ulric was taken off in a separate ambulance to me. My mother had contacted his parents to let them know he was on his way to our local private hospital. As the paramedic from my ambulance introduced herself to me as Leigh, my mother interrupted her. "I've called Grayson to come deal with the horses. What happened, Phoebe?"

"Ulric hurt Alto," I lied. "We were having a race to the end of the field and he couldn't stand the fact I was winning. He stuck something in Alto's thigh," I cried again, and it was through my guilt at what I'd done to my horse, but they weren't to know that.

"The idiot boy. I'll make sure Margot knows exactly why he's ended up being blue-lighted to Richstone Royal." She told us she'd make her way to the hospital in her car and left us to it. Leigh might have missed the frustrated shake of my mother's head in my direction, but I hadn't. Even though Ulric was to 'blame' for the accident, my mother was still disappointed in me. If she'd been concerned, I'd have been amazed, but it still hurt that even when finding me injured she was more interested with how it might have damaged relations with the McDowells, rather than my bones.

I was helped into the back of the ambulance and

went dizzy. I was in a lot of pain even though I could put weight on everything.

"Let's get you a catheter in and some lovely pain meds pushed through your system," the freckle-faced paramedic smiled at me warmly. "You'll feel a whole lot better then." She and her colleague, who had been driving the ambulance, helped to get everything set up and then I was hooked up and we were on our way to hospital.

Once there, the paramedics wished me well and I was transferred to a ward and my own lead nurse, Linda. No one could tell me anything about Ulric other than he was having his own tests, and no one knew where my mother had gone.

After taking a history from me, Linda went off and came back holding a plastic pot.

"Okay, Phoebe," she said. "Before you go for your X-ray and CT scan, I need you to go do me a urine sample so I can run a pregnancy test."

"Oh, I'm on the pill," I told her.

"Yeah, we still test everyone, so do you need a hand getting to the bathroom?"

I began to shuffle off my bed, wincing, "No, I can make it. Even if my left thigh and arm want to protest heavily."

Slowly, I made my way to the bathroom, taking the pot from Linda's hand as I passed her. My limbs protested with every movement.

Lowering myself onto the toilet seat made my eyes water, but I managed to do the deed and placed the pot where Linda had asked. A short while later Linda took the pot and said she'd be back soon.

Getting back on the bed, I got into the best position I could find, leaning more onto my right side. They'd warned me that I needed to stay awake until my tests were complete, so I let myself think about everything that had just happened.

I should have felt remorse for what I'd done to Ulric. He could be dead for all I knew. But I felt no sympathy for anything that had befallen him. He'd gotten what he deserved as far as I was concerned. Just like he'd pushed his foot down on the accelerator and put pressure on Daniel, I'd pushed the pin and put pressure on Alto. After that fate decided his outcome.

I'd already seen he was hurting and as I pictured his whimpers, I smiled to myself.

Now he felt pain, just as I did about the loss of my friends. Though my pain was inward, it was every bit as acute.

There was a knock on the door of my private room and a male doctor walked in, identifiable first by the stethoscope hanging around his neck. He was followed by Linda.

"Hello, Phoebe. I'm Dr Mayhew, and I've come to talk to you about your tests and discuss the best plan of action going forward. How are you feeling?"

"Like I fell off a horse."

"Indeed." He smiled kindly. "I should imagine you are very tender. Would it be all right for me to do a physical examination to check you over?"

"Of course."

I'd already had some tests like my blood pressure taken by Linda, but the doctor checked me over thoroughly, examining my arms and legs and pressing down on my abdomen.

I started to panic that I'd ruptured some vital organ.

Finally it was over and he told me I could relax. "So, Phoebe. I do believe that you are just heavily bruised from your fall. I don't think you have any broken bones or cracked ribs, but we shall let you know what things to look out for."

"So I don't need an X-ray?"

"No. We're not going to do an X-ray, but I am arranging for you to have an ultrasound."

"Oh okay, does that look at things more thoroughly?" I didn't understand the difference.

"Phoebe." Dr Mayhew paused. "Are you unaware that you are pregnant?"

It was like for a moment I'd entered an alternate reality. I'd heard his words, but they were clearly not for me. "I'm not pregnant. I'm on the pill. There must be some mistake."

The doctor shook his head. "Your urine test came back positive, and I've examined your abdomen. There is no mistake. I estimate you are around nine weeks pregnant."

My heart thudded in my chest. But then a knock came to the door and my mother's face appeared.

"You have to keep this confidential because I'm eighteen, right?" I checked.

"Of course."

"Just tell my mother everything is fine but you're keeping me a little longer for observation."

The doctor frowned but nodded.

The nurse opened the door, and my mother strode through, ignoring the nurse completely and holding out a hand to the doctor. "Daphne Ridley."

He took her hand and shook it. "Dr Mayhew. I was just informing your daughter that while I believe there are no broken bones, I want to keep her here under observation overnight, especially after she received a bang to the head."

"Whatever you think best, doctor."

He looked at me and then to Linda. "We shall leave you for a moment and Linda will be back later to make sure you are comfortable and to check your blood pressure."

"Thank you," I said, trying to communicate my thanks for their silence with my eyes.

I was pregnant? How? I mean I knew how the whole sperm and egg situation occurred, but I was on contraception. I'd not missed any pills and I'd still had my light periods. Surely there was some mistake? I had put weight on, but that was because I'd decided limiting my diet could suck it after Flora's death. She'd always been made to watch her weight and in the end being thin had served her no purpose, so I'd comfort eaten in grief and thought to hell with a few extra pounds.

I looked at my stomach. It wasn't that different. It didn't look like there was a baby in it. The doctors had mixed me up with someone else and when they did the ultrasound they'd realise.

"Are you being vacant due to banging your head or are you purposefully ignoring me?"

I stared up at my mother. "Sorry, I'm a bit out of it with the painkillers. Have you seen the McDowells?"

"Yes. Ulric has broken ribs, a broken collarbone, a fractured right wrist, and multiple broken bones on his right hand. He won't be sitting his exams anytime soon and I doubt will ever draw or wield a paintbrush again. Margot is in bits."

"What about Richard?"

"He's upset, but he's also incensed about another of Ulric's impulsive decisions. He sends his apologies and also said if Alto and Bonny needed veterinary care, he would of course cover the costs. Needless to say, that's the McDowells crossed off our list."

I narrowed my eyes. "Don't let me keep you if you need to go update the potential husband spreadsheet."

Scowling, my mother went in her bag and brought out my phone. "I thought you'd want this in order to let your friends know you're in hospital. They'll know what to bring you more than I do. Let them know they're free to pop up to the house to get anything you need up until two am. Then I'll be locking up for the evening."

I looked at the clock on my phone that said it was currently thirty minutes past midnight.

"Right, I'll be off. I'll see you back at the house tomorrow, I presume."

"Thank you for coming and for bringing my phone," I said begrudgingly.

"Actually Grayson had it sent in a taxi. He found your belongings when he went to put the horses away. Are we so rich you can just leave Tiffany in the stables?"

"I had been planning on returning, Mother."

"It was still there for anyone who happened upon it. You really do need to become more understanding of just how difficult it is to run a household and to take care of everything. And now I have to go and face your father who's moaning about the company again."

"Oh?"

"It'll be nothing, I'm sure. I spoke with Eddie and he didn't seem unduly concerned about anything so I'm leaving them to it."

With that she left me in peace. Although not a minute later, Linda walked in.

"Right, Phoebe. Usually, ultrasounds can wait but given your fall we're taking you straight down there. There'll be a gentleman here shortly to wheel you down to the ultrasound department where the sonographer is waiting. In the meantime, I need you to drink this water." She placed a jug in front of me and a glass.

"I'm not pregnant. They're going to do whatever they do and then ask you to go find the patient that is pregnant."

"Water," she ordered me, then she left the room.

Around twenty minutes later, the porter came to collect me. He introduced himself as John and chattered amiably to me until we reached the room. Then a lady in scrubs came out asking me to enter a room to change into a hospital gown. The door then opened from the other end into the ultrasound suite.

I knocked when I was ready, and she brought me through.

"There's been a mistake," I told her, and she frowned as she looked through the files. "What mistake? Everything seems to be in order here."

"I'm not pregnant. I take contraception and I've had periods."

The sonographer sat beside me. "Phoebe. Your notes are here. The urine test was positive, and the doctor has examined you and been able to estimate the length of your pregnancy. You can still have slight periods and you can get pregnant while on the pill. Have you forgotten to take any?"

I shook my head.

"Have you been on antibiotics, or had sickness or diarrhoea? That can affect the efficacy."

"No, nothing like that. Nothing at all." Then I remembered something, and the world seemed to tilt on its axis. I remembered drinking after my father had beaten me up and throwing up on my parents' rug. Oh God, no.

"Let's take a look, shall we?" the sonographer said, noting my no doubt paler expression, and I nodded, now subdued and no longer protesting.

She rubbed gel on my stomach after warning me I might find it cold and then she began using the wand, pressing it over my belly. Although she'd told me it would be slightly uncomfortable, especially given my full bladder, I was too busy searching the screen looking for evidence that the doctor had been telling the truth.

"There you are, Phoebe," the sonographer said, pointing to a grainy image on screen. "That's your baby."

28

Liam

It had been killing me not to text Phoebe while she was on her date, but I didn't want her to think I didn't trust her. However, I wasn't about to wait in moping while she was out, so I texted Marlon and Brett and went to meet them in The Crown.

"We should be studying, not drinking," Brett stated moodily. "We're not all naturally intelligent. Some of us have to work for it."

"No one forced you to come out," I told him.

"Someone has to be here to referee if you two decide to have another punch up."

"I'm taking it steady tonight," Marlon announced. "Can't believe we only have days before our exams start. Then we move on, hopefully to much better things."

"God, I hope so. I want some fresh pussy and some prospects," Brett agreed.

Marlon was going to the nearest university to Sharrow still. Brett had applied for several places as he didn't know where he wanted to go, but he wanted the opportunity to move away from Sharrow. Brett's private life was complex. His father had got his secretary pregnant when Brett was fourteen. Not only did he have an almost four-year-old brother, but his father had since married his ex-secretary who already had a daughter. Darcy was seventeen. They hated each other. Each blamed the other's parent for the affair that split their families up. His own mother was now remarried and happy and Brett smelled freedom. But he was also loyal to us, so he'd not made any decisions yet.

"I'll raise my glass to fresh pussy," Marlon said and they chinked glasses, both looking at me and grinning.

"Look at Mr Whipped," Marlon quipped.

"Fuck off, I am not," I shot back.

"Then why have you checked your phone eight times already since we sat down?"

"It's acting up. I'm not sure it's working."

A few minutes later, Marlon excused himself to visit the bathroom, and Brett went to the bar to fetch more beer. As my phone rang, I leapt on it.

It was an unknown number, but it could be Phoebe.

"Pussy-whipped," Marlon sing-songed down the phone.

I turned in the direction of the bathroom to find him guffawing, and then looked at Brett who was shaking his head at me.

"Fuckers," I said when they came to sit back down.

"Your phone is perfectly fine and just admit you like the girl."

I ignored them, taking a sip of my fresh pint, and wondering what kind of time Phoebe might get back from her date.

"He's probably showing her his etchings by now," Brett teased after seemingly reading my mind.

"I'll break his fucking fingers so he can't draw again if he touches her," I growled.

They just laughed some more.

This time we managed to spend the evening without an appearance from either Lisette or my temper, although I didn't think it would have taken much to set me off. But the others kept purchasing beer shandies and keeping us relatively sober.

We were eventually thrown out at twenty past eleven and as I bid my friends goodnight and wandered back over the bridge, I'd still not heard from Phoebe. I swiped to open a text, my fingers hovering over the keys. *No, Liam. No texting after alcohol, remember?*

By the time I walked in my front door it was just after midnight and I figured I wasn't going to hear from Phoebe now. She must have decided to go straight to bed or something. My mind wondered what could have kept her from texting me, and fed up of being mentally tortured I reached for the barely touched whisky bottle I had in the drinks cabinet.

I was startled awake by my ring tone and grasped for my phone, not looking at the screen too closely as I let my fingerprint answer the call.

"Yeah?"

"Liam? It's Renee. I'm sorry to wake you, but there's been an accident."

I sat up straight. My vision swam and I gripped the bed in an attempt to get my balance.

"What?"

"I'm guessing you were out tonight, because the ambulances would have gone past your door. Phoebe and Ulric were involved in a riding accident."

"Is she okay?" I was already trying to get off the sofa, but my inebriation meant I swayed and banged into the coffee table.

"Son of a fucking bitch, that hurt," I exclaimed.

"Don't you go hurting yourself too. Phoebe needs you in one piece. She's fine, just bruised, but she wants to see you. I told her she could stay with me tonight because they've decided she doesn't have to stay in overnight after all as long as she has someone to watch her. But she wants to stay with you. Get ready and I'll send my driver to you. She doesn't want to alert her parents to the fact she's coming back home."

"Okay. I'll get ready," I stated and we ended the call.

I sat on the sofa wishing the room would stop spinning. Coffee. I needed a coffee, and to splash my face with cold water.

Despite my best intentions, I was still unsteady when I got into the car Renee had sent, but I did my best to act sober. I'd brought a reusable mug of coffee with me and hoped this one did the trick, though I was feeling a little nauseous due to the car movement sloshing all the liquids inside me.

Renee stood in the reception area, coming out to the car as I arrived. She glared as I walked towards her. "Just as I thought from talking to you. You're wasted. You should have told me. Phoebe needs someone who can look after her. You can barely stand up."

"I'm trying. I'm drinking coffee. I just need a little time."

"Why are you drunk on a school night? Especially given we have exam revision in the morning." Renee's hands went to her hips.

"Because she didn't text or anything. She was out with him all night and didn't contact me once."

Renee ran a hand through her hair and shot air down her nose audibly. "Hospital canteen *now* for some food and drink. You're not coming within an inch of my best friend until you can make a sentence without slurring your words. I'll text Lucie and let her know we'll be there in a while."

I followed Renee into a small canteen where there were no staff working but filled vending machines. She got me a fresh coffee and a couple of pasties. Realising I was now ravenously hungry, I wolfed them down.

"So you got drunk because you'd not heard from Phoebe?" she clarified.

"Yeah."

"But she could hardly break off from her fake date to text you, could she?"

"But it went past midnight and I'd still not heard from her." It sounded like a pathetic whine even to my own ears.

"Because she was here, in hospital," Renee's voice rose.

"I know that now," I groaned, "but I didn't when I got back from being out with Brett and Marlon. They'd been winding me up and I just figured I was better blocking it all out."

"I'm guessing the apple didn't fall far from the tree after all," she said.

I swiped the coffee cup off the table, the coffee remnants spilling all over the floor. It had felt more dramatic in my head, but a paper cup didn't do a great deal.

I wasn't expecting the resounding slap that came across my face.

"Sober up and grow up," Renee said. "I'll phone my driver back. Just go back to the bungalow. You're no good to my friend like this. She needs someone reliable."

"I'm not going anywhere without seeing her." My tone was firm.

Renee tilted her head as she stared at me, mulling things over. "It's a mistake, Liam, but if you insist, my friend could do with seeing the reality of who she believes can care for her."

"Oh, is this the true, Renee Anderson? Is a rat no

good for your riches friend?" I narrowed the gap between us. "Phoebe can make her own decisions."

"She can. I completely agree. Let's go," she said, pointing her head out of the canteen door. She turned back around. "And for your information it's not where you come from that makes you no good for her. It's how you're acting right now. Phoebe needs people she can depend upon, and currently that's not you."

I did my best to concentrate on walking, knowing I needed Phoebe to see that I cared about how she was. That I was pleased she was okay.

I followed Renee into the room, seeing Phoebe laid on the bed looking pale. Her face lit up when she saw me, and her smile dazzled me.

"You are so fucking beautiful," I said, stumbling into Lucie on my way to Phoebe's side.

"Hey, wait a minute." Lucie said, grabbing my arm, "are you drunk?"

I snatched my arm back, "Get your hands off me. I need to get to Fifi." I slumped onto the side of the bed and Phoebe almost leaped out of the way.

"What the fuck's up with you? What's going on?" I looked at the other two. "Something gone down here tonight? Been talking about me? Or has Ulric managed to convince you to stick with your own kind?"

"Paranoid much?" Renee snapped. "Phoebe's moved out of your way because she's heavily bruised, you idiot."

"Why's he here in this state?" Lucie asked her.

"Wouldn't accept my advice to return home, even though I offered to call my driver back, so I decided

Phoebe should see him for herself. He's an argumentative drunk tonight."

"Who the fuck are you calling a drunk?" I yelled.

"Get out, Liam," Phoebe shouted, and I turned around, frozen in place, looking at the girl who'd made me feel I had a future.

"Huh? But I've come to look after you."

Her face was a stone-carved statue. "I said leave. Before I get security to throw you out."

"But I think I love you, Fifi."

She flinched and then turned away. "I'm not going to talk to you while you're drunk. Take Renee's offer of a driver and go back to the bungalow."

I couldn't believe it. I'd bared my soul and told her I thought I loved her, and she'd looked away. Hadn't said it back. Hadn't even acknowledged my words.

"Have I just been a game to you? Some rich bitch's plaything?"

The look on her face sobered me up faster than any amount of black coffee could have done.

"Get. The. Fuck. Out. Of. My. Room." I watched a tear run down her face.

"Phoebe, I didn't mean it. Just give me a chance to explain."

The door opened and a nurse walked in with a security guy. "What's going on here? May I remind you this is a hospital. We have patients trying to sleep."

"I called Phoebe's boyfriend, but I didn't realise he'd been drinking. I'm so sorry," Renee told her.

"I'll be quiet from now on," I said, but it fell on deaf ears.

"Right, son, we'll have you leaving here quietly, or not. Your choice," the typically burly security guard widened his stance.

I nodded. "I'll take the car, Renee. Thank you."

She sneered. "The offer's withdrawn. Find your own fucking way home." She turned away from me. I followed the security guard and then I called for a taxi, knowing that when I got home, I'd drink a whole lot more even though it was the worst idea in the world.

When I woke up, at first, I wondered why I was on the sofa. Then I looked at the empty whisky bottle and my discarded mobile phone. Clutching my head, I dragged my phone towards me and looked at the front. It said 09:26 and I realised it had been text notifications and the phone ringing that had made me wake up.

Marlon: Just heard about last night.

Brett: You've got until ten am to be at school and then I'm skipping class and coming round. If your antics fuck up our place here, you'll be worrying about more than a sore head from beer. I'll kick your fucking head in.

With horror, I remembered the call that Phoebe had been in an accident. But what had happened after that?

Sitting up, I waited for my brain to start remembering. But I only saw fragments. Yelling at Renee. Snatching my arm away from Lucie. Phoebe's look of disgust and disappointment. A security guard making sure I didn't walk back inside the hospital.

What the fuck had I done?

I texted Brett.

Liam: I think I've really fucking blown it. I need you, man. But first, go find Renee or Lucie and find out EXACTLY what I did last night.

Brett: Jesus Christ. Renee isn't here. She's stayed home with Phoebe. I'll grab Lucie at break and then I'll be over.

Liam: Thanks. I don't think there's a way out of this for me though, man. What I do remember. It's real fucking bad. I'm waiting for Daphne to tell me I'm gone.

Brett: Sit tight, don't assume, and wait for me to get there, and for fuck's sake don't do anything stupid.

It was a bit late for that. While my phone was in my hands, I opened up my messages to Phoebe and found messages from the night before.

Liam: Phoebe. I didn't mean it. I'm sorry.

Liam: Just answer me. I swear I didn't mean what I said.

Phoebe: This is Renee. Phoebe is trying to rest. I'm turning her phone off. Stop texting.

Liam: Just tell her I'm sorry.

But there were no more replies.

The thing was, I now couldn't remember what I'd been apologising for.

29

Phoebe

As soon as he'd left, I'd broken down in tears. What the actual fuck? I'd never seen Liam like that before. Drunk, disorderly. Completely out of control. And to say the things he had?

The glimmer of hope Liam had offered me in a life beyond Richstone had been dulled by his unpredictable outburst.

Destroyed.

And now there was more than just me to think about.

When my friends had come to visit me on the ward, I'd immediately told them both I was pregnant, and I'd sworn them to secrecy. The only secret I still kept from them was that of me and Flora overhearing the rats and that one I would take to my grave.

Both of my friends had told me I had options. That I didn't need to have it. While I knew that, I also knew that

I was keeping my baby. Had known it the moment I'd seen it was real. This baby was a good thing in my life. A positive. A chance for me to be an amazing mum and to love unconditionally. I no longer cared where I ended up living, as long as I could care for my child. Dating back to my previous periods, the sonographer had dated me at twelve weeks pregnant and my baby was due around November 28th.

As soon as they'd told me I was pregnant, everything else had become largely insignificant. If my parents hated me, fuck them. My own baby would never know my rejection. The only thing I couldn't anticipate was Liam's reaction. Sure, he'd be shocked, but then what would he think about things? I'd seen his softer side of late and imagined him falling deeply in love with our baby. Dreams in my head that might have been plucked from fairy tales read as a child because the reality was very different.

The reality had turned up to the ward drunk.

The person I wanted to care for me had been obnoxious and incapable.

Showing me I didn't know Liam Lawson at all.

I didn't care how apologetic he was. Right now, I was focusing on healing from my accident and looking after my baby.

There was a whole heap of guilt and regret wrapped around the accident. I could have killed my baby. I was so intent on revenge; I lost all common sense. Ulric was a waste of breath, but by doing what I had I'd proved I was no better than him.

And I needed to be better.

Needed to be an amazing example to my baby. I placed my hand on my stomach protectively.

My mind kept circling back to Liam saying he thought he loved me though. I repeatedly told myself that he'd said it drunk and had no doubt used it as a way to get round me.

What an absolute mess everything was.

Renee knocked on my door and then came in with some breakfast: beverages, toast, and pastries. I made myself have an orange juice and some toast even though my appetite was lacking. After I'd eaten, she passed me my paracetamols. I didn't want to take them, worrying about their effect on my pregnancy, but the doctors had told me I'd be in too much pain without them.

"Thanks for staying off with me and for the use of this room."

"Anytime. I mean it. I don't want you going back to live with your parents, Phoebe. What if your father kicks out again? It's too dangerous."

"Yeah, and Eddie's hardly around these days. He's away a lot with the business."

Renee passed me my phone. "I turned this off last night because Liam wouldn't stop texting, but now you've had a decent night's sleep and some breakfast you might want to catch up on messages."

I took it from her and switched it on. After a minute my phone began to ping with notifications.

"Eddie's texted. He's been trying to get a hold of me. I'll just call him."

I got the answer back that he was 'busy right now' and so I went through my messages. I opened up the thread from Liam and read through all the apology messages. There had been nothing else since the early hours.

Other text messages were 'get well soon' ones from people I knew from school. I placed the phone at the side of me feeling dejected.

"Shall I get the books out? We could do some revision?"

I shook my head. "I'm not in the mood. You don't have to stay here with my miserable face. Go do your thing."

She stared at me like she wanted to say something but didn't know if she should.

"Out with it. Whatever it is," I demanded.

"I was so angry at Liam last night, Phoebe. He got drunk because he couldn't bear the thought of you out with Ulric. That he didn't know what was happening. I couldn't understand that lack of trust in you. Also, him acting like a petulant child when he's gonna be a dad pissed me off."

I shrugged. "I've seen him beat the shit out of a grown man, make a girl give him a blow job. He's openly admitted to me that he's damaged people with knives before. Is this the person I want as the father of my child?"

Renee came closer and sat on the bed at the side of me. She stroked my hair back from my face and pushed it behind my ear.

"Liam already is the father of your child. And while I don't condone violence, why did he do these things?" She got up and refilled her coffee cup and returned to the bed. "I spent a long time thinking of this last night because I'd never seen anyone like that before. Liam seemed, well, feral. But he's not from here. He's from a place where you do have to fight for survival and a couple of months in Richstone as a student isn't going to change that. He hit his mother's boyfriend to protect her. He did what he did to Ivy to protect him and you. Last night he couldn't deal with you being out with Ulric. And although he wants to trust you, you're the person who showed his video at school. I know last night he'd never intended to be leaving the bungalow. Drunk out of his brains, he tried to drink coffee and sober up, but it all went wrong." She took a large gulp of coffee. "I'm not saying his behaviour was in any way acceptable because it wasn't, but I think he was insecure and felt vulnerable because of the situation and the alcohol. He said he thought he loved you. You can't ignore that."

I sighed. "Right now, I'm just getting myself physically recovered, and then I will talk to Liam. I need time to think, and he needs time to be remorseful about the fact he was rude to my friends. I'm not ready to talk to him about the baby yet. It's going to further complicate an already messy situation."

"Then don't tell him right now. When you feel better, decide whether you're going to give him an opportunity to apologise or make a clean break. You know I'll help you if you want to leave in secret."

My eyes filled with tears. "You'd do that?"

She nodded. "I would. Although you know he'd sit me in a room with a knife to my throat to get the address out of me, don't you?"

I laughed at the same time as tears ran down my cheeks.

"Yeah, he would." I sniffled.

We chatted a little more until my phone rang: Eddie returning my call.

"Phoebs, it's happening. Get out of the house because shit's going down."

My brow furrowed. "But I'm not in the house. I'm recovering at Renee's."

There was a moment's silence. "Recovering from what?"

"Eddie. I was in a riding accident at home last night. I'm just bruised, but I was in hospital until the early hours. Did they not tell you?"

"No, and I've been in meetings with Dad all morning. What the actual fuck? Are you okay? Do you need anything? I'll leave here now. I'll kill that fucking man."

"No, I'm fine here at Renee's. I'm just resting. It's a waiting game while the bruises fade. Now tell me, what's happening?"

"I'd arranged a shareholders meeting this morning. Dad thought it was to appeal for them to invest more in the business, but it was actually for Hector to storm in. He presented his offer to take over and the shareholders were unanimous in a vote towards it. Then he summoned

Dad to a meeting. Dad left puce in the face. Hector followed and I believe has gone to the house."

My stomach fizzed with nervousness and excitement. "Shit, it's really happening."

"Oh, I have to go. Hector is calling me. Speak soon, and do not go anywhere near our parents."

"I'm going nowhere."

I ended the call and sat back and shrugged my shoulders at Renee.

"Tell me everything that's happening," she said.

An hour later Eddie called me again. "Hector wants to speak with us in person. I've told him about your accident and where you are. He wants to know if he can meet with us there."

I quickly asked Renee.

"Yes, that's fine with Renee. She's going to get the garden room ready. I can make my way down there gently."

"Okay. We'll be there in about an hour."

"See you then."

I turned to my friend. "I'm so nervous. What if Hector hasn't been able to conclude the deal with my parents? Life will be unbearable."

"It won't because I've told you I'll get you out of here," she said.

I reached over and squeezed her hand. "I love you, Ren Anderson."

"Right back at you, Fifi Ridley."

An hour later I was nervously awaiting the arrival of my brother and Hector. Eddie arrived first, leaping out of the car and rushing towards the building. He wrapped me in a gentle hug. "You sure you're okay?"

"Yes, just stiff and sore."

"Man up then. I'm like that before and after a shagfest," Eddie winked.

"Eddie!" I laughed.

He tipped up my chin. "See, it got a smile on your face. Now let's hope Hector's going to continue to keep it there."

As Hector's car arrived in the driveway, it looked like we were about to find out.

Hector walked slowly over to us, briefcase in his hand. He greeted us all and then took a seat, accepting Renee's offer of a coffee.

Eddie and I were no doubt looking at him like gold diggers at the reading of a will.

"Your father has just signed over his share of the business to me."

I let out a sigh of relief and saw Eddie do the same.

"Your mother turned up at the house trying to throw her weight around, but she soon realised it all came from the rocks she'd placed around her own neck. Faced with the truth about her relationship with her abusive husband coming out, she was keen to make a deal."

I held my breath.

"It's been agreed that I also buy the house and the bungalow."

"Oh."

"I've given them a financial deal which gives them the chance to start again somewhere else. I suggested out of the U.K. Your mother says she has headhunting offers from various schools and I told her she would be a fool not to make the most of it. But mainly I told them none of us gave a shit where they went as long as we didn't have to set eyes on them again. Your mother is handing in her notice at Richstone effective immediately and so I need to go talk to the governors and see about potentially bringing Drummond in temporarily as cover."

He smiled. "This morning I've secured a business for which I have a CEO in place who I know will bring it up to being a force to be reckoned with, and a new property I'm getting for a bargain price that I'll immediately put on the market for rental as soon as the purchase goes through. And we're all rid of your parents. You will of course need to arrange to have any of your belongings removed from the house at your earliest convenience."

"My horses," I exclaimed.

"I'll go arrange for them to be brought and stabled here with mine." Renee rose to her feet. "Please excuse me, but given what Phoebe's parents are like I believe this is an urgent matter to attend to."

"I also need to leave now actually," Hector said. "There is much to do. Take the rest of the day off, Eddie, to be with your sister. I'll be in touch."

When Eddie and I were left alone, we smiled tentatively at each other.

"Let me know what you want, and I'll arrange for it to be packed."

"I'm just sore. I'm coming with you," I told him.

"Huh, I don't th—"

"Eddie, I want to see them destroyed. Even if every step I take causes me deep discomfort, I want to see them one last time as I go and get the few things I give a shit about."

"You need to bring Renee with you and get Lucie to come up after school. I'll arrange for packing boxes and for someone to come and take your things here."

"Liam needs to know that he has to vacate the bungalow."

"You can call him, can't you?"

"Erm, yeah, sure."

"I'm not happy about you coming to the house, but I understand. How about we get a bottle of champagne to celebrate seeing the back of the bastards?"

"We can, but I'll not be joining in," I said. Then I told him he was going to become 'Uncle Eddie' in a few months' time.

30

Liam

I was like a cat on a hot tin roof waiting for Brett to arrive. The sound of tyres screeching on gravel had me running to my window, just in time to see Daphne Ridley race up the drive. Had something else happened to Phoebe?

Slipping my trainers on and a black hoodie over my t-shirt, I made my way up towards the house, hanging back around the trees. Daphne strode out of the car, slamming it shut behind her. Oh, this wasn't something sad, Daphne was furious. However, once she entered the house there was nothing more to see, so I made my way back to the bungalow, annoyed at not knowing the cause of her temper.

And then a familiar car headed up the driveway. Hector Sackville's. I realised that the decimation of

Daphne and Maxwell Ridley was upon us. Things were changing, but Phoebe wasn't here with me to discuss it.

I'd fucked up.

And now if Hector's plan came to fruition, there was only one thing left for me to do.

To leave the bungalow and return to Sharrow Manor.

Brett arrived shortly afterward.

"Has there been any gossip at school today about Daphne?" I asked him.

"Nah, why?"

"Something's going down now. She's just raced up the drive followed by Hector Sackville. Anyway, come through and tell me the worst."

And he did.

"The accident is all anyone is talking about. Ulric is fucked. His gloating around being a future Monet or some shit is toast. The rumours are it'll take months to heal and intense physio just to use the hand again. Lucie said he'd shoved a pin in Alto in order to win a race and it spooked both horses."

My knuckled turned white, I clenched them so hard. "It's a good job he's already in pain and ruined or I'd be going to find him to make him that way," I grumbled.

"You need to focus on your own behaviour. After Renee phoned to tell you about the accident, you turned up drunk, were rude and obnoxious and were thrown out by security."

"I guess that's what I was apologising for then." I sighed.

"Yeah, or it could have been the fact that you asked

Phoebe if you were a game to her. Accused her of changing her mind and wanting Ulric."

I felt the blood drain from my face. "I said what?"

"You questioned her feelings, right after declaring that you felt you loved her."

I leaned over with my head in my hands.

"I don't even remember it, Brett. Not any of that. Just bits of yelling at people."

"Sounds like you were a class act. Lucie said Phoebe is resting at Renee's and you should let her get on with it, and just carry on trying to apologise by text until Phoebe grants you an audience."

"Fucking hell," I roared, throwing a cushion because I needed to throw something, but didn't want to have to tidy up pieces of broken ornaments and that was without the fact they could be valuable. "I thought I'd done it. I thought I'd got Phoebe and got the job with Richard after I passed my exams. Saw a fucking future. What an idiot. People like me don't get happy ever afters."

Brett clapped his hand on my shoulder. "Liam, you've just had an argument. Everyone does. You'll sort it out. It's only the fact that she's recovering from the fall that means she's not here smacking you around the head."

"Do you think so?"

"Yeah, I do."

I picked up my phone. "So I apologise again and again, and I wait."

"If you want to get the girl, you sure fucking do."

I swiped open my screen and typed.

Liam: Brett has just filled me in on my

**despicable behaviour. I can only keep apol-
ogising.**

I kept it like that and sent it. But there was no reply,
even after I saw the 'read' notification.

Brett was just leaving to go back to school for the afternoon session when Eddie's car went past the bungalow.
Phoebe was in the passenger side of the car. Our eyes
met, but then she looked away staring straight ahead.

Sorting this out was going to be harder than I
thought. I felt helpless. Not only was she in recovery and
I'd not been there for her, but now something was going
on at the house. I sent her another text.

**Liam: I don't know what's going on up at
the house, but if you need me, you only have
to call. Even if it means nothing is solved
between us, I'm here for you.**

But again it went unanswered, although this time it
also remained 'unread'.

31

Phoebe

I'd read Liam's message just before I passed the bungalow. When I caught his eye, I knew he wanted answers, but right now I had nothing to give him. Right now, all my attention was needed for this final showdown with our parents and to make sure I left unscathed.

We exited the car and Eddie took my arm as we walked into the house. The sound of arguing could be heard coming from the sitting room.

"You were nothing without my money, Daphne," my father said. "You came from trash."

"Without me, you'd have ended up in prison," my mother yelled back. "So you can either give me half of everything and we can just go our own way, or I'll fight you in court, even if it means there's not a penny left for me to win after legal fees at the end of it. I get fifty percent and I'm not waiting for a divorce to get it. I want it now."

There was the sound of a large crack, followed by a scream, and the words, "Stupid fucking bitch. I'll teach you your place, shall I?" We rushed forward into the room, to see our father's fists raining down on our mother. She hit the floor and he started kicking. It was brutal and she curled up. She begged and cried, and I'd seen it all before. When I'd been there myself.

Neither of us stepped forward. We weren't putting ourselves in the line of fire for her. But I did reach for my phone.

"Police and an ambulance please," I said. "My father is beating up my mother as we speak."

My father realised then what he was doing. Stopped, the haze of violence punctured. My mother's eyes were swollen shut. I had no doubt she had punctured ribs, and a sliver of blood ran from her cut lip.

"Oh my g— oh fuck. Oh, Daphne. I'm sorry, I'm..."

"Save it for the police, Father," I told him. His head snapped around to face me and eyes wild, he ran forward. Whether it was to hurt me or to try to escape I didn't know, but all I could think about was protecting my baby. I needn't have worried. Eddie stepped in front of me, brought his fist back and then flung it forward into our father's face. Bone crunched as blood splattered from his nose. As he crouched down, Eddie got his boot and kicked him several times until he laid incapacitated.

"When they ask, I did it to get him off Mother," he

said simply. I nodded and then I walked to the doorway to await the police.

"It's over. We're free of them," Eddie said as we closed the door behind the police who'd just interviewed us.

"Do you think so?" I queried. "I mean, if she prosecutes him, she could call us as witnesses."

"Okay, so maybe there are a few loose ends, but see it as the final nail in the coffin of Maxwell Ridley. He lost his business due to no confidence and then beat up his wife. Anyway, Daphne knows she can't say he was hitting you too without people asking why she didn't do anything about it. It could all come out yet about her being his therapist. Personally, I think she'll get that financial package she was looking for of fifty percent up front and it'll never see a day in court."

"Yeah, you're probably right. It annoys me though that she gets a decent amount of money and can carry on her illustrious career."

"The woman has clearly never been happy. She's no winner."

"Good. I never want her to be happy."

"Are Renee and Lucie coming over to help?"

I nodded. "Yes. Thank goodness all my stuff is still here. I thought Daphne might start a bonfire just for kicks. I'm selling everything and making a nest egg for me and my little one. I don't care anymore what anyone thinks, Eddie. I'm done with this place."

"Me too, sis. I'm going to get myself a place in London seeing as that's where I'll be working in my fantastic new job. Have to say, I never thought I'd end up working for Hector Sackville."

My face paled. "Oh shit. That means in the future you could end up working for Ivy."

Eddie laughed. "I know she's a bitch but when she eventually takes over the reins she'll be focused on business and I'll have shown I'm indispensable. She once came onto me at a party anyway, so I'm sure she'd be putty in my hands if the situation ever actually arose."

"You are so full of yourself."

"If you've got it, flaunt it, sis. I flaunt it and haven't had any complaints yet."

We heard voices and Renee and Lucie appeared outside the door. Marjorie must have let them in. Gosh, Marjorie and the rest of the staff. I knew that though they might lose their jobs here that they'd soon find employment elsewhere. They were all so competent. But I couldn't worry about other's people's futures, I needed to focus on my own.

"We're here, ready to be ordered around and we've brought someone who might be able to help with your nest egg," Lucie said. Bells stepped around them. "You just let me know what you want to sell, babes, and I'll organise it all. Plus, I brought garment bags, clothes rails, and boxes and tissue paper for all your things. They're too nice not to be sorted and packed properly."

I burst into tears. So much had happened in such a

short space of time and my hormones were fighting with the pain in my body and the mess in my head.

But my brother was here, and my best friends were here, and right now, they were what I needed around me.

Until I had the strength to go to see Liam.

We slowly sorted through all my belongings and it was incredible to look at how easily I parted with the 'luxury' items I owned. Even with all the ultra-saleable things gone, I still had lots of clothes, shoes, and bags, and really, what did I need? When it came to it, I doubted I'd take anything more than what I could fit in my car, and I would sell the Audi and change it to something cheaper and more practical and once more add to my savings account.

As it was, we filled my car, Lucie, and Renee's with as much as we could. Things I could use in a new place like bedding, quilts, and pillowcases. My rug and mirror. I took down my curtains. Gradually, the room looked less like my room and more like a stripped guest room. The furniture there, but the personality stripped.

"We'll see you back at mine," Lucie said, and her and Renee took the last of the things they were carrying and made their way out of the building.

I stood in the doorway and stared at the room I'd grown up in. Where when I was little, I thought I'd had a fabulous life, only for the dream to sour as my mother milked every opportunity as I grew up.

Then I closed the door and walked down the stairs.

Marjorie hovered in the hallway and watched me approach with tears in her eyes. "I wish I had known what was going on. I would have taken you away from here, Phoebe."

"It's all okay now," I said. "But what about you? Where will you go?"

"I'm staying right here. We all are. Mr Sackville is including us with the rental price. Said we had nothing to worry about."

I smiled genuinely at the woman who'd kept me well fed over the years. "That's wonderful. They'll be lucky to have you. Take care, Marjorie."

We embraced for a final time and then I walked out of the house and towards my car. I didn't give the house a last glance as I was glad to turn my back on it.

Opening my car door, I threw the final items I'd brought down with me into the passenger side and threw my handbag in on top, closing the door.

The sound of gravel crunching underfoot came from behind me and I knew without turning around that Liam was there.

"Can we talk?" he said.

I pointed to the bench situated within the flower beds just a short walk away. "I'm in a lot of pain and need to get back to Renee's so I can have my next lot of painkillers so I can't be long."

He nodded. "Okay."

We walked over and Liam took off his coat and put it down on the bench in order to cushion the seat for me.

"How are you feeling?" he said.

I huffed. "Depends as to what your question is about. Falling off a horse? My parents finally getting their come-uppance?"

"All of it, I guess. But first, you physically."

"I'm bruised down my left side and so I'm sore, but I'm okay. Bruises fade." I couldn't help but be a little short, partly from pain, and partly because I was still pissed off at his behaviour.

"I know I fucked up big time, Phoebe, but don't give up on us now. Not when we're so near to getting the fresh start we want."

I didn't know what to say that to that so I went with the fresh starts topic. "Bells is helping me sell my most valuable clothing. She reckons I'll probably come away with around ten to fifteen thousand pounds."

"That's good. So what's happened with your parents? Are they gone?"

"Yes, I intended to come see you about that. Hector has bought the house... or made a deal to anyway. Hence my belongings in the car. It means you have to move out the bungalow.

He nodded his head. "That's fine, we knew that was a possibility. I'll get packed and go to Brett's."

I was starting to get uncomfortable on the seat and tired. "Look, Liam. I know we need to talk about every-thing, but I feel exhausted. I just want to get back to Renee's and rest, so can we do this in a few days when I've had chance to heal a little physically?"

Those slate-grey eyes that usually sparkled with his

charm, dulled slightly. "Sure." He hesitated. "Are we done, Phoebe?"

"I hope not," I said honestly, my voice quiet at first, but then I spoke clearer. "I hope that actually we're only just beginning."

A smile broke out over his face then, like sunshine peeking through on a cloudy day.

"Oh thank fuck for that."

"We're a long way from okay right now. There's a lot to talk about," I said.

He lifted his hand and pushed my hair behind my ear.

"I'm in no rush, as long as I know there's a chance we can work things out. I am so sorry for what I did. My behaviour was inexcusable."

I shrugged my shoulders. "I just caused someone to fall off a horse and crushed their dreams. I'm no innocent."

His eyes widened. "You caused it? The accident?"

"Yup. Didn't expect to hurt myself, but Ulric's ruined anyway. One minute I'm glad about it and the next I feel like it's made me no better than him."

"Fuck. Everyone thinks he caused it."

"Good. You need to know about the business offer from his father. I overheard Ulric talking to Richie at school. It was to get you out of the picture. The wining and dining of me was all to keep his reputation sweet until he got his university placement."

Liam's eyes flashed with fury and his jaw set.

"So Richard hasn't been impressed by my aptitude at maths, just saw a way to move a threatening chess piece?"

"It's Richstone in a nutshell, Liam. Games, games, and more games."

"I will get him back for this," he spat out.

I grabbed his hand.

"No, Liam. Now we leave them to it, and we start again somewhere else, before it ruins us too."

2

Liam

I wasn't happy about Phoebe driving to Renee's and so I made her call George to take her, and I drove her car there and let George drive me back to the bungalow.

Packing up my few belongings, I knew I'd miss the place. It had been somewhere I'd been able to relax and find myself. Now I'd be back to a sofa at Brett's which wasn't ideal for anyone, especially someone sitting exams.

But coming from Sharrow Manor, I knew how to adapt to new situations and a couple of hours later Brett turned up for me in his BMW to help me move to his.

"You don't seem as sullen, which is interesting given you just lost your riches residence. Have you spoken to Phoebe by any chance?"

"Yeah," I grinned, "and although she says there's a lot we need to talk about, she did say she hoped we weren't done."

5

"That's great news, mate."

It really was. I felt like a huge weight had been lifted off me.

"Fancy going for a quick pint later?" Brett asked as he drove me to his.

"No thanks, though I'll have a Coke. I've decided I'm going teetotal."

"Fuck off," Brett started laughing, but then he checked out my face, and realised I was deadly serious.

Alcohol had fucked up my mother's life and it had almost messed up my own. There was a simple remedy and that was not to drink any more.

"You'll be turning vegan and meditating next," Brett whined.

The days that followed encompassed tiptoeing around Brett's while trying not to get in the way and revising like crazy. I texted Phoebe simply to just check in with how she was and said I would be guided by her about when we finally talked.

I sat my first exam on the following Wednesday, meaning the countdown to leaving school had truly begun.

And then Phoebe sent me a text.

Phoebe: How about we go away this weekend to Brighton? Do what we originally planned before I fell off a horse? We could

stop overnight rather than just go for the day?

My heart soared.

Liam: Sounds great. Are you booking, or shall I?

Phoebe: I'll find somewhere.

Liam: Okay.

For the first time in a long time, I began to feel an unfurling of hope. I'd tried to bring myself around to the possible future of student loans and university digs and being by myself, but it wasn't what I wanted deep inside.

I wanted to take a chance with a girl who I'd thought would be a potential ticket to wealth and who turned out to make my life richer in so many other ways.

I learned how badass my woman was when she drove to Brett's in her bright red Audi and beeped her horn loudly.

Kids stood on the street, moving in on the vehicle as I walked down the path.

"You rich, lady?" one of them said.

"Nope. I've got to sell this car soon to pay some bills, so I thought I'd enjoy picking my boyfriend up in it."

"Your boyfriend is Liam?" Another asked.

She looked at me and grinned. "Yeah. See you later, kids. When I drop him off tomorrow you can have a closer look at the car if you like?"

"God, yeah."

I threw my bag in the boot and got in the passenger side and she drove off. "Like fuck are you showing those brats this car tomorrow. They'll strip it while you're there. It'll be stood on bricks before you've blinked."

She laughed. "They're just excited kids."

I shook my head. "You still have so much to learn."

Her face fell and I felt bad. "I guess I'm not being fair, some of them might genuinely like a chance to look at a nice car, but I just worry that stigma about the riches could put you in harm's way and you're only just recovered."

"I know."

"You're looking good though. Healthy."

"Renee's been feeding me up and spoiling me. She's worse than Marjorie."

We agreed that while driving we wouldn't talk about anything too serious. Phoebe's mind needed to be on the road.

"So what hotel have you booked us into?"

"A gorgeous one that looks out over the sea front. I know we're saving, but I felt like this time we should have a nice room and enjoy the view and some comfort.

The drive took us about an hour, but eventually the car turned onto Brighton sea front and I got my first look at the sea while we waited in traffic. Phoebe drove us into the hotel's underground car park and then we made our way upstairs.

The hotel's reception was vast with an enormous,

carpeted area set out with tables and chairs where patrons could relax.

"Good morning, how can I help you?" The friendly lady behind the reception desk enquired.

"I have a room booked under Ridley, with early check-in from eleven," Phoebe said. It was now ten minutes past.

She clicked in onto her computer screen, checked a couple of things with her including taking her car registration and a credit card imprint, and then we were offered two keys and shown how to access our floor.

I carried our bags up to the lift and eventually we pushed the door open on our room. Phoebe had booked us a suite. Two bay windows looked out over the sea, the brilliant sunshine from the windows both warming the room and covering it in an amber glow.

There was a small circular table with two comfortable chairs in front of one bay window, ideal for relaxing with a glass of wine or a beer if I hadn't declared myself teetotal. This was opposite the bed. In the centre of the two bays was a tea and coffee making facility, and in front of the other bay window was a larger circular table for dining with four chairs. At the opposite side of that was a living room area with a sofa and a built in TV. There was the usual hotel desk/dressing table at the left side of the bed.

It was perfect.

Phoebe looked tired as she sunk down on the bed. "You okay?" I asked. "I was going to suggest we went somewhere for lunch, but maybe I could just pop to a shop and get us some sandwiches?"

"Would that be okay? I could do with a nap to be honest. I, er- I didn't sleep well."

I understood. She'd been apprehensive about our trip.

"There's plenty of time for that walk on the beach. You relax and I'll go see what's out there and grab something nice for us to eat."

She nodded and I left her to it.

I found a nice beachfront café who were happy to pack me some supplies and then I made my way back to the hotel. It was the first time I'd been to Brighton and I already liked the hustle and bustle of the place and its general vibe. I looked forward to us exploring further.

When I returned, Phoebe was under the covers and emitting little snores. Carefully, attempting to be as quiet as possible, I put the shopping down and then I stripped off and climbed into the bed alongside her, putting my arms around her sleeping form. It wasn't long before the warmth of her body soaked into mine and I fell asleep myself.

"What time is it?" Phoebe said, stretching under the covers and rubbing at her eyes.

I turned to look at my phone on the bedside table. "Just after three."

"Fuck, I've missed half of our first day here." She

attempted to sit up, but I wrapped my leg around her and held her in place.

"You needed to sleep. You've just been through a lot. We can come back to Brighton anytime. Anyhow, we have the rest of the day, and tomorrow yet. You've only been asleep a few hours."

Her stomach rumbled and I looked down towards it. "I think I'd better get some plates out for those sandwiches. Why don't you go splash your face with some cold water and then come get something to eat?'

"Sounds good."

And so that's what she did. She looked much brighter by the time she left the small bathroom and sat at the tiny dining table in the corner of the room.

"I got cheese sandwiches, ham sandwiches, a cheese and onion quiche, a couple of slices of cold pizza, some olives, and some kettle chips."

"I'll start with some quiche," she said.

Phoebe demonstrated a hearty appetite by sampling everything I'd bought, and then sated, she sat back in her chair, letting out a long happy sigh.

"That was lovely. I feel so much better after a sleep and something to eat and drink."

"We can let our food settle a while and then go explore?" I suggested.

"Sounds like a plan."

Silence settled between us for a moment. This was it now. The time when we talked about everything that had happened lately.

"I think we should talk now," I said.

"Yeah, you're right. It's as good a time as any."

"You go first," I said.

"I feel like since Flora and Daniel died things just changed between us," Phoebe admitted. "We'd just started being a couple. It was all very new and very different given who we were as people, and then we were blindsided by what happened to our friends."

"Yeah. I didn't want it to change things," I replied, "but how could it not?"

"I was filled with hatred," she admitted. "I mean, before their deaths, I already resented my parents, loathed Ivy, and this just exacerbated everything. I then hated Ulric and I hated you. I lost myself among the hate. So fixed on this bad person I felt I now was inside. Like I would avenge Flora and ruin everyone, and then everything would miraculously feel better." She looked out towards the window. "But in reality, I felt triumph for a very small amount of time and then I just didn't care, or I felt guilt."

"Because you're not a bad person, Phoebe. Not really. You've shown you can be when pushed, but it's not who you are deep inside and I'm glad. I've been there. Done things I'd rather not have done and seen things I'd rather not have seen. Things that made me turn myself to stone. To stop caring and stop feeling. You were the one who told me that I wasn't who I thought I was, that I cared about my friends. When Daniel died, I felt so much guilt, but at the same time I realised I was capable of love because I'd loved him."

"I wanted to ruin you, Liam. Hated the fact that at

night I couldn't sleep unless I was wrapped in your arms. Blamed you."

"As you should. I brought us all to Richstone and I'm the one who had the idea to blackmail you all. We've already discussed this. I don't want things between us to end, but if you need me to leave, I would do that. For you. I'd do anything for you, Phoebe. Haven't you worked that out yet? I'm here in Brighton, hoping we can fix things, and hoping we can plan a future."

"Well, this is where we find out, isn't it?" Phoebe drew out a long breath. "Because I have something to tell you that will change our future sharply once again, and you might just decide you don't want it after all."

"I'm not following." I felt my forehead scrunch up as I tried to read Phoebe's face, but then she said the words I had never expected in a million years.

"I'm pregnant."

33

Phoebe

L iam sat in a stunned silence. I decided to fill it by
telling him the circumstances of my being sick and
it making my contraception fail.

"So there you go. You came to Richstone planning to
get a riches pregnant and you've achieved your aims."

I left him a few minutes longer. He still didn't
respond, just sitting there with his hand to his forehead. I
felt like I could see the million and one thoughts flicker
past his features. I knew he needed time. Knew how I'd
felt when it had been confirmed to me. Like the Waltzer
was spinning and you just needed someone to stop the
ride for a moment so you could reset your equilibrium.

"I just want you to know, Liam, that I don't expect
anything from you. I know it's a huge shock and it gets in
the way of everything we said. But I'm keeping the baby.
That's one part of our future we won't be deciding on

together. I'm keeping it no matter what your opinion is. But I understand you might not feel the same and that's okay."

"I need a minute or two," Liam said, and he got up out of the chair, walked into the bathroom and locked himself in.

I sat there for a moment not knowing what to do. He'd not said a word about the pregnancy. Not given me any indication as to what his feelings were. *Yes, he did,* my mind chided at me, *he just told you he needed some time.*

I would give him some. I wrote him a note to say I'd gone to get some fresh air on the seafront and that I'd be back later, and then I put on my shoes, grabbed my bag, and I quietly made my way out of the room.

I walked down the promenade for a while taking it all in. It sounded crazy, but I didn't want to walk down the beach without giving Liam the opportunity to walk with me. For it to be a first for us. But if he decided he didn't want me if I only came as a package deal with our baby, then I would walk down this beach strong and alone and vowing to stay that way.

I'd been outside around twenty minutes when I saw him heading towards me. My body tensed up as if to protect itself.

"Can you have ice cream?" he said unexpectedly.

"I- I think so."

We walked and picked our flavours and then Liam beckoned towards the sand. We made our way onto the beach, my feet sinking in the sand and we carried on walking forward until the sand got wetter and firmer and we could walk more easily.

"My mother regretted having me so young," he said. "Whenever she was drunk she told me how I'd ruined her life. How my birth had trapped her before she was ready."

I took a deep exhale, waiting for him to tell me it wasn't a good idea to have it. That the time wasn't right for us.

"We spoke about it when I went to see her the other week, before our visit. She didn't know that when she drank so much her truths spilled out like vomit. She told me that she loved me, but she wished she'd been able to have me at the right time."

Taking my hand, he pulled me in front of him and looked me directly in the eyes. "If you're keeping our baby, Phoebe, you won't ever regret it. You will make that choice to commit yourself to being a loving mother who puts that baby first. Before yourself, before me, before anyone, and you will never make it feel like it was a mistake."

"I wouldn't do that, Liam. I'm not your mother."

"I'm sure my mother thought that when she was young, too." His hand stroked down my cheek. "I know you've already had a lot of time to think about things, but I ask you again to spend time thinking hard about it all. Not because I don't want it, because I do, but because if you ever make the kid feel shit about itself, I'll take it and you'll never see either of us again."

My head ricocheted because in the same sentence he

said he wanted the baby, but then threatened to take it away from me.

I couldn't help it. I laughed. An absolute rumble from my feet to the top of my head because this was Liam Lawson in his full glory.

"What's so funny?"

The more annoyed he got, the more I laughed.

"Welcome to fucking women's hormones," he mumbled.

I finally managed to get myself under control. "Liam, I already said I was having the baby with or without you. It's my number one priority, and with the parents I've had, don't you think I might have my own rules on how loved it's going to be?"

He kicked the sand. "Yeah, well, I still needed to make my point."

"And your other point? You want the baby?"

"Yeah." He nodded. "It's fucking ridiculous. We have barely any money, no prospects at the moment, and haven't even been on a proper date. Seems the perfect time to start a fucking family."

That did it. It set me off laughing all over again. But this time Liam joined in too.

He grabbed my hand and we walked across the sand. "Take it all in, Phoebe. This is the thing you've talked to me about. Enjoying the beach, listening to the sea."

I did, and it wasn't the romantic notion I'd had in my head. It was a guy and a girl and an unknown future, but the sun shone down on us and I could only hope it was the start of things to come.

Afterward, we sat outside a café on the sea front, and I went into my handbag and pulled out the small ultrasound photo the sonographer had printed for me and I passed it to Liam.

Although the picture wasn't clear, I pointed out to him what the sonographer had described to me. His eyes searched every part of the picture.

"Wow. This is surreal. I mean, you've said you're pregnant and here's the evidence, but my head's still like, 'am I dreaming?'"

"Yeah, I still feel a bit like that myself. It's not like I've a massive bump or anything and I'm not having any symptoms: no sore boobs, no sickness. I'm just getting tired."

"But you're feeling okay now still, after the sleep?"

"Yeah, I'm fine. Enjoying the sea air."

"Well, just let me know when you want to go back to the suite and we'll go."

"Funny you should say that, because actually, we'll need to make our way back to my car soon."

His eyes questioned me. "What for? I think I'm full for secret reveals, so can you just tell me what's happening?"

"I arranged to go see a house," I said.

"*Phoebe*," Liam scolded, his arms folded over his chest.

"I just wanted to be nosy. It's not like I've said we have to live there."

"We wouldn't be able to afford to live there unless it's

a garden shed," he huffed. "It's not fair to waste people's time like this."

I pouted. "Let's just go with an open mind and then we can talk about things later. You did say I could look around the residential areas."

"Yes, the streets, not actually go in the houses," he said, exasperated.

I looked at my watch.

"Come on then," he gave in, "And then, I'm deciding on what we do for the rest of this evening, because you are being a bad, bad, girl, and it's about time you learned your place."

"Oh yeah, and what's that?" I asked.

"Underneath me, of course," he winked. "Or on top, or at the side, or on your knees."

"Yeah, yeah, I get the point. Okay, we go see the house and then you take over. I'd hate to threaten your masculinity, bad boy."

He pulled me in towards him, taking me by surprise, and then he crushed his lips to mine. My body responded hungrily, and my lips parted wanting more.

He broke off the kiss, gave me a smug smirk, and we walked back to the hotel car park.

The house wasn't the exact one of my dreams, but it was pretty, and a reasonable rental price for its location, just fifteen minutes from the seafront. On a quiet cul-de-sac, it was semi-detached. The house was an attractive looking property with some red brick to its façade and large windows. There was a cute little gate at the front entrance although it was a dirty grey colour, with a small front garden, and a garage.

A lovely older couple greeted us, who explained it had been their home for years, but they were now moving into a bungalow nearer their daughter and had decided to rent the place for a year or two.

"Come on in and let's show you the place," the woman who introduced herself as Marion said.

There was a small kitchen with wooden cabinets, and I realised I was going to have to learn how to cook. Life was going to be very different after having everything done for me. Yet, I couldn't wait for my independence, even though I knew life was going to be tough, especially learning everything at the same time as having a newborn.

Liam seemed to be auditioning for some movie role, doing his best to charm the couple and asking the right questions about the place. He announced we were expecting and looking for a place to bring up a baby, which got Marion fussing around me telling me what a wonderful home it had been for her own children. The rooms had all been freshly painted in neutral tones and out to the rear was a small patio area and a small lawn with some overgrown shrubs at the outside borders. As I watched Liam laughing and chattering, a pang came in my chest at how this would be the dream reality, us starting life together in this house.

Eventually, the tour came to an end and we thanked

the couple and said we'd be in touch as soon as we'd 'had a chat about things'.

As we got back in the car and I began to drive away, Liam sighed and rubbed the back of his neck. "Don't book another, Fifi. It hurts that we can't have that."

"What if I said that maybe we can?" I told him.

"I'm not following. We don't have anywhere near enough money," he replied.

"Flora's mother visited me at Renee's the day after my accident," I said, and I began to recount the visit as I drove us back to the hotel.

I'd woken terribly sore and glad of paracetamols. All I could do was be patient. Renee had already been in around four times fussing around me. I'd begged her to go back to school, but she said she'd arranged for any work to be sent to the house and no longer needed to go in for anything but our final exams.

When the knock came to the door and Renee popped her head around the frame once more, I knew my "Hi," was strained. But Renee's face wasn't wearing her usual exuberance either.

Victoria Chadwick looked thinner and paler than ever, but as she saw me, she smiled a caring and comforting smile and took a seat at the side of my bed, laying down a bunch of flowers and some chocolates on the bedside table.

"I heard the news, Phoebe. About the accident and about your parents. Derek got hold of Eddie at the publishers. He told us about your parents. I had to come. My dear

Phoebe, why did you never tell me? I would have taken you in as my own."

"I don't know why I kept it to myself. Scared, I guess. But they're gone now."

Victoria put her hand over the top of mine. "But what are you going to do? You have no home."

"I'm leaving Richstone after my exams. I'm going to find somewhere peaceful. Somewhere there isn't this elitist competition all the time. A fresh start."

"And are you going to university?"

I shook my head. "No. I've lost all interest in education. I'll finish my exams, but I actually had an idea for a small business I'm going to try. Something I can do from home." I told her about my plans to start renovating old furniture. As soon as I'd suggested it to Julie Lawson, the thought had consumed me, and I'd been looking at the process online. I couldn't wait to get started and see where it took me.

"It sounds promising, if you think you'd be good at it." Her gaze went inward momentarily. "Flora would have probably joined you. She always did like doing people up, maybe she could have moved onto furniture."

"How are you doing?"

"It's hard. I'm not going to lie and say it isn't. Derek and I have grown closer. He's ceased his membership to the sailing club and sold the boat. We're also thinking about moving away, but not too far, because I don't want to be too far away from Flora. But somewhere a little smaller, without all the memories of her. It's too much." A tear fell down her cheek, but she quickly wiped it away.

343

"Anyway, the reason I came is this." She went into her handbag and brought out a cheque for two hundred thousand pounds made out in my name.

"What the hell?" The words escaped my mouth before I could stop them, but I was shocked.

"I had so much saved for Flora. For her education, for her wedding, for her first home, for her first baby. She'll never need any of that money. She would want me to make sure her friend was financially okay when left with nothing because of her diabolical parents."

I shook my head vociferously. "I can't accept that. I get some money when I'm twenty-one. Until then I'll work something out."

"Phoebe, this is not a time to be stubborn. It's a gift. But if in the future you are ridiculously rich in your own right and want to pay it back, then donate the amount to a charity you think Flora would have liked and let me know. But I insist you take it. I've lost my daughter and I won't let her friend worry about her own survival. Spend it on a fresh start. On rent. On food. On some furniture in need of update. Put some in the bank for emergencies, but I'm begging you to take it."

Nodding, I took the cheque from her. "One day I will pay it back."

"That's up to you. It's not a requirement. All I'm interested in is that you're okay. Please let me know when you're settled, Phoebe. I don't want to interfere. I just need to know you're all right. There's been too much tragedy already."

We chatted, we cried, we hugged, and then Victoria Chadwick left me to rest.

And my rest was all the sweeter for knowing I really could make a fresh start somewhere new.

I finished my recollection just as I pulled back into the underground car park. I turned off the engine and turned to Liam.

"So you see. We can rent that house. But that's a decision we need to make together, and we don't need to decide now. So over to you, Liam Lawson. Time for you to organise the rest of the day."

34

Liam

I'd seen Phoebe's face light up as we entered that house and it frustrated me that I couldn't get it for her. My frustration grew ever larger as I chatted to the old couple and was greeted like their equal. Like someone who could live in a house like that and raise a family in it.

And now Phoebe had just told me that it was indeed a possibility.

While the stubborn, proud part of me wanted to say we weren't using a penny of Victoria Chadwick's money and I would find a way, the other sensible part knew that even if I managed to achieve my own dreams it was going to take time. If not for the baby I would have argued we made our own way without help, but the pregnancy had changed everything.

I would take someone's charity if it meant my child got the best start in life. It was that simple.

We went back to our hotel suite and I told Phoebe to change into something nice and I went on the internet and found a decently rated restaurant nearby. Thankfully they had a space available and so I made a reservation for eight-thirty.

I went over to Phoebe and sat alongside her on the sofa.

"Phoebe Ridley. I would like to ask you out on an official date this evening."

Phoebe chuckled. "I would be delighted."

I'd booked a bistro so that there was a broad selection of food to choose from as I didn't know what Phoebe fancied to eat.

It was a nice restaurant with a good ambience and what I liked about it most was that it was in the middle of what I was used to and what Phoebe was used to. It seemed fortuitous as we sat there, that in Brighton we had found the perfect middle ground.

"So tonight we can only discuss first date things," I told her.

"Okay," Phoebe grinned. "I'll start. What's your favourite colour?"

"Black. What's your favourite smell?"

"Your aftershave. Why do you wear the bracelets around your wrist?"

I lifted my wrist up and stared at the frayed braids. "I went through a phase at school at sixteen. Made us all have them. The others cut theirs off the day after, but I always had to be different, so I kept mine on. They're not going to last much longer, but I just can't remove them. Not yet."

"You can still keep them even if you do. I'll frame them for you."

"You'd do that?"

"Yeah, of course."

"Thank you."

"You're welcome."

We carried on asking each other questions the whole way through the meal and it settled something inside me. We weren't here being the rat and the riches; we weren't here being the grieving friends of Flora and Daniel; and we weren't here being the people worrying about the future with a baby coming. We were just Phoebe and Liam out on a date.

I loved every minute.

"Okay, last question," Phoebe said as I paid the bill and we got up ready to leave.

"Yes?"

"Do you put out on a first date, or do you wait a certain number?" Phoebe asked with a wink.

"I suggest we go back to the hotel and I'll let you find out," I answered.

As soon as we were through the hotel door, shoes and clothes were discarded and we fell on the bed in a tangle of limbs.

I pulled off her underwear and soon we were both completely naked. My hands smoothed over Phoebe's creamy, soft skin, taking in her plumper breasts and then caressing her stomach.

"I still can't believe our son or daughter is in there," I marvelled. I knew then that while this was all earlier than I'd have wanted, and completely crazy, that I was all-in.

The bad boy from Sharrow Manor was about to turn soft as shit, because if Phoebe didn't already own me, the baby inside her belly definitely would.

Leaning down, I kissed the flesh just under Phoebe's belly button.

"We're going to be okay," I told it and then I looked up at Phoebe. Her eyes were wet with tears, but she wiped them away and then she said,

"That's good to know, but now you need to focus on what's a little further down."

Lowering myself down the bed, I pushed her thighs apart and snaked my tongue around her clit. Phoebe's juices flowed. By the time I pushed inside her she was so fucking ready. I moved within her over and over with an increasingly faster rhythm until her eyes closed in ecstasy.

"God, yes," she screamed as she shook around me. I emptied myself inside her, knowing I could fuck her over and over and it would never seem enough.

Her eyes opened and she startled a little when she found me staring into them.

"I love you, Phoebe Ridley," I told her.

She smiled. "I love you too, Liam Lawson."

I kissed her mouth hungrily and then breaking off, I said, "Let's take the rental."

"Really?" Phoebe almost squealed.

"Really. I want to know if we're okay to do a little painting of the place and then if we can get it early, we could come down at the weekends in between the exams and get the place ready. As soon as our exams are over, we can move in. I want to train as an accountant still, but once that's done we'll buy a place, Phoebe, and pay that money back to the charity in Flora's honour."

She nodded and kissed me and then there was no more talking for a long while.

The next morning, we rose leisurely having ordered a room service breakfast. Then we phoned the couple, who were delighted to hear we wanted the place, and arranged to pay a deposit, which I insisted on settling out of my savings.

"I can't believe we're going to live there," Phoebe jumped up and down. When she'd stopped, I swept her into my arms and spun her around.

On our way home, we drove past the place again, and Phoebe and I got out for a minute or two, snapping some photos. I wanted to show my ma. We would only be an hour away from Sharrow Manor, but it was enough of a distance for absence to make the heart grow fonder. I needed to forge my own life and my ma needed to live hers, whether she finally found a way out of her misuse of alcohol or not.

Despite my telling Phoebe to not come back to Sharrow Manor, she ignored me completely, dropping me back outside Brett's door. Of course within seconds kids were around the car again. I climbed out of the passenger seat and gestured to the five of them.

"Right, you lot. If you want to look at the car there are rules. You take nothing, and you say thank you to Phoebe for showing it to you, because I told her not to, but she won't listen. We clear?"

They all nodded and I kept a close eye on them as they took turns to sit in the passenger seat, and rev the engine. They excitedly chatted with us about luxury cars and Phoebe once again told them that the car was being sold.

"So you're from Richstone?" one of the younger boys said.

"I am, but I'm moving to Brighton. I'm not rich anymore."

"Huh, I thought all the riches were bitches, but you're nice," he said.

"Yeah, she's fabulous. Now time's up and you all need to fuck off," I ordered.

They groaned but left and then I pressed Phoebe up against the side of the car and kissed her.

"If you can work on the 'fuck off', I think you're going to be a great parent," she giggled.

"Get yourself back to Renee's and text me when you're home," I ordered.

She saluted, moving out of my arms. "I've had the best time," she said, before climbing back in the car. Then she drove away.

Brett opened the door to me. "Looks like it went well then," he said.

"Fancy a pint?" I told him. "Coke for me of course, but I think you'll need a cold one with everything I have to catch you up on."

"You might want to rethink your abstinence," he replied. "Daphne came back and left a parting gift."

35

Phoebe

I knew I'd not paused for breath since I'd got back to Renee's and I'd taken the tension in her face as a friend's reservation about thinking I was jumping into things too fast.

"Come on then. Tell me what you think about my fresh start."

"I think it's come at the perfect time," she said, and then she began to tell me about my mother.

Daphne had been back to collect her belongings from the house after her release from hospital. Apparently, the locks having been changed, she'd had to phone Hector, who'd sent Ivy to meet her with the keys and oversee she only took her personal effects and didn't douse the place with petrol and then discard a cigarette.

But my mother had had one final hand to play and in

uniting with my enemy, had given Ivy the video of me on my knees with Liam's cock in my mouth.

I guessed karma had come full circle as Ivy circulated the video like fire on dry grass, stating that unlike the fake video, this was one hundred percent legitimate, and I'd got Liam to make the hoax clip of him and Ivy to deflect from the real one.

Not long after she told me, Liam texted me asking if I knew.

Phoebe: Know and don't give a damn because we no longer have anything to hide!

Liam: That's my girl!

"At some point I'll come face to face with Ivy and she'll see that no matter what she does, she can't get the better of me," I told Renee.

"Well, she's having a party to celebrate the end of the exams and everyone is invited. Feeling brave?" Renee asked with a look of mischief in her eyes.

"I'm feeling brave as a lion and Ivy's going to hear me roar."

I concentrated on finishing my exams and ignored all the gossip that followed me around. Ivy was present as I waited for a couple of my exams, doing her usual saying scathing things within hearing distance instead of confronting me outright. I heard about my 'time here coming to an end, along with the rats', that without

Daphne's guidance I'd forgotten salad existed. I kept my head down and let her think she'd won.

And then the exams were done, and so was I. The party was tonight, and then afterwards Liam and I moved to our new home. We'd gone from strength to strength as a couple over the past few weeks, but we always kept our motto of 'one day at a time' and so far, no one from Richstone had seen us in public as a couple—until now.

Now almost seventeen weeks pregnant, I wore a pale-lemon strappy sundress that hugged my newly emerging bump, along with a pair of cream sandals. Liam wore one of his old t-shirts and jeans. We were done pretending to be anything other than what we were.

Initially, I was surprised that we got through the door of her party, but then I saw Hector, who beckoned us into a room that turned out to be his study.

"I'm sorry, Phoebe. It appears Ivy has not learned all of life's lessons yet and decided to air your video without thinking of the consequences. I presume you have some for her?"

"Of course."

Hector opened a cupboard and drew out a small black holdall. "There's twenty thousand pounds in there for you to not physically hurt her."

"And that's why I like you, Hector. Because you already know me well enough to know that I'd turn down your money if you asked me to just walk away altogether."

"In a perfect life, Phoebe, you'd have been the perfect person to start at my company. Alas, we know that could never work. But I know that whatever you do decide to do, you'll be fine. You have resilience, and that will stand you in good stead."

"You have my brother. Take care of him."

Hector smiled. "He's already proving himself worthy. Shares are up with the deals he finalised and the business is already on a strong road to recovery. I'll definitely be keeping him around."

I took the holdall of money, because my principles had gone when the pregnancy test showed positive. An extra twenty grand in my bank account was nothing to turn my nose up at. It was taking money indirectly from Ivy, and who knew? Maybe one day, when Hector was no more, and if my brother became a force to be reckoned with, we could still bring down Ivy Sackville if she stayed poisonous. Time would tell.

For now, I would take my leave of Richstone. Just as soon as the party ended.

———————

Liam and I joined the main party walking hand-in-hand and we greeted friends, while ignoring those who jeered. The ones who felt they'd put up with the rats all they had to and could now expect them to disappear back to where they came from.

I'd spotted Ivy but she hadn't seen me or was pretending she hadn't. Too busy acting like the Queen she thought she'd once again become.

Casey joined us all, giving first Liam, and then myself a hug.

"Is it done?" I asked her.

"Easy as pie," she replied, and we shared a satisfied smile.

Lucie and Renee kept fussing around me all the time, hugging me close and getting teary.

"I'm only going to be an hour away," I protested.

"I know, but we might be further away once we decide on our university placements," Lucie sulked.

"There are holidays, and it's only for a few years. We're best friends forever," I said. Liam overheard and pretended to make a puking motion.

"You wear friendship bracelets, so you can shut up," I retorted. He answered by sticking out his tongue.

"We knew the rats coming to Richstone would change things, but I did not predict you having one's baby," Renee said. She waited a moment and then looked at me. "Did Sarah hear that?"

"With the speed at which she's running in Ivy's direction I'd say so," Casey said. "God, my sister is a stupid bitch with no mind of her own. A complete sheep."

"She might be looking for a new flock after tonight," Lucie said, giggling.

Brett had already said his temporary goodbyes to Liam earlier and had set off to stay with his father for a couple of weeks of the summer break. He'd said he had no interest whatsoever in being around Richstone any longer, though he'd vowed to keep in touch with Lucie and Renee via future get-togethers or if they ever needed a friend. Marlon had his own party to go to at Sharrow and had informed us he'd be coming to see us in our new place in a week or two whether we invited him or not.

"This baby is playing havoc with my bladder tonight," I said. "Excuse me while I just visit the bathroom."

Moving away from my friends, I made sure that Ivy saw me leaving on my own. I waited in the queue for the bathroom and after a few minutes made my way inside, relieving my bladder, and then exiting to wash my hands.

Surprise, surprise, there she stood.

"Phoebe Ridley. How the mighty fall," she gloated. "I mean look at you. You're broke, homeless, and now I hear you're pregnant to a rat. Good God, could you stoop any lower?"

I mock gasped and pointed to her neck.

She smoothed down the material there. "Oh yes. Your bee necktie. Sarah brought it to me. Finders-keepers, and we all know I'm the true Queen here anyway. Your attempts at de-throning me were pathetic." She leaned into me, "How does it feel to see that I have everything and you have nothing?"

I smiled back, something she wasn't expecting if her sour lemon sucking mouth was anything to go by. "It feels pretty fucking amazing. Because actually I have a new home. I'm with a man I love, and I'm having a baby. I've lost my place in Richstone, but I've found my happy ever after, whereas you have to do your daddy's bidding, a slave to whatever you're ordered to do. You'll not be able to make an independent choice until his death."

Her mouth downturned even more.

"So really, who's the winner here and who's the loser? You're a pathetic puppet whose daddy owns the strings and the best you can do is take my necktie? Enjoy my sloppy seconds to remember me by while you're living your miserable existence, no doubt still belittling others so you can try to make yourself feel better about the fact you are in fact, no one special."

She lifted a hand as if to slap me and I brought up my own, which held a switchblade. I thrust it up against her throat, just above the necktie.

Her eyes were wide.

"Don't even think about making a move that could have a detrimental effect on my baby." I growled out, pressing the blade enough to know it would prick a little and sting. I watched the few small beads of blood rise and I smirked as Ivy grew paler. I'd taken money to not physically hurt her, but as far as I was concerned this was just a warning of what I was capable of doing.

"I'm going to take this knife away from your neck and you're going to leave this bathroom. If you tell anyone I'm carrying it, I'll come for you one night when you're asleep. Liam taught me exactly how to use it." My eyes narrowed at her. "Nod your head with your agreement at leaving quietly."

By now, people were banging on the door, asking what was going on in there.

Slowly, Ivy nodded her head.

I took my hand away, ready to protect myself at any cost if she made one wrong move. But she didn't. Instead, she bolted out of the bathroom. I slammed it shut behind her into the next girl's face and locked the door again.

Washing the blade under the hot tap, I placed it in my bag inside my tampon holder, giving it another use now I didn't need it for its original purpose.

Then I walked out of the room and back to Liam. We said goodbye to everyone and left the party.

But we didn't go far. Sitting in my car in the Sackville's car park, the holdall now safely in the boot, we went through all the material the microphone hidden in the necktie had given us and edited it into a nice compilation, and then we sent the audio file to Renee.

Afterward, she told us how she stormed the stage just as Ivy was about to give her speech and played out the complete bitch fest we'd recorded. Ivy had spent half the night talking to The Poisons about how wonderful she was and about everyone else's faults. Now, 'everyone else' had got to hear her opinions.

It would certainly make life a lot more difficult for Poison Ivy. And I wasn't even done with her yet...

I had one last visit to make before I left Richstone. I'd called Margot McDowell and asked if I could say goodbye to Ulric and see how he was doing. That I had a gift to give him before I left.

Richard had sent Liam a text a few weeks ago saying

that due to unforeseen circumstances he could no longer offer him an internship. He'd clearly decided that if Liam raised the issue of Daniel's death now it would be old news. He hadn't contacted me since my parents left; no longer interested in the girl with no prospects. What he'd forgotten, and would learn fast, is that if you cast someone into the shadows, you couldn't see them in the dark.

"Margot. Thank you so much for letting me surprise him," I air-kissed both her cheeks. "I just thought he'd be really low at having to miss the party and I had this present for him." I waved the wrapped rectangle I carried.

"He is, but like I said to you on the phone, I didn't think being around hundreds of drunk teenagers celebrating was the place to go with a hand in a frame. He has to be so very careful."

"I won't keep him for long. I just didn't want to leave without saying goodbye."

"Dreadful matter with your parents. Are you still in touch with them?" She might be giving me a look of sympathy, but Margot was clearly looking for first-hand gossip.

"Absolutely not. You saw what my mother was like when we came for dinner, and I'm sure you've heard rumours about my father. He did beat me; it was all true."

"Oh, Phoebe. Well do take care. I wish you well. So Ulric's room is..."

I left her and made my way up to his room where he was still recuperating.

Knocking on the door I waited for the, "Come in," and then I entered.

"Phoebe. Fuck, I did mean to get in touch," he said, alarm in his expression.

"Don't worry about it," I waved off his excuses. "I'm just here to say goodbye."

"Goodbye?"

I moved closer and took a chair at the side of his bed.

"Yes. I'm leaving Richstone for good. There's nothing here for me anymore. I'm sure you know all the gossip, but I'm not here to chat about myself. I'm here to chat about you."

"I can tell you're pissed with me, but, Phoebe, I swear I didn't do anything to Alto."

"Oh, I know you didn't," I took a hair pin out of my bag. "Because I did it."

Ulric scrabbled further up his bed, as if the pin in my hand was a threat, having to move carefully because of his own hand.

"Oh, don't worry. I'm not here to do anything else tonight. I just came to give you this back."

Putting the pin back in my bag, I unwrapped the gift in my hand revealing the portrait of Daniel, Flora, and their baby which was now framed. "Only this will be the last original artwork by Ulric McDowall, won't it? I'd hate to part you from it, so let's put it here on your bedside table where you can look at the family you basically murdered for a while."

Ulric trembled.

"I heard what you said to Richie. Every. Damn.

Word. The truth about what you thought about me and my friends. And that's why you'll never draw again. I also know what your father's role in keeping Liam and I quiet was, and so now I'm going to deal with him."

I saw Ulric look at his phone.

"Touch that before I leave and I'll re-crush that hand, and stab the other one," I told him.

He looked up at me, his eyes glittering with hatred. "You're a bitch who has nothing. I'll still be rich, no matter what."

"Remember your famous last words," I said as I got up to leave.

"Bye, Ulric. I hope you get the life you deserve."

I made my way back downstairs and went to find Margot, who was in her living room.

"You off now, Phoebe?"

"I am. Thanks so much, Margot. Before I go though... I have a very delicate situation to talk to you about."

She looked wary and put the Pomeranian down from her lap.

"What's Ulric done now?" Her eyes alighted on the slight curve of my stomach and I saw the foreboding in them.

"Oh, it's not Ulric. It's about Richard. I debated saying something, but if it was me, I'd want to know."

"Take a seat, Phoebe," she sighed, patting the sofa next to her.

Going into my bag I took out some photographs. "Are you sure you want to see these?" I asked.

"I doubt it's anything I haven't seen before," she said sadly.

It was time to reveal the discovery I'd had to fight to hold back in my mouth all week.

"I had a meal with the Chadwicks last week and on my way back, I passed the marina. It was late and I was surprised to see Ivy Sackville headed that way. Excuse my language but she's a hateful bitch I don't trust an inch, so I parked up and I followed her." I passed Margot the first photo.

"She met Richard. I'm sorry."

The photos clearly showed Ivy and Richard up close and personal. His hands in her hair. Their mouths together.

I knew why Richard would do so, trying to further himself by learning a Richstone rivals' secrets. What Ivy was doing with him I had no idea and didn't really care.

"You deserve better," I told her. "Better than your son too. They'll destroy you and believe me I know what that's like. Get out of here, Margot. Take your dogs and go. That's my advice." I handed her the rest of the photos. "Hector Sackville received the same photographs earlier tonight too."

That had been Lucie's last task for me at the party. To seek out Hector and to tell him that I felt he deserved to know the truth about his daughter. And that a set-up of insider trading might be just the ticket to rid himself of Richard McDowell for good.

I leaned in and hugged the devasted but resigned

woman next to me on the sofa. She sank into my embrace for just a minute before pulling back and looking at me.

"Thank you, Phoebe. You'd better be on your way."

I nodded.

After leaving the house, I got into the car where Liam had sat patiently in the passenger seat, ready for in case I needed him.

"Is that it? Can we now leave Richstone?" he said.

"Just one more thing," I replied, going back into my bag.

I took out the pistol and pointed it in his face.

Marlon

It was only ten-fifteen, but I had no more patience for the party at Michaela Chapman's house. There was ample supplies of bud and alcohol, but nothing settled me right now. Daniel was gone forever, Liam was moving away and moving on, and Brett would be at his father's for the next few weeks. It left me here in Sharrow Manor, adrift.

I told my friends I was fine. They didn't need to hear that life at home wasn't great. That everything centred around my little sister. I loved her dearly but felt like a ghost in my own home. My mother was so happy, I didn't feel like I could say anything. My stepfather was a good man. Had kept me fed and watered since they'd got together.

The sooner I went to my uni digs the better, and so I

prayed I'd passed my exams. I'd still be close to home, but at least I'd have some independence.

Though I told myself not to, I found my feet walking the path I knew led to the Handley's house.

I didn't expect to find Lisette on the doorstep trying to get away from her husband.

Before I even realised what I was doing, I'd run down to, and hurdled the gate, grabbing hold of Reid Handley, pulling him off her.

"Marlon, no," she said as I pulled back my fist ready to launch it into Reid's scrawny face.

I saw her nose ran with blood and forgetting Reid, I pulled off my t-shirt, balling it up and offering it up to her nose.

She grasped it and held it there for a while.

"I had it under control," Reid snapped. "You can leave now."

"I'm going nowhere until I find out what's happening." I placed my hands on my hips, my legs in a widened stance.

"Whatever," he said. "Perhaps he'll listen to you," he told Lisette. "I'll be fixing you some tea and a cold compress."

Lisette took the t-shirt away from her nose. "What are you doing here, Marlon? You need to leave."

"Has he hit you?" I growled.

"No. I just got a nosebleed."

"Then why were you on the doorstep arguing?"

She sighed. "He was fussing. I just needed some space."

"I don't believe you," I said. "I don't believe you at all."

"It's the truth," she snapped. "I'm going inside now. I'm sorry about your shirt; I'll replace it."

"I don't give a fuck about the shirt. I give a fuck about you."

"Ssh," she looked in the direction of her house. "I told you. It was a mistake. It's over."

I scoffed. "You tell yourself that, but I don't believe you about that either."

Walking back down to the gate, I knew where I was headed. The Crown. Time to drink until I lost feelings, because it hurt too much to have them.

Liam

Had I really said that Phoebe didn't have it in her to be a bad girl? I knew after tonight that I never wanted to get on her bad side again. She'd decimated her enemies and now had a gun held at my face.

She pressed the trigger.

BANG.

The red flag with the black printed on words fell down in front of my eyes.

"Is this my warning of what will happen if I ever mess you around?" I queried with a raised brow.

"I bought it potentially to scare Ivy with," she laughed, throwing it into the car well. "Are you ready to get out of here?"

"So fucking ready," I told her.

We'd sorted the house out almost completely the weekend before, and so only had a few last things in the boot of the car, including our extra twenty grand. We drove to Brighton reflecting on the events of that evening.

"I cannot wait to start our new life and to never have to set foot in that place again," Phoebe said.

"I feel the same way, though I'll still have to visit Sharrow Manor to see my ma."

Phoebe squeezed my hand. My mum had been so happy when I'd told her about the baby and showed her the photos of the new house. She'd made new vows of giving up drinking to be a fabulous grandma, but I couldn't trust her words.

When we pulled up outside the house Phoebe gasped.

Because there, after I'd asked Marion to organise a little favour for me, was a shabby chic painted cornflower-blue gate.

To signify, hopefully, the start of dreams coming true.

EPILOGUE

Four years later

Danielle Florence Lawson owned me, and she knew it.

"Daddy, Daddy, again, again," she ordered, and like a fool I let her climb on my back once more while I pretended to be a horse.

"Dani, leave poor Daddy alone; he's been working all day," my wife protested.

"It's fine," I said.

Phoebe leaned down and gently tugged me up by my chin. "There'd better be energy for another ride later." With that, she went back into the house. The one we'd just bought from the couple who'd originally rented it to us.

"One last trot around the garden and then it's time for a bath and a bedtime story," I warned my daughter, and then I took off around the garden once more, delighting in her little whoops and yee-haws.

Wondering if I could get her mother to make similar noises later.

THE END

Read about Marlon in Beautiful Broken Boy. Coming 2021.

Release updates will be in my newsletter so sign up now to get the latest on Richstone.

www.subscribepage.com/AngelDevlin

For the description move past the following playlist.

PLAYLIST

Goodbye, Billie Eilish
See You Again, Whiz Khalifa ft Charlie Puth
Use Me, PVRIS ft 070 Shake
Losing My Mind, Charlie Puth
Queen, Shawn Mendes
Days Gone, Nathan Whitehead
New Me, Ella Eyre
Stitches, Shawn Mendes
Good As Hell, Lizzo
Look What You Made Me Do, Taylor Swift

ABOUT ANGEL

Angel Devlin lives in Sheffield, UK, with her long-suffering partner and son, and her beautiful Whippet furbaby.

When she's not thinking up dark and dirty book scenarios, she spends her time looking at the house thinking 'oh my god, what happened' and hoping it's a tornado and not the fact her head was too busy in her work. Then she takes the dog for a very long walk.

She also writes paranormal romance and dark suspense as Andie M. Long.

FOLLOW LINKS ARE BELOW

Instagram: @andieandangelbooks.

Reader group
www.facebook.com/groups/1462270007406687

Facebook
www.facebook.com/angeldevlinbooks

Other Angel books with delicious bad guys/downright
dirty billionaires
Buy on Amazon:
www.amazon.com/author/angeldevlin

BEAUTIFUL BROKEN BOY

Marlon:

I pretend I'm fine and everyone believes me.

They believe that the person who lost his best friend, the person invisible to his own family, the person who is lost to himself can somehow be okay.

But she sees it. Lisette Handley recognises my broken pieces and calls them beautiful. Tells me I can be whole again.

Lisette should be off-limits, forbidden. She's married and teaches at Sharrow Manor, the deprived and struggling school I attend.

Our broken pieces can only hurt each other more, yet we can't resist.

Casey:

I know he's lonely and looking for comfort.

He calls to me because I'm lonely too.

But he's in love with another woman. It's complicated.

So I'll be Marlon Rowe's friend, his confidante; even though he tries to push me away because I come from Richstone. The place he holds responsible for his friend's death.

I should stay away from him, yet I can't resist.

There's more tragedy to come.

More secrets to be revealed.

As the worlds of Sharrow Manor and Richstone cross once more.